OF THINGS NOT SEEN

A GHOST'S MEMOIR

BOOK 3

OF THINGS NOT SEEN

A GHOST'S MEMOIR

BOOK 3

ROBERT J. MCCARTER

Little Hummingbird Publishing
Flagstaff, AZ

Of Things Not Seen
A Ghost's Memoir, Book 3

Cover image from pixabay.com and © Lymedia | Dreamstime
Back cover image ©iStockPhoto.com/J_GriffithPhotography

Version 1.0, August 2017
ISBN: 978-1-941153-97-0

Find out more about this book at: www.ShuffledOff.com
Visit Robert's website at: www.RobertJMcCarter.com

Published by:
Little Hummingbird Publishing
P.O. Box 23518
Flagstaff, AZ 86002
www.LittleHummingbird.com

Little Hummingbird Publishing is a division of Arapas, Inc. Find more about Arapas at: www.Arapas.com.

For my Mom. I love you and I miss you. For Carolene and Gayle—my life is better for having known you and poorer for no longer having your beauty and strength in my life.

Editor's Note

Unlike the previous "A Ghost's Memoir" books, this one is not arranged as "transmissions" as they came in from the SECI chamber. It was written by Jesús Dominga. His style of writing is very different than JJ Lynch's and we often would ask Jesús to add details or fill in the blanks (particularly about his childhood).

Because of this, we decided a normal chapter style was more appropriate. These words are Jesús's and he is aware of the changes and edits we made to make the story more cohesive.

Tamara Watson and Jin Shi
Tucson, Arizona
May, 2014

Part 1

La Familia
(The Family)

"Now faith is the substance of things hoped for,
the evidence of things not seen"
Hebrews 11:1

Chapter 1

"BLESS ME, FATHER, FOR I HAVE SINNED," I WHISPERED to Father Finnegan who sat placidly in the other side of the confessional booth. "It has been seven months since my last confession. In that time I have felt anger towards my killer, and since I found him and brought him to justice, I have found myself in a place of deep despair, a place of confusion. I have begun to doubt my faith."

Father Finnegan took a deep breath and sighed, his thumb moving his rosary beads smoothly along his index finger as his mouth moved silently in prayer. His hair was grey, with only a hint of the red that was there when I first met him, and his face was deeply wrinkled. He didn't say anything.

"I'm a ghost, Father," I continued, moving my face right up to the brass confessional screen so I could see him clearly. "I sit here, I see you, I speak to you, but you can't hear me. You can't tell me how to confront this crisis like you helped me so many times before. You can't tell me to do Hail Marys or Our Fathers. You can't assign me an appropriate act of contrition. You can't..." I trailed off, fighting back the tears. I longed for the life that was past, for the body that let me communicate with the living, for the faith that used to seem so unshakable.

"Sister Dominga is up there in her room dying. I am down here, dead, wishing you could hear me. There is another ghost, a strange woman, who keeps appearing in Sister Dominga's room. She is probably there now. I don't know who she is. I don't know what she wants.

"I have left my ghost friends up in Tucson and walked here to Mexico City, walked home. But I have no one to talk to. I have no one to help me. I can't leave Sister Dominga, but I don't think I can stand this. The Bible doesn't talk about souls in my state... It doesn't mention ghosts. What does this mean, Father? What can I do? I am so confused, I..."

A woman, large and middle-aged, walked into the confessional. I didn't want her to sit on me, nor did I want to hear her confession, so I flew up and out of the confessional. As I did, I heard her say in Spanish, "Forgive me, Father, for I have sinned," and I heard Father Finnegan reply in his Irish accented Spanish, "I will hear your confession, my child."

I felt a sharp pang of jealousy that such a simple act of comfort was now beyond my reach. I slowly flew out of the church and into the nunnery, back towards Sister Dominga's room.

I didn't know what I was doing or what I needed, but I did know that I would be there when Sister Dominga died. If she, by some chance, became a ghost upon her death, I wouldn't let her go through it alone. Not after all she had done for me.

I flew slowly to the old wooden door of her room. It was

thick and scarred with age and use. I stood there listening—was the other ghost in there?

I heard her voice, soft yet strong as she whispered to Sister Dominga. "I am here, Grandmother. I am here. I heard your call and I came. I will show you the way if you need. I will be here for you." Her words were in Spanish with an accent that I couldn't quite place.

Grandmother? Did she say Grandmother? Sister Dominga was a nun, she had been a nun almost her entire life, how could she be a grandmother? She had been like a mother to me, rescuing me from the streets and saving my life, teaching me, raising me, how could I not know she had a child, much less a grandchild?

I wanted to rush in, to demand an explanation, but I pushed that impulse down. I had surprised this ghost before, and she would disappear if I rushed in. So I moved slowly through the door until I could see her. She was petite and slim with long black hair that was braided in the back and skin a shade lighter than mine. As soon as I was far enough through the door for me to see her, her head turned towards me and our eyes met.

Those eyes made me feel just a little bit alive, and they scared me too. They were blue, shockingly blue, ice blue, the kind you see reflected in the depths of icebergs. Her gaze penetrated me. I just knew that she saw deep into my soul and could see my doubt and my weakness.

This was the third time I had seen her and the longest she had stayed.

"My name is Jesús," I said. "I just want to talk."

She continued to stare at me, her lips turning down into a frown, her head moving slowly back and forth. With a gentle "pop" she was gone.

I STOOD AND STARED AT SISTER DOMINGA FOR THE longest time. Her face drawn and pale, her breathing slow and unsteady, her eyes closed, looking like they would never open again. A soft moan escaped her lips and I feared the worst. I was here because I needed her, and in case she needed me. And what if she did need me, could I even help her when I didn't know how to help myself?

I longed for the round-faced Sister Dominga with the hard, uncompromising eyes that hid an endless capacity for compassion. I wished she would open her eyes and give me one of her looks, the kind that used to make me scared and excited. The kind of look she gave me as a boy that said she knew exactly what I was up to and that I would not get away with it.

I stood there and felt the doubt that had brought me to walk from Tucson, Arizona, to Mexico City. It was like a disease, a cancer, a darkness inside me, eating me from the inside out.

The mystery of the other ghost, calling Sister Dominga Grandmother, was maddening, but it was drowned out by the noise of my own doubt and fear. I had been back for three days and done nothing but watch Sister Dominga, wander the church and the orphanage, and hope...

But I didn't know what I was hoping for. A dying woman to wake up? My doubts to magically disappear? To suddenly know what I was doing with my afterlife?

I had been here before, bereft of faith. I had been down low, much lower than this, and had survived. And it was Sister Dominga that had saved me body and soul.

"How can I do this without you?" I asked her. She had been like a mother to me, and it was always the mothers that had brought me to faith.

When I spoke, I saw the smallest change in her face. A slight relaxing of her now gaunt features, as if the pain that plagued her had eased for a moment.

"My first memory is of Mass," I continued, studying her face. "It was around 1972, I was maybe three, my mother had dressed me in my best shirt—which was admittedly not much back then—and walked me to the church. I remember all the people, beautiful in their suits and dresses and shiny shoes. I remember the hard wooden pews, and how my mother had me kneel on the padded bench when she did."

Sister Dominga let out the smallest of sighs and I felt a tear run down my ghostly cheek. Maybe there was something I could do for her, some small way I could help her while she still lived. It was like the tiniest sliver of sunlight after a terrible thunderstorm.

"You want to hear my voice?" I asked her. "Does that help somehow?"

She didn't answer, but I could feel it. I could feel just a glimpse of the woman who had saved me and raised me. I could feel her longing for company, to not feel alone as she passed from this world. I could see her, in her coma, physically relax.

I laughed, a brief awkward bark. A tiny bit of the pent-up pressure I had been feeling for the last several months escaping. This I could do. This would help Sister Dominga. This would help me.

WHEN THE DEACON CAME AROUND SWINGING THE THURIBLE full of incense, I remember that scent was so sharp and strong that I wrinkled my nose and sneezed, the smell of frankincense overpowering me. I moved closer to my mother;

the man in his white vestments scared me. He looked so old and so serious. Like if I didn't do what he told me I would receive much worse punishment than the scoldings my mother gave or the spankings my father gave.

I slid still closer to her on the pew, enjoying how I could slide on the polished wood. I might have turned it into a game, but my mother took my hand and held it tightly.

Her hand was warm and so much bigger and stronger than mine. She looked down at me, a thin smile on her face. I needed to be quiet—she had told me before we had left. I needed to behave. I bit my lip and nodded so she would know I knew what she wanted. Her smile became full and wide and she gave me a small nod before turning her attention back to the deacon with the old brass thurible.

My mother was so beautiful. I remember staring up at her and thinking there was nothing more beautiful in the world than my mother. She had light-brown skin and big brown eyes. Her black hair was swept up in the back and piled on top of her head. She wore a blue dress, worn, but the best she had. She sat with her spine straight, her eyes on the priests.

She felt so strong, so true, like nothing bad could ever happen to us just so long as my mother could go to Mass. She prayed all the time, for our health and well-being, for God to give her and my father another child.

I didn't know it then, but in that church as a three-year-old boy, I was experiencing faith. Faith in my mother.

She was smart and beautiful and could do anything.

Faith came easy. Faith came naturally. It has not been easy or natural since then.

"S<small>TART AT THE BEGINNING, AND DON'T LEAVE ANYTHING</small> out, Jesús."

Sister Dominga would say that to me when I came back to her orphanage with a black eye, a split lip, or a guilty look on my face. She had a knack for listening and would always seem to know when I was leaving something important out. She would stand there, her arms crossed, her lips pursed, her eyes relentless until I spilled the essential facts.

Start at the beginning, and don't leave anything out.

That was a long time ago, when I was a boy, when I was such a terrible mess. My family had been killed, I had been living on the streets, and was nearly beaten to death when Sister Dominga found me. She saved my life, she got me off the street, and eventually, she saved my soul.

Sister Dominga ran a small orphanage called *Orfanato de San Miguel Arcángel* (the Orphanage of Saint Michael the Archangel). It sat in Miguel Hidalgo, one of the sixteen boroughs of Mexico City. Just an old brick building behind a humble city church, the *Iglesia de San Miguel Arcángel* (the Church of Saint Michael the Archangel).

When she found me, nursed me back to health, heard my story, I was eleven years old. I was older than the kids they usually took in, and way too old to be adopted. So my role there was a bit different. Sister Dominga wanted me to act as a big brother to the other kids, watching over them, making sure they followed the rules. I saw my role a bit differently. I saw myself as their protector. I wanted to make sure no one ever did to them what had happened to me.

The one thing we didn't have any trouble with was my role as storyteller. There were anywhere from six to eight boys there at a time, and we all slept in the biggest room of the old building, beds lining all the walls. When it was time for lights out, I would read stories to the younger boys. I would first read them in Spanish, and then in English. Sister Dominga loved it that I knew English so well and thought I should pass it on to the other boys.

When I first got there I had this habit of reading the ending first. Sister Dominga would give me the books, something like Hansel and Gretel, or a Hardy Boys mystery. I would always skip ahead and read the ending before I sat down to read it to the boys. I wanted to know how it would end so I could do a better job of reading it. That's what I told Sister Dominga. But she knew better—I skipped to the end so I could brace myself for what was coming. It's just the kind of life I had lived.

And here, now, as I stand here trying to figure out how to tell my story, I would love to jump to the end. But I can still hear Sister Dominga telling me to start at the beginning and don't leave anything out.

I talked this over with JJ, my ghost friend, who's done this whole memoir thing before. I told him what Sister Dominga used to say and asked him what he thought. He looked me over with those intense blue-grey eyes of his and said, "Yeah, that works, as long as you leave the boring stuff out. Stick to the story you need to tell."

I have to tell this story. Not that I think my life is all that interesting. Maybe it is, I don't know, though. It's my life, so it's completely normal to me.

So, no skipping to the end. No leaving out anything important. JJ tells me it takes some guts to do this. I believe him. I hope that I am up to the challenge.

My name is Jesús Manuel Rivera Dominga. I was born without the Dominga on the end. I added it once I was an adult to honor Sister Dominga and what she meant to me.

This is for you, Sister Dominga.

Chapter 2

MY FATHER'S HANDS WERE BIG AND ROUGH AND HE ALWAYS had this musky, sweaty smell to him.

About the same time I was going to Mass with my mother, I would sometimes go to work with my father. It was a rarer thing, but sometimes when my mother couldn't watch me, he would take me.

My father was a short man with broad shoulders and a barrel chest. In the early days, he had a big mustache and often had several days' growth of beard.

He was a stone mason, working with heavy rock all day long. He was strong and quiet, and seemed to love his work.

The day I remember when I was very young was a Saturday. We were in *Naucalpan* (one of the boroughs of Mexico City) working on an outdoor patio in one of the big houses up on the hill. The house seemed like a castle to me, with big wooden doors, tall ceilings, and large paintings on the wall. We didn't go in, I only glimpsed these wonders from the outside, but it seemed like a magical place. I wondered who could possibly live there and have so many beautiful things.

My father was smoothing out sand in a wooden frame, getting ready to lay in the large pieces of flagstone.

"Papá?" I asked quietly. I knew he didn't like to be disturbed when he worked. My "job" there was to bring him things when he asked.

"Yes, Jesús. What is it?" he said in his thick English. My father almost always spoke to me in English. He wanted me to learn it well. To him it was a symbol of a better life.

"How did they get all that?" I asked, my gaze going to the window and the riches within.

He shrugged his broad shoulders and looked back to his work. He pulled the piece of wood across the uneven sand creating an area of flat, even sand that just begged to be played in, but I knew better.

I moved towards the window, it was the largest window I had ever seen, very wide and much taller than me. The sill of it was low enough that if I just moved one of the potted plants that rested there and jumped up, I would be able to see right into the house and get a better view.

My father grunted as he picked up a large piece of tan flagstone and moved it towards the flat sand. I looked at him and marveled at how strong he was, how big his arms were, at how the muscles in his neck bunched. The sight distracted me from my quest to see better into the house for a moment. It was clear to me then, there could be no one stronger in this world than my father.

After he got the piece of flagstone into the sand, I turned back to the window. It had a collection of cacti on it, some of them I had never seen. They were full of sharp needles, colorful flowers, and bright greens all in a row. I found one plant, a small barrel cactus, that I thought would be light enough for me to move. I reached up and started to move it towards the edge of the sill. It made a scraping noise and I turned and looked, but my father was intent, studying the assembled flagstones, looking for the next piece to lay.

I slid it farther, my arms stretched up above me. I just had to see fully into that house. As I got it to the edge of the sill, I realized it was heavier than I had thought. I tried to get a grip on the clay pot, but it was glazed in a bright blue and slick. Fear spiked through me as I realized the pot and large cactus was going to fall on my head.

"¡*Dios mío*!" my father cried, as one strong arm grabbed me and pulled me away, with his other hand he managed to get a grip on the lip of the pot. His hand arced down with the pot as he arrested its momentum, the sharp needles of the barrel cactus penetrating the skin of his arm. He set both the pot and me onto the ground and I saw the look of pain on his face.

"¡*Lo siento*!" I cried, telling him I was sorry.

"English," he said as he gritted his teeth and slowly pulled his arm away from the cactus, the barbs of the needles doing more damage as they pulled away from his skin.

"Sorry, Papá. I am most sorry," I said. "I wanted to see."

He nodded slowly as he plucked some of the larger needles out of his skin. The smaller hairlike ones, I knew from experience, were too small to come out and would bother him for a long time. Small droplets of blood formed where the large ones were pulled out. My stomach lurched and my heart pounded.

"Papá, I... Please..." I stammered.

He looked up at me and smiled. "No problem. Next time, you ask." He then grabbed me with his uninjured arm and lifted me so I could see into the house. The floor was made of glittering stone tiles, the inside door to the room was carved with a rearing horse. There was a colorful woven rug on the floor, and furniture made out of leather.

I gasped at the sight of it. Such wonders, such magic, I was sure wizards or princes lived there.

My father chuckled at my reaction, but put me down, put the cactus back, and said, "Enough."

He went back to his work, the pain of the injury I caused him seeming to be nothing at all.

Then I had faith in my father. Faith that he was strong enough to meet any challenge and that he could protect me from any danger.

THE STORIES I WAS TELLING SISTER DOMINGA HURT. NOT because they were bad stories or about bad things, but because they brought into sharp contrast the difficult things that were going to happen. These old, old memories of my childhood were not anything I had thought about in a long time. And, I think my ghostly form aided in this. JJ and I have discussed how the ghost's memory is better than the living. JJ said it has to do with the "meat" being gone and "not getting in the way anymore."

Whatever the case, the vividness of these memories as I told them was shocking.

"It's funny," I said aloud, "but as a ghost I can't smell at all. But as I sit here and talk about that pungent incense as I went to mass with my mother or the powerfully musky scent of my father as he labored, it is almost as if it's real. As if they aren't long, long gone." Again Sister Dominga visibly relaxed when I spoke to her, so I kept articulating my thoughts.

"I am so confused. But this seems to be helping, this

talking to you. So I will keep doing it, it is the least I can do after all you did for me." I felt some relief that I was able to help, even in a small way. Without thinking much about it, I moved my ghostly hands underneath Sister Dominga's head and summoned the "warmth."

It's hard for me to tell you what the warmth is. It is something Banquo, my ghostly mentor, taught JJ and me about. Actually, JJ used it to great effect in several situations, but I had never tried until now. It required that I be calm and clear and let go. Just be present. Just allow love to flow through my hands into Sister Dominga. At first it felt horribly awkward. How was holding my hands near her going to help? I was a ghost. I couldn't really help her. I couldn't even touch her. But then I felt the smallest sensation of warmth in my hands. It felt... Well, it was shocking at first. Temperature is another thing that ghosts don't experience, so feeling something akin to the heat of sunshine on my skin was surprising and delightful. I laughed and smiled, something that had been rare for me lately.

I moved closer, stepping into the bed, my ghostly form overlapping with it, so I stood right next to her. I put my right hand under her head and my left hand under her back where her heart was. I felt the warmth again flowing through me and into her. Sister Dominga took a deep breath and sighed. It was a small thing, but it made my heart sing. This was somehow easing her suffering, and for that I was grateful.

As I stood there, I thought about the warmth. It felt like it was coming from outside of me, like it wasn't a part of me, like it was from...

I cut the thought off. I wasn't ready to contemplate where the warmth came from. I was confused about the fact that I was still a ghost, that I was still stuck on Earth, that I hadn't heard the Call (it happens when a ghost moves on—more on this later). So I just relaxed and let the warmth flow and kept telling my story.

"So where were we?" I said. "We were talking about faith. About how as a child I had faith in my mother and faith in my father. But that simplicity of my early childhood didn't last all that long."

Chapter 3

NOW THAT I THINK OF IT, WAS IT REALLY "FAITH" THAT I had in my mother and father?

What is faith?

Doesn't it have to be devoid of proof to be truly faith? I had faith in my mother's faith, and had ample proof of how it made her stronger, how it kept her steady. I had faith in my father's strength, which was evident in nearly everything he did.

Was that faith? I think it was, but what happens to my faith when I see evidence that contradicts those views of my parents?

And maybe this is my essential issue: confronting the remains of a faith that has been proven to be unsound. I had great faith in what would happen when I died and... well... nothing of the sort happened. I am here. I am a ghost. I have not been taken home.

But back to my mother and father. As a child, I sort of had blinders on. My mother, while very religious, was also very superstitious—those things used to seem very different to me, but I am not so sure anymore. My father, while a hard worker, didn't make much money, desperately wanted a better life, and drank too much tequila. I, of course, was not aware of all this when I was three or four, but time and maturity has made it obvious.

"Come, Jesús, we must go now," my mother said. Her eyes were wide and she spoke rapidly.

"Where are we going?" I asked. I had been playing with some blocks, constructing what I thought would be a grand tower on the floor of our one-room house, while my mother cooked at the stove. Her brother, my uncle, had just been over, and they had talked in hushed tones.

"To church," she said, grabbing my hand and pulling me up. Her leg brushed against the colorful blocks and toppled my tower.

"No!" I cried, upset about my tower and not even thinking about church.

"I need my Jesús to go to church with me," she said, yanking my arm uncomfortably and crossing herself with her other hand.

I began to feel her desperation and started to cry. Something was wrong with my mother, something only church could fix. This trend became more pronounced as the years passed. My mother would have to go to church more and more, and if I wasn't in school, I would have to go with her.

My blocks forgotten, I kept glancing at my mother as she pulled me out the front door of our casita onto the narrow dirt road that led to it. She walked quickly, her eyes staring forward, her grip tight. She still wore her white kitchen apron over an old pale-yellow dress. There was a smudge of flower on her cheek—a white stain on her brown skin.

"Uncle Francisco?" I asked quietly as I tried to keep up with her.

"Yes," she said, sharply. "He... Uncle Fran has... well..." she stuttered and stammered for a few more strides before stopping and squatting in front of me. "He did something, Jesús. We must go light a candle and pray. Can you be my big man and help me?"

I nodded solemnly. I knew how to pray. My mother had often told me that Jesús Christ and I had the same name, so he had to listen when I prayed to him. "What should I pray for?" I asked.

Her brow briefly furrowed and moisture sprang to her eyes. "Pray for his soul," she said in a whisper. "Pray he finds his way."

My mother then stood up and started her fast walk towards our church. As we walked, I started mumbling a prayer, "Jesús, please watch over my Uncle Francisco. Please help him. Please help my mamá." I said it over and over while we walked to the church, while my mother lit a candle, while we kneeled before the altar, while we walked out of the church.

After it was over, my mother seemed calm and back to her normal happy self. I smiled because I knew my prayer had already worked.

SISTER DOMINGA LET OUT A DEEP, SHUDDERING SIGH. The warmth that I felt flowing through me, into her, was surprisingly strong. It felt sacred, it felt holy, it felt like communion.

For a moment after I had stopped talking, it was perfect—this bright sharp moment of beauty and peace. I had been lost in my story, deep in my past, and had forgotten about everything. That Sister Dominga was dying and that I was broken, my faith gone.

As the present tumbled onto me, the warmth fled, and I felt alone again.

When my faith was strong, I never felt like I was alone. There was always God there with me, watching over me, helping me. And the times when I didn't have faith, the feeling of aloneness has often been overwhelming. After my parents were killed... after the gang of boys I spent some time with, the Muchachos, left me for dead... and then there with Sister Dominga.

Pain crept back onto her face and I stepped back out of her bed. Right then the door opened and a nun entered. "How are we today, Sister?" she said.

She was short and round, wearing a simple white habit, consisting of a loose white dress, a white coif on her head, a wool belt, and her rosary beads hanging from the belt. Sister Helen. "Time to tend to you, dear. We must keep you comfortable." I moved farther back as she brought a basin with warm water and a sponge over to the table next to her bed. "You do look better," she commented as she looked at her face. Sister Dominga didn't look as good as when the warmth had been flowing into her, but she didn't look as bad as when I arrived.

I floated out of the room. I never stayed for her care. I couldn't bear to see how the most base of her physical needs were dealt with. Keeping her clean, changing her clothing and bed pads, feeding her... I couldn't watch.

So I left and contemplated my past and what I would tell Sister Dominga next.

UNCLE FRANCISCO ALWAYS HAD A READY SMILE AND A booming laugh. When he came to visit he always brought me a piece of *leche quemada*. It literally means "burnt milk," but it is a caramel candy with pecan halves on top. I loved them. Francisco was tall and lean and had lighter skin like my mother.

My mom and Uncle Francisco were *criollo*, of pure Spanish decent. My grandparents had immigrated to Mexico from Spain. My father was *mestizo* with a strong dose of Mayan. I, of course, had no idea what any of this meant as a child, but in Mexico lines were drawn between the criollo and the mestizo. The criollo tended to be more affluent, had a greater representation in government, and tended to have better jobs. As it seems to happen all over the world, many lines were drawn around race in my home country.

My mother's family were proud of their heritage and did not think my father was an appropriate mate for her. Not only because of his mixed blood, but because of his lack of an education and his simple trade. They thought him below her. They had basically disowned her when she married my father, and my mother had to give up a lot to be with him. She was used to nice things and enough money. Their early life together had little of each.

Uncle Francisco was my mother's only contact with her family. He would come around every month or so, give me my piece of *leche quemada*, talk to my mom, drink with my father. I loved his visits. He was full of amazing stories, wore fancy clothes, and had this thin, well-trimmed mustache that I found fascinating. And he would never speak in English. His Spanish was fluid and flowing, and oh so dramatic.

One day he came and shared tequila with my father. I didn't really know what it was then, but I knew the strong smell and I knew how it could change my father. "Juan, I have a job for you," Francisco said to my father, his long frame draped over one of our kitchen chairs. My father's face brightened. He had been home more lately, work being slow, and everyone seemed very serious about it. "I am redoing the courtyard in my restaurant, and I need a job done, such that will be talked about far and wide. I will spare no expense on materials, it will be the jewel of my establishment!"

My father nodded his head slowly, "Thank you, my brother, you can count on me."

Francisco's eyes narrowed and he leaned close to my father. I was on the floor not far away playing with a wooden truck and they were not paying attention to me. Francisco whispered to my father, but it was the kind of loud whisper that men that drank tequila often used. "I need someone I can trust, someone that can keep quiet."

My father nodded solemnly and filled their glasses with more tequila. "I am your man, Francisco." I saw a hunger in both men's eyes as they clinked their glasses and drank. My uncle's hunger I did not understand, but my father's I had an inkling of. It was the look he had when he so carefully practiced his English, and insisted I do the same. It was the hunger he had for a better life, the desperation he felt to prove himself worthy of my mother to her family.

At the moment, of course, the four-year-old me didn't understand this intellectually, but I could feel it.

I could feel change coming, and it scared me.

Chapter 4

THE DAY OUR LIVES TRULY CHANGED IS SO CLEAR TO ME. I remember dirt under my bare feet. Dry and fine, cool to the touch, the kind of dirt that fills your nose so that is all you can smell. I was four years old. This is where it all started.

I was standing there being inspected by adults. My father was there with his stubbly face and mustache and my mother with her bright brown eyes, wearing her best dress. There was another adult; a man in a clean, unwrinkled white suit with a red tie. He had a wide smile and very white teeth.

They were talking about me, but I didn't really understand what they wanted. It was adult talk. I just knew that I was the center of attention. I stood tall and smiled back at the man in the suit.

My father asked me to say hello. He said this to me in English. I looked at the man and said, "Hola, Señor. Buenos días."

My father frowned and shook his head. "English," he said. "Talk to Mr. Langold in English."

"Hello, Mr. Lan-gee," I couldn't manage the pronunciation of his last name. "How are you today?"

English and Spanish weren't that different to me then. Words were words. It wasn't until I grew older that I understood that the differences in languages go far beyond the words and reflect much of the cultures that created them.

The man squatted and said, "I am just fine, Jesús. How are you?" He spoke his words in English, slowly and carefully.

"¡Bien!" I said, clapping my hands together. My father gave me a look, so I added, "Fantastic," and everyone laughed.

My father and Señor Langold walked into our house and started talking. My mother came over and put her hand on my shoulder. She was shaking a little bit. I knew what was happening was important, I just didn't know why. I peered into the open door of our little house. It was made out of cinder blocks with a tin roof—a simple rectangle with one room.

I saw my father grab a bottle of Tequila. He took out two glasses and filled them, giving one to Señor Langold. They clinked their glasses and drank the amber liquid.

I stepped towards the door, but my mother caught my hand, pulling me away. "Want to go to the park?" she asked in Spanish. While my mother could speak English, she preferred her native tongue, and that is what we spoke when my father wasn't around.

The playground was a long walk away, but I loved the swing and eagerly agreed.

I looked back at the two men in the house. The bright sunshine made it hard for me to see them clearly, but I could see how my father looked at Señor Langold, and it made me uncomfortable. The look he gave Señor Langold was the kind of look I gave him—hanging on every word, eager to please, somehow innocent.

That look scared me.

I started to ask my mother, but she pulled me towards the park and my worries were soon forgotten.

I RARELY LEFT SISTER DOMINGA'S ROOM WHILE I SAT VIGIL. The only time I felt comfortable leaving was when Sister Helen was there tending to her.

When I left, I would mostly wander into the church. With its high vaulted ceilings, tall stained glass windows, altar, and statue of the crucifixion up front. It was in many ways your typical Catholic church. It was old, but so was Mexico City.

I could have wandered the halls of the little orphanage, or I could have gone outside and wandered the neighborhood, or I could have spent time in the rectory, or the quarters for the nuns and priests, but I didn't. I always ended up in the church, staring at the life-sized statue of Jesús Christ on the cross.

It was hallowed space, and even though I couldn't feel my faith, the space kept calling me. My questions kept taking me there.

"Why?" I asked the statue of Jesús. "Why haven't you come for me? Why am I still here?"

It was a Thursday evening and the church was deserted. I could feel the quiet that only an empty place of worship can hold, but it wasn't soothing. It bothered me profoundly.

"Why?" I asked again, my voice louder. I could feel my confusion slipping to anger. "I have believed. I have done my best to be a good person. *¿Por qué? ¿Por qué?*"

The statue with its crown of thorns, with its pierced hands and side, did not answer, did not move, did not provide me with the answers I sought. It was inert, a piece of painted wood, what was I expecting?

My gaze went up as I looked at the ceiling of the church and I caught a flash of movement and thought I heard a soft, mournful moan—or maybe laughter, I couldn't really tell. It was just a flash and then it was gone.

"Oh, my. Now you've done it," I heard a voice say behind me.

I whirled around and saw a man standing there. He looked like a Mayan native. He stood there wearing a plain white shift, with a deeply lined brown face, and the telltale transparency of a ghost. He gently moved his head back and forth.

"What have I done?" I asked, taking a step back.

"Disturbed the lurkers," he said, pointing his finger straight up towards the high arched ceiling.

"Lurkers?" I asked. I was more than a bit off balance. When I first arrived I was surprised not to see any other ghosts besides the woman in Sister Dominga's room. I thought a place like this would be filled with them, having offered comfort and solace to many. I figured ghosts would come here when they died. But I hadn't found any until now.

"They are spirits that are stuck," the man said and then pointed at me. "Kind of like you?"

I stood there and stared. First at the Mayan man and then up at the ceiling where I caught another glimpse of what now seemed to be ghosts.

"Who are you?" I asked.

"My name is Yochi."

"What are you doing here?"

"What do you mean?" he asked, looking around the church.

"This is a Catholic church, you're dressed in traditional garb. You don't seem to belong."

He smiled. "This was not always the conqueror's church. Once my people worshiped on this ground."

When he smiled I saw missing teeth, and I felt my heart lighten in a strange way. For a moment, everything seemed OK.

"See, Jesús, all is not so bleak as you imagined." With a gentle pop he was gone.

I stood there for a moment looking around, confused, and then said, "Wait! How did you know my name?" I thought I heard laughter echoing among the rafters of the church and I felt my heart lighten. But then I heard a noise from above and caught movement up there again. A chill went down my spine and I headed back to Sister Dominga's room. I wasn't ready to meet the "lurkers," whatever they were.

Chapter 5

AFTER THAT FIRST MEETING WITH SEÑOR LANGOLD, OUR lives began to change. My father, who had been working as a mason, started doing something else. When he came home with his clean shaven face and his white shirt buttoned to the top, I asked him what he did all day.

"Business," he said to me. I looked at him puzzled, trying to come up with an appropriate question, but before I could, he asked, "What did you do today?"

"*Escuela*," I said, but my father frowned and I searched my memory. Keeping English and Spanish nouns separate was hard. I bit my lip until I remembered. "School! And play!"

My father smiled and laughed, pulling me into his lap and giving me a hug. My fingers found his upper lip, which was now bare. It scared me the first time I saw him without a mustache, and I still didn't like it. My fingers rubbed against the roughness of the day's stubble.

Soon we moved to a house with a separate bedroom, a real kitchen, and a bathroom. My mother and father seemed very happy about it, so I was happy about it. It was close to a much bigger park, so that was what counted to me. Not long after we moved, my father started wearing a tie, and coming home from "business" later, often missing the noontime meal and siesta. I missed him.

My mother seemed happy, though. She started having new dresses to wear, and had friends over. They gathered in the kitchen in a tight clump, drank sangria, and made tamales while laughing and talking. I don't know exactly what they were talking about, but it seemed to be about their husbands. I didn't understand all their words, but it made me feel a bit scared. I did know that they would never talk like that with their husbands present.

My mother decided that I would be her *vendedor*, or salesman. She dressed me in new clean clothes and we walked up the hill to a much nicer neighborhood where the houses were several stories high with red clay shingles and carved wooden doors.

She had a rusty, squeaking cart she pulled, loaded with tamales. When we found a good house, she gave me a basket with a dozen of them and sent me to the door. We had practiced what I should say.

"Hello, señorita," I would say in Spanish. "Fresh tamales, the best in town. I helped make them myself." I would then smile as big as I could and hold the basket forth. My mother would put fresh rosemary in the basket from our garden, so the scent of the proffered basket was enticing.

Sometimes they would slam the door, sometimes they would smile down at me and politely say, "No, thank you," and sometimes they would ask how much. When that happened, my mother would walk forward and I would watch in awe at the negotiation. Just like my mother would do at the market, but this time she was the one saying how hard she had worked and what a struggle it was to feed her darling boy.

I liked it when she referred to me as her "darling boy." When our sales went well, my mother would buy me an ice cream on the way home.

While we lived in that house, which was still small, I think we were at our happiest. To my parents, having some space and a garden and a separate kitchen was such a luxury. To me, their happiness fed directly into mine.

I think we lived there for about a year. It couldn't have been much longer, because everything changed on my fifth birthday.

SISTER DOMINGA KNEW MANY OF THE STORIES THAT I WAS telling her, but they helped her so I kept telling them. Her breathing would slow, her face would relax, and sometimes she would let out a sigh.

I was eager to come to the point in the story where Sister Dominga entered my life. I wanted to tell her how much she meant to me, how she had changed my life, but I didn't. I started at the beginning and didn't leave anything out.

Besides, there was another reason to tell the tales. As I spoke them I felt that other ghost near. I never saw her, but I could feel her. She was listening. It was my hope that the telling would call her forth and I could find out why she called Sister Dominga her grandmother.

I paced around the small room. Sister Dominga and her bed dominated it. Her face was so changed from when I met her, even from the last time I had seen her. She was wasting away, slowly dying, her face far past gaunt. She was old. I'm not sure how old, but I would say at least seventy-five.

Her long hair—which I had rarely seen—was wisps of white forming a chaotic halo around her head. She had been difficult to look at when I first got there, but I was beginning to get used to it.

I kept expecting to see her soul separate from the body that clearly was no longer serving her. I kept expecting her ghostly form to start talking to me.

Other than the bed, the little room held a small dresser, a wooden desk, a window, and a large crucifix.

I stopped in front of it and looked at the image, the man, my namesake, nailed to the cross. I had been taught he died for our sins, that he had a place for the faithful, that heaven awaited us.

I crossed my arms and stared. The symbols of my faith now seemed to taunt me. This wasn't heaven I was in. And, while I hadn't been perfect, I had done my best. I had lived the most righteous life I could.

Even my name taunted me. Jesús.

In Tucson, among my ghostly friends up there, I make a big deal about the pronunciation of my name. I insist that they pronounce it *Hey-Zues*, not *Gee-Zus*. My explanation was I didn't want to be confused with the guy on the cross. But, the problem is, down in Mexico, *Hey-Zues* is the way Jesús is pronounced. Whether you are some street urchin or the son of God.

I know my mother named me Jesús hoping, even when I was a baby, that I would become a priest. She would have hated the life I led.

I was about to go back to Sister Dominga when I felt something. It wasn't much, just a chill running down my left side. I turned quickly, hoping it was the mysterious female ghost, but instead I was greeted by a gape-toothed grin. Yochi.

"She can hear you," he said, nodding towards Sister Dominga.

I nodded in agreement. What he said didn't make me glad. I wasn't surprised. Her physical reaction led me to believe she could hear me on some level.

"So can that one," he said, nodding towards the crucifix.

"What? How do you know?"

"Open heart always heard," he said with a grin. I turned to look at the crucifix, and when I turned back, the little man was gone. Could Jesús Christ hear me? Was he witness to my pain and doubt? To my sorrow and uncertainty?

I shook my head, trying to clear it of all those heady thoughts. They really didn't have a place here. I went back to the bed and started telling Sister Dominga more stories.

Chapter 6

WHEN SOMEONE IS ON THEIR DEATHBED, LIKE SISTER Dominga was, the first question that comes up is usually: what happened? We ask this as if our mortality is a surprise, something we didn't expect or plan for. She's dying. But why?

This was the first question I asked myself when I got back to her. I found her in her room unconscious, her face thin and drawn, her eyes closed. But I wasn't surprised. I had felt something drawing me back down this way.

I was eleven when Sister Dominga found me. I remember her seeming so old, certainly older than my mother. She must have been in her mid-forties. That was almost thirty years ago, no real reason to be surprised that she was dying.

I can imagine the conversation she had with the doctor.

"I am sorry, Sister," the doctor would have said. "There is nothing more we can do for you medically."

Her face, still a bit round then, would have briefly fallen before she took a deep breath, nodded once, and said, "Good. It is time I go home."

Sister Dominga was unshakable in her faith. Sister

Dominga was my rock, my anchor. I knew that if I just told her about the crisis I was going through she would give me one of those serious side-glances and say just the right thing.

But Sister Dominga was done talking. She was going home.

As the days wore on, as Sister Helen tended to her, as Father Finnegan visited her, as the nurse came daily and checked on her, I kept listening for a diagnosis. I kept wanting to know why. But no one said much. They treated Sister Dominga with care and tenderness, but no one really talked in her presence. And I understood that too. Sister Dominga valued silence. She had done many silent retreats in her time at the church.

One day when I had had enough of it, I waited until Sister Helen was there and flew down to the cathedral. Since I had first encountered Yochi, I hadn't gone there much. The mystery of the lurkers kept me away.

When I got down there, I came up short. Yochi was there, as I was hoping, but next to him was Banquo. Their heads were close together and they seemed to be having an intense conversation. I couldn't hear their words, but judging from their expressions it was something serious.

I stood there for a minute watching them. I was mostly raised in a church by nuns, it was a foreign thing for me to interrupt my elders. At one point both Banquo and Yochi looked up at the ceiling, which I had been pointedly avoiding.

I saw a flash of movement and looked back down. I didn't really want to know what was going on. I was there for Sister Dominga, not to deal with mysterious ghosts lurking in the ceiling of the church.

After a time, the conversation ended and Yochi disappeared with a soft pop. Banquo walked over to me.

"How are you?" he asked. His face was full of compassion, which just made it clear to me how poorly I was doing. I had been in Mexico City for about a week and hadn't seen Banquo during that time.

I shrugged my shoulders.

He nodded and gently put his hand on my arm. He did it right, his hand modulated to match my ghostly form so I could feel him. He guided me to the center of the church and he looked straight up. "You need to do something about this."

Banquo was my teacher. He had found me in the morgue in Tucson, he had taught me how to stay out of the bardo (your own personal hell), how to cut the cord that had tied me to my dead body, and most everything else I knew about being a ghost. He was a mentor and a father figure. I held him in the highest respect.

"No way, man!" I exclaimed. He had caught me off guard.

Banquo leveled his penetrating gaze at me. When he looked at you like that, he was doing more than looking. He was being "Aware" of you, sensing your feelings, trying to understand you. It's really not that different than the look Sister Dominga gave me when I was a kid and just as uncomfortable.

"I am here for Sister Dominga," I said.

He nodded. "I know, and you know that she has some time left."

"Yeah," I said. I knew that she did. Whatever was happening was happening slowly. It didn't feel like she was going to die anytime soon.

"And you need something to do."

I shook my head. "I need answers, Banquo. I need to understand why I am still here, why I am still a ghost."

Banquo smiled gently. "And this will help." He again looked up at the ceiling of the cathedral. "I can feel it."

Banquo just stood there, his grey eyes unwavering, his arms folded and resting on his large stomach. This "feeling" he talked about is better described as "Awareness." Ghosts are much more aware of intangible things than the living are. With the weight and the density of the body gone, our ability to be "Aware" grows.

Banquo had started teaching JJ and I about this before I left for Mexico City. Awareness of Self, Awareness of Others, Awareness of All. Those are the threefold lessons of Awareness.

So, Banquo's "feeling" was based on his finely honed sense of Awareness. Banquo always seemed to know things.

I sighed and nodded, letting myself look up at the church's ceiling. It wasn't that fancy... well, for this neighborhood in Mexico City it was, but on the scale of Catholic churches, not so much. The beams were large, made out of polished wood, supporting the smooth finish of the ceiling. It was plain and elegant and strong.

I looked around, there were a few parishioners sitting or kneeling in pews. I could hear low tones coming from one of the confessionals, an old lady with long grey hair was lighting a candle and mumbling prayers.

"It's odd that there aren't any ghosts here," I said. "I would think it would be full of them."

"Exactly!" Banquo said, thumping me on the back.

I then looked back up at the ceiling and glimpsed movement. It wasn't much, just the briefest of flashes. Not a ghostly form that I could tell. I relaxed and let myself feel, become Aware of what was up there. My teacher was here, and that calmed me, helped me remember what he had taught.

I began to hear a murmuring, like voices carried on the wind. The tone of it was mixed, happy and sad woven together into a jumbled whole. I felt a chill go down my spine and looked back at Banquo.

"They... they are up there. It's not right."

He nodded grimly.

I rubbed at my ghostly mustache. A gesture I had when I was alive, and one I developed after death once I'd gotten good at managing my ghostly form. "Um... This might be a silly question...."

Banquo smiled and said, "Go ahead."

"Ahh... why don't you and Yochi take care of this? Why do you need me?" I shuffled my feet. I didn't want to question him, but I felt strongly my place was with Sister Dominga.

"Both Yochi and I have other responsibilities, and you need this."

I sighed. "OK, how do I do this?"

Banquo smiled and nodded. "Use your Awareness, you'll find your way." And with a pop, he was gone.

Chapter 7

I COULD SMELL THE ALCOHOL ON SEÑOR LANGOLD'S breath. I wrinkled my nose in a gesture that was probably considered rude, but I was five and it was my birthday. He had come close when he handed me a present, his breath hot, his smile big, his teeth straight and white. "For Juan's little man," he said, far too loudly. I could see the red tracing of capillaries in his bloodshot eyes. When he sat back down on a lawn chair, he put his arm around my father and said, "Family is everything."

There was a lot that was happening at the time that I didn't see, or if I did see it, I didn't understand it. For example, I saw my mother cross her arms in front of her and lean away from my father when Señor Langold put his arm around my father. I saw the silly smile on my father's face at the older man's affection. I had also smelled the tequila on my father's breath earlier.

Señor Langold and he seemed to always drink tequila when they were over at our house.

I carefully opened the package, doing my best not to rip the paper. It was a silvery color and smooth and beautiful. I knew my mother would find a use for it. Señor Langold said, "Just rip it open, boy." Those seated around our backyard echoed this sentiment.

I didn't, though. I slowly worked the tape and got the paper off in a single piece and folded it up and set it aside like it was a prize, before turning my attention to the package. It was just a rectangular cardboard box that fit comfortably on my lap. No labeling or hint of what was inside. I paused, feeling the weight of it, shaking it gently. "He is careful, Juan," Señor Langold said to my father, his voice too loud. "He thinks before he acts... that is good."

I cut the tape holding the box closed with my thumbnail and carefully opened the box. I was excited to see what it was; I knew that Señor Langold was rich. I was also nervous; there was something about him that I didn't like. Didn't trust. His smile seemed to come too quickly. His appearance was always perfect. His eyes often a bit too wide.

Shortly after he first appeared and my father started working for him, I asked my mother about it. My father had been an *obrero*, a simple laborer, a mason. He had been like many of the men in our old neighborhood.

"He was working at your Uncle Francisco's fancy restaurant in Miguel Hidalgo, repairing some tile," my mother said. "Señor Langold was having lunch and choked on a piece of pork. Your father slapped him on the back, saved his life. He says we are family now." The look on my mother's face was complicated, more than I could understand at the time. What I could tell was that she wasn't entirely happy about it.

When I opened the box, I gasped. It was black and beautiful and the boy in me loved it. I pulled it out and held it gently in my hand. It was a plastic gun, the kind the police used in the shows on our new TV. The smile that spread across my face didn't last long. My mother surged up from her seat, ripped the toy gun out of my hand, and went into the house with it.

My father spoke rapid apologies to Señor Langold before rushing after my mother.

Something changed that day. It took another few years before it all played out.

As a rule, ghosts seem to like roofs. You don't have to worry about getting in the way of the living, the weather is no longer a concern, and the views are better up there.

When Sister Helen would come to tend to Sister Dominga, one of the places I would retreat to would be the roof. Not the cross at the apex of the church, but the peak of the clay-shingled, steeply inclined roof. I would sit there and watch our corner of Mexico City go by. Kids playing in the orphanage's tiny yard, cars on the streets, people moving through their lives blissfully unaware of me.

The tough part of this "free" time was that I could think. And my thoughts kept careening back to my current state— a Catholic ghost.

And in some ways, my quandary seemed to be the quandary of the Mexican people. Spaniards and Indians, Catholics and indigenous cultures. We are a mix of this and lean one way or the other depending on the circumstances.

Take *Dia de los Muertos*—Day of the Dead. It takes place on November 1st and 2nd in conjunction with the Catholic holidays of All Saints' Day and All Souls' Day, but it is linked backed to an Aztec festival dedicated to the goddess Mictecacihuatl, where for thousands of years our people came together and celebrated their ancestors.

The two celebrations are superimposed over each other. One European in its origins, the other native. One more "civilized," the other more "primitive."

And I think I feel that. This civilized side, and this primal side. They sometimes work well together and sometimes they seem to be at war.

My thoughts drifted to Yochi. I wondered how he reconciled being a ghost in a building that houses a religion that has, to a large extent, supplanted his. I was gathering myself to go look for him when he appeared with a "pop."

"Well," he began without preamble, "I don't try to reconcile it. I am what I am. The church is what it is. I exist and so does it. What is there to reconcile?"

I found myself accepting the oddity of the conversation. Banquo had never done something like this, but with my knowledge of Awareness, it was certainly possible.

"But my faith... It doesn't speak of ghosts, it doesn't explain my state."

"When you go outside and see a storm brewing, do you believe the weatherman that it will be a sunny day, or do you believe your own eyes and nose and know that it is going to rain?"

"Are you saying that since I am a ghost, my faith is wrong?"

Yochi smiled and shook his head. "I am saying that what is, is. That when what you are experiencing contradicts what you were told, either you are perceiving incorrectly or what you were told was wrong."

This interchange I found both very confusing and very comforting. I didn't know how to make sense of what he was saying to me, but the fact that an older, wiser ghost was taking the time to console me gave me hope.

"You are what you are, Jesús. Believe what you believe." With a small nod of his head and a "pop," Yochi was gone.

I shook my head and smiled, looking back down on the busy street below. I tried to apply what he had just told me. "I am a ghost," I said quietly. "I believe in a religion that doesn't believe in me."

Whenever I was away from Sister Dominga, a piece of me stayed with her. Well, not literally, but a piece of my Awareness. I felt a shift and knew that Sister Helen had left. It was time to go back and continue my story.

AFTER MY FIFTH BIRTHDAY PARTY AND SEÑOR LANGOLD'S gift of a toy gun, things changed rapidly.

My mother and father began to have loud fights, the sounds of passionate Spanish echoing through our house as I hid in my room.

My father started being gone more and more, and my mother became depressed.

At five, I didn't fully understand what was happening, not in terms of who and what. But I did fully perceive what was going on emotionally. My parents were mad at each other and unhappy, and it all revolved around Señor Langold.

Since the first sign of trouble that was clear to me was that toy gun, I began to worry that what was going on was my fault. That I had somehow caused it. That if I hadn't been so delighted in the gift, my mother would still love my father and we would be happy.

I began to long for the days when my father worked with his hands and had his mustache. I missed our one-room shack. I began to hate seeing my mother in her fancy dresses. At first they had made her so happy, now she was so sad.

We soon moved up the hill to one of those big houses we used to sell tamales to, and for a few weeks I had hope.

My mother sat me down on my bed to tell me about the move. The bedspread had a cartoon mouse with a cape on. Mighty Mouse. My mother had bought it for me after we got our television and I fell in love with the show. When my parents would fight, I would hide under it and pretend I was on adventures with the superhero mouse.

"We are moving," she began, a smile on her lips.

I looked at her seriously. The last time we moved things had gotten better and then much worse. "Why?" I asked.

"Your father is an important man now. He needs a house that properly reflects his status."

I nodded. Important people had big houses, everyone knew that.

"And the movers will be coming next week. I need you to be a big man and help out."

I nodded gravely. If people were being hired to help move us then my father was truly important. I was determined not to let him down.

She nodded and stood up, smoothing out her skirt. It was white with blue flowers on it. "Some boxes will be delivered tomorrow. I want you to pack up your toys this weekend."

I nodded, and as she left I said, "Mamá?"

She turned back to me, leaning against the doorframe. "What is it, Jesús?"

"What does Papá do?" I knew that he worked for Señor Langold and did something terribly important, but I didn't understand what it was.

She blinked rapidly and bit her lip. "He's a business-man," she said, her voice tight. She turned and left, ending the conversation.

It was the same answer they had given to me before, and the way she said it this time, it made my belly hurt.

Chapter 8

PARENTS LIE TO CHILDREN. I AM SURE THEY HAVE GOOD reason, and not having been a parent it is not for me to criticize. But I can tell you that as a child, I didn't like being lied to. Sometimes when your parents lie to you, you know it right away. It feels unsafe, as if the ground were moving beneath your feet. But when you find out a lie that your parents told you long after, one on which you built up your confidence in them, well... the ground just doesn't move beneath your feet; your metaphorical world starts tumbling down around you.

I used to love to play hide and seek, especially after we moved to the big house on the hill with its two floors and many rooms. I would do it with anyone, anytime, anywhere. I liked the feeling of being in a small confined space, of hearing the frustrated seeker pass by me again and again. I felt like I had a superpower, like Mighty Mouse, and I was invisible, which is why they couldn't find me. And I loved that feeling of being invisible.

That feeling—being invisible, unnoticeable—would soon play an important part in my survival. It's odd how the things we learn when we are very young often reverberate throughout our lives.

And that feeling is one that I now feel most of the time as a ghost. I am literally invisible to the living around me. And it is not a feeling that I dislike. If I can't be seen, I can't be hurt. But that sensation that came with my imagined invisibility is one that I remember distinctly as a child. It was like an invisible shield that I was projecting, something I was doing with my mind so that it was difficult to see me. That sensation made it feel real to me.

Anyway, when I wanted to feel that feeling and I couldn't find anyone to play with me, I would play at being invisible on my own. I was growing curious about what my parents did when I was not around... what they were like, who they were. I was about six and we had been up on the house on the hill for a year or so. That house had many marvelous places to hide.

It was another form of hide and seek. I would "hide" and "seek" out others, and try to do it without them noticing.

We had a sitting room that my mother had filled with beautiful furniture. I approached from the hallway that led to the stairs and heard their low voices. I couldn't hear what they were saying, but I could hear the tone—serious and urgent.

My mother got up, saying something about getting more wine. My father was slumped on the couch; it was upholstered in a brown fabric with copper tacks holding it down at the edges and polished wooden feet.

I could barely see his head, so I moved low and quiet across the tan tile floor and got behind the couch. I could hear cupboards opening in the kitchen and my father letting out a weary sigh. I couldn't fit under the couch, but I put my arm, a leg, and as much of my torso as I could squeeze in under it. In my boy's mind, I thought the less of me visible, the more invisible I could be.

From under the couch I saw my mother walk back into the room. She was wearing shiny black shoes with heels, a piece of jewelry with blue stones around her ankle. She sat on the couch and I could hear the pouring of wine.

"What are we going to do?" she asked. Her voice was low, but I heard her clearly.

"There is nothing we can do," my father said. He sounded defeated, which was strongly at odds with the faith I had in his strength and power.

"But..." my mother said, sounding scared. "There must be some way out."

My father laughed. It was a dry snort, only the beginnings of a laugh and ended up sounding choked. I began wishing I wasn't there. They didn't want me to hear this and I suddenly didn't want to hear it either. "One does not leave the cartel," he said. "Ever."

I, of course, knew what the cartel was. Even at six years old I knew, and the knowledge that my father worked for them was like a slap in the face. I almost cried out.

I could see both of their feet underneath the couch. My father was leaning forward, putting weight on his feet, as if ready to spring into action. One of my mother's feet twitched nervously, the heel coming up and then tapping down on the tile.

"I wish you had never saved Señor Langold's life," my mother said quietly. "I wish we still lived in our little casita. I would give all of this up for..."

"That man would have murdered Señor Langold, right

there in the middle of Francisco's restaurant. What was I to do?"

They had told me Señor Langold was choking and my father had slapped him on the back. At first I was confused by the lie. My father had been a hero. He had protected Señor Langold from a bad man.

"You have a good heart, Juan. You did the right thing. I just wish..."

"That he hadn't died?" my father asked, loudly. I bit my lip hard to keep myself from crying out. "That I hadn't hit him so hard? That his head had bounced off of soft carpet instead of hard tile? That Langold hadn't taken care of the police and brought me into the cartel? That..." My father's voice ended in a strangled sob and I felt my heart break.

"Hush," she said in a whisper. "You'll wake Jesús." My mother sighed and I heard her pouring more wine in her glass. She still went to church a lot, but she had taken to drinking a lot, too.

"I didn't mean to kill him. I didn't mean for any of this to happen."

My parents kept talking, but I wasn't listening anymore. I was putting every ounce of energy I had to making myself invisible. My heart was pounding so loudly that I was sure that they could hear it, I was sure that they would find me out.

When my parents finally went into the kitchen together, I snuck upstairs as quietly as a mouse and crawled under my covers, pulling them over my head.

Chapter 9

THE SUN WAS COMING UP, PEAKING THROUGH THE BLUE curtains of Sister Dominga's room. I moved to it and gazed outside. I didn't want to keep telling the story, despite the benefit to Sister Dominga. We were headed into dark territory, and even though I had spent years trying to heal the scars from that time, I was reticent to venture there again.

Outside, the neighborhood was starting to wake. The corner grocer was opening up, unlocking the metal security door and getting ready for business. A few cars drove down the narrow street and a couple of laborers strode purposefully towards their jobs.

They made me think of my father. The way he was before everything changed. Intellectually, I find regret to be a waste of an emotion, but right then it was heavy upon me, and mere thoughts could not banish it.

"What happened then?" I heard a voice ask. The voice was female and she spoke softly, but there was a hardness or maybe worldliness to it.

Shocked, I spun and saw her. The ghost that had called

Sister Dominga Grandmother. Her eyes still unnerved me—they were the pale blue you see reflected in icebergs. She had a black shirt on her slim form with her arms bare, a tattoo of a running lynx decorating her right shoulder. That told me something. You don't see a lot of bare skin with ghosts, it's hard to do. She must have mastery over her ghostly form; it was crisp and only slightly transparent. The tattoo was in black and greys, but so vivid I expected it to move.

I looked at my own form and found I was a wispy mess. I had been lost up here alone in Sister Dominga's room, and had let my discipline go. It's one of the essential lessons Banquo taught us: Form matters. A sloppy looking ghost is a sloppy thinking ghost. It's kind of the same as the living bathing and wearing clean clothes. Too much time not looking after yourself takes a toll on you mentally.

"Umm..." I stammered, as I looked up from my firmed up ghostly form back into those eyes.

"Your father, did he extract himself from the cartel?" She spoke to me in Spanish, and her voice had an accent. She sounded a little like someone who had learned Spanish in the States, but I couldn't quite place the accent.

"No, he didn't," I said, watching her carefully. I had questions I wanted to ask her, but I didn't. I was afraid she would disappear again. I thought of her as this wild animal and that any sudden move might spook her.

"Well... what happened? Grandmother and I like hearing your story."

"How... how can she be your grandmother?" I asked.

Her mouth opened as if to speak and just then the door to Sister Dominga's room opened and Sister Helen came bustling in. "Good morning, Sister," she said. "It looks like God has blessed us with a beautiful day."

With a pop, the other ghost was gone and I flew myself up to the roof.

MY LIFE CHANGED AFTER THAT NIGHT WHEN I HEARD MY parents talk about the cartel—fear became my companion.

Up until then I had had faith in my father's strength and my mother's piety, and a very innocent faith in a God I didn't really know. After that, I feared that my mother's praying and my father's strength would not be enough, so I was left with the God I didn't really know.

I began asking my mother to take me to Mass. This pleased her to no end, but she didn't really know the cause. I kept the secret of what I had heard, and they kept up the lie. My father was a "business" man. But of course, supplying drugs to the gringos up north was a huge business. I didn't really understand that then, but I did know that the cartels were something of a boogey man—a great, undefined evil that had spread its tentacles throughout our society.

There were often stories of people being hurt, or worse yet, killed because of the cartels. When I was very young, when we lived at our dirt-floored, one-room house, I remember all of us dressing in black and walking to church for the funeral of one of our neighbors. He had stood up against the cartel. They had shot him down in the street.

I feared for my family, I feared for myself. I prayed hard.

"Mamá?" I asked quietly one day after we had left the church. The one we went to then was a beautiful white church, Assumption of the Blessed Virgin Mary Church, with a tall clock tower and an even taller bell tower. When we had left our little one-room house with the tin roof, we had left our odd round church with the grade school behind it and moved to a bigger, nicer, richer church.

This church was a thirty-minute walk away from our house. There was one half that distance, but it was not as beautiful as our new church.

"Yes, Jesús," she said. I remember her red lips and the smell of rose water she had put on that day.

"If I pray hard enough and long enough, will God answer my prayer?" I knew that not all prayers were answered. People, so many people, were suffering, and I didn't think it was just the ones that didn't pray.

My mother stopped and squatted down facing me. A frown formed on her beautiful face. "What is it that you pray so hard for?"

I licked my lips and thought hard. I couldn't really tell her what I had overheard, but maybe I could tell her something. "I wish we could go back to our little house. When Papá had his mustache and worked with stone and I got to help. When..." I looked away, my face, I am sure, betraying the fear I had been trying to hide.

Moments ticked by as I studied my shoes, my heart pounding in my chest. I was sure that I had given away too much, that she would know that I knew, that I would be punished for playing my invisibility game with them.

My mother made a strange noise, deep in her throat, like a scared animal. She drew me into a hug and squeezed so hard I was afraid she would hurt me. "I pray for this too," she whispered, a shudder going through her body. She let go of me and pulled my chin up with her hand. I could see tears floating in her brown eyes, but not yet escaping. "Let's go back to church, you and I," she said, her voice growing strong. "We will pray together for this."

I was surprised. My mother who loved her big garden and her fancy dresses and her beautiful kitchen was going to pray for a life that had seemed too small for her. She held my hand tightly as we went back to the church.

The fear I was feeling doubled that day. My mother was more scared than I was about my father and the cartel.

Chapter 10

I KNEW I HAD THE OTHER GHOST HOOKED. SHE HAD BEEN listening as I told stories to Sister Dominga and now she had to know more. This surprised me and pleased me. I think, like most people, my life seems entirely normal to me—it's my life, after all. I felt a distinct pleasure that she found it interesting.

After Sister Helen was finished, I went back to the room and sat with Sister Dominga, my hands under her head and back letting the warmth flow, but I didn't start my story back up.

I could see that the warmth eased her pain, but not as much as it did when I told her stories. So, instead of telling stories of my past, I started recounting episodes of Mighty Mouse, a cartoon I watched when I was a child and we lived in the big house and had the incredible luxury of a TV.

I liked Mighty Mouse because he was brave and strong, and yet so small. As a boy, I was small for my age, and most everyone in the world was bigger than me. I also liked the show because it made me laugh. He had his yellow tights and red cape, they sang silly things in serious voices (like

Mighty Mouse singing, "Here I come to save the day!"), and whenever he did something amazing, the voice telling the story said, "What a mouse!"

Even though what I was telling Sister Dominga was silly, it still seemed to bring her some relief, so I didn't feel bad about stopping my story.

As I did this, I extended my sense of Awareness and I could feel her, the other ghost. At first my proverbial heart skipped a beat—the presence I felt was right behind the large crucifix that hung on the wall. I remembered what Yochi had said about being heard in regards to the crucifix, *open heart always heard*. I stopped talking in mid-sentence dumbfounded. Was God there listening? What kind of fool was I to doubt my faith?

But a moment later, I realized the presence behind the crucifix was the ghost who called Sister Dominga Grand-mother. This was where she hid when she listened to my stories. I felt the fool, and even though I was dead, my cheeks blushed brightly.

I took a deep ghostly breath and pushed that silliness away. If God was listening, then of course, I wouldn't be able to feel His presence in a single location. God was every-where. And if God was everywhere, why hadn't he taken me home yet?

My embarrassment twisted into anger, and I heard Sister Dominga groan. The warmth had stopped, and looking at her, I could see the pain growing on her face. I was now hurting her, not helping her. I couldn't bring my pain, my doubt to her.

I stepped back and saw her face relax noticeably. Not as much as when I was clear and the warmth is flowing, but better than when I was full of doubt.

"Don't follow me," I said in the direction of the crucifix and flew straight up to the roof. When I had been telling Mighty Mouse stories, I had been trying to goad her into making her presence known. But when I told her not to follow me, I was serious. While the mystery of her intrigued me, I was in no mood.

Except for those early years, I was never a wide-eyed innocent when it came to religion and faith. We are getting to the point in my story where it will become clear why. But I had found, with Sister Dominga's help, a practical and realistic way to be in the world, and faith was a large part of it.

And there, up on the flat roof of the nunnery, as a ghost, I had lost it. The Call had not come to me, nor had the bardo. The latter really confused me. I was so upset, and yet the bardo didn't come calling either.

JJ and Banquo have talked much about the bardo. The term comes from Buddhism and refers to a hellish place that many ghosts descend into. They are the ones that are gape-jawed and appear to be in great pain—kind of the classic view of the wispy, tortured ghost. The bardo is one's own personal hell where you face your fears and doubts.

So, any rational ghost would be glad the bardo didn't come calling for them. But right then I was a little less than rational and felt disappointment that God didn't seem to want me and neither did the bardo. That I was stuck in this ghostly world with no way out. I had done what I thought needed to be done—brought my killer to justice—so why was I still a ghost? Why was I still here? What kind of punishment was this?

"Are you OK?" a voice asked. The voice was gentle and

light, like a spring breeze. She spoke in Spanish with her odd accent.

I looked, and there was the mystery ghost, her face betraying deep concern.

My ghostly form was wispy again, and I tightened it up. Something Banquo called "getting dressed." I certainly didn't want her to see me like this.

"Yeah, fine," I answered, the anger in my voice obvious. I answered her in English. Not really intentionally, but something told me she would be more comfortable with that language.

I saw the smallest glimpse of a smile on her face as she nodded. "But, you are not fine," she said, switching to English. In that language she spoke with a mild accent also, and because of the odd nasally inflections, I doubted that English was her first language.

I just stood there blinking. I wasn't fine, but I certainly didn't want to say it. I'm not sure why, but saying it out loud would somehow make it more real. Bigger. Harder to deal with.

"Your stories help her and help you. Maybe you should stop talking about mice and tell your story."

I nodded. She was right, I knew it. It was the only thing that was helping me keep it together. There had been so many questions that I had had for this ghost, but I was too much of a mess.

I flew back down to Sister Dominga's bedside and started the warmth. The other ghost joined me and stood in front of the crucifix this time. A dim part of me was pleased at the progress.

I looked at her and she nodded at me encouragingly.

I looked down at Sister Dominga's face and resumed my story.

Chapter 11

JJ WARNED ME OF THIS. HE TOLD ME THERE WOULD BE parts of my story that I didn't want to tell, and that those parts were often the most important. And as I think on it, this may be a part of my story you don't want to hear. Seeing my past clearly, knowing who I am now, where my life has taken me, this all seems inevitable. It had been almost two years since my mother and I had prayed for a simpler life, but nothing had really changed. As an eight-year-old child, this didn't seem inevitable or fate or anything like that. It just seemed violent, and horrible, and cruel.

It was a Saturday in September, the rainy season was beginning to taper off and everyone was spending more time outside. My mother and I started the day as usual, going to Mass at the Assumption of the Blessed Virgin Mary Church, saying prayers, hoping the looming danger of the cartel didn't find us.

I was in a mood that day. I hadn't slept well, plagued by nightmares of this clown chasing me with a knife, saying "*Ven conejito, ven.*" He was calling me a little rabbit and telling me to come to him. He had glowing red eyes and I remember the sound of his big clown shoes slapping against the floor as he chased me through the cathedral of the big, fancy church we went to.

"*Conejito...*" he whispered as I shook under a pew, his feet right in front of my face. "*Ahí estás,*" he hissed as his face came into view. His breath smelled like rotting garbage as he reached out and grabbed me by the neck and pulled me out from under the pew.

"Please! Please, don't hurt me," I pleaded, feeling a warm trickle spread through my pants and run down my leg. "Please!"

"I'm not going to hurt you," he said, a terrifying smile on his face. "I've come to take care of you, *conejito*. You and I, we will be great amigos. We will be inseparable." He then stood me up on the stone floor and tenderly straightened out my best white shirt, the one I wore to church. "See," he said, "I won't hurt you."

He still held the glittering knife in his right hand. It was shiny, like a mirror. On it, I could see another clown sneaking up behind me, another glittering knife in his hand poised to plunge into my back.

I woke up screaming, my mother holding me tightly, telling me that everything was OK. Once I realized it was a dream, I held her tight and cried and cried.

Once I had calmed enough to tell her the dream, she had me get dressed and we rushed off to church.

"Feel better now?" she asked as we walked back.

I shook my head. I could still see that clown in my mind, the glittering knife, the clenched-jaw grin.

"Prayers didn't help, Jesús? They must have, how could they not help my Jesús?"

My name was starting to become an issue for me. Some

of the kids had begun to tease me, coming to me and "pray-ing" for things, like a new bike or a toy they coveted. It was insulting and my mother emphasizing the divine nature of my name really rubbed me the wrong way.

"How do we know what prayers God will answer?" I asked, my voice too loud. "How do we know if he answers the right prayers?"

"Jesús?" she said, slowing down and looking at me.

"How do we know?"

She smiled, but her brown eyes looked sad. "We don't know, my son. We do our best to be righteous, to follow God's edicts, but he decides, we do not."

My mother's simple statement of faith made me mad. What kind of system was this, where there was so much fear, so much suffering, so little certainty. "And so you were not worthy of another baby?" I asked. I was old enough to know I was being cruel. My mother had prayed long and hard before I was born, and although she had desperately wanted another child, God had not given her one. It was a grief she always carried.

Her eyes narrowed, and her mouth formed a straight, hard line. "What has gotten into you today, Jesús?"

"Why didn't God give you another child? No one prays harder than you do. I've prayed for God to give you another child for years. Why?"

She blinked several times, tears springing to her eyes. "It is not for us to ask. It..."

"Why?" I said loudly, passersbys staring at us.

She took me by the arm and pulled me up the street until we came to a small street that was free of pedestrians. "What is this, Jesús? Tell me now."

That street smelled like rotten garbage, which reminded

me of my clown dream. I started to cry, the fear from the dream that had not yet left me.

"Please," she said, "talk to me."

I nodded and wiped at my tears. "If... if God didn't grant you another child, how... how do we know He will protect us from the cartel?"

Her eyes went wide, her hand going to her mouth. She had thought I didn't know, that the lie was in place, and somehow protecting me. But I knew and had felt a sickening vulnerability since I had found out.

"How... how long?" she asked.

"Winter before last," I said slowly. "I was playing my invisible game, and heard you and Papá talk about how he saved Señor Langold's life and killed a man, what he does for him, what you are both afraid of."

She nodded and smoothed out my shirt again. "Well, I guess you are old enough now."

I felt my heart swell with pride, but it did nothing to ease my fear.

"The thing you must remember," she said, "is that your father is a good man. He didn't want this, it happened to him."

I nodded slowly. I knew my father was a good and strong man. I just didn't know if he was good and strong enough.

"But we must not let him know," she said quietly. "He has enough concerns, let us keep this one between us. Can you do that for me, Jesús?"

"Yes, Mamá." I knew the look my father had on his face when he came home from his "business" trips. His eyes heavy, his frown deep, his need for tequila stronger than his need for his wife and son.

"That's my boy," she said, as she put her hand on my

back and guided me back to the main street and towards home.

I felt a burden lifted off of me. Now that my mother knew that I knew, now that she knew we were both praying for the same thing, now that I didn't have to pretend around her, I was sure things were going to get better. God had sent me that horrible dream so that I would finally talk to my beautiful and wise mother. Everything was going to be fine.

I was just a child. I was so naive.

I BLINKED, COMING BACK TO REALITY FROM THE DEPTHS of my story. In my memory I could still smell the rose water my mother used to wear. I could hear the fabric of her dress as she walked me quickly back home. I could feel the sun on my skin.

This ghostly life felt hollow and insubstantial in comparison. And for good reason. It was.

I looked around the room and found that my ghostly companion was still there. She had come a step closer to Sister Dominga's bed as I had told my story. She was staring at me, her blue eyes looking right through me. It made me uncomfortable.

"My name is Jesús," I began. "But you must know that by now."

She nodded but didn't speak.

"I used to be a bounty hunter. I died when one of my captives stabbed me in the eye with an ice pick." I was executing the ritual I had learned in Tucson. Ghosts generally shared cause of death when they met.

Her brow furrowed briefly, but she didn't say anything else.

"What is your name? How did you die?" I wanted to know, but what I wanted to know more was why she called Sister Dominga Grandmother.

She bit her lower lip and took a step back.

I met her eyes and held them. I opened myself up to Awareness. I was expecting to feel her fear, but that wasn't quite it. I felt that she was shy and cautions, but not scared. She was... I looked away and back down at Sister Dominga. I had felt this deep, abiding faith in the mysterious ghost, and it made me feel ashamed and jealous. She had the kind of faith I used to have, that I wanted to have, but it felt different than my own tattered faith. It was somehow broader and more diffuse, but strong nevertheless.

I am growing in my ability to sense things, using the Awareness training Banquo has taught us. But it is a tricky thing. It's kind of like an enhanced sense of intuition. You feel it more than know it, and it is not always translatable into words. But the kind of faith I felt coming from her deeply humbled me.

"Maybe you should continue," she said. "Something bad is about to happen, isn't it?"

I looked back up at her and nodded. She was hungry for the story, that I could feel too.

Chapter 12

As fall turned towards winter, I spent my time at school, church, or playing with friends. Without thinking, I started to spend less and less time at home. My father wasn't there much, and my mother...

Well, since I had shared what I had known about my father and the cartel, something had changed between us. She seemed her normal, cheerful self, but I would catch her at odd moments staring at me, a look of deep worry on her face.

At first I tried to allay her concerns. "It'll be OK, Mamá," I would say. "I pray every day. This is a prayer God must answer."

She would then smile with her lips but not with her eyes and say, "Of course. If we both pray hard, how can He deny us?"

But I could feel the lie when she told me that. She wasn't sure if our prayer would be answered.

I kept praying, but I didn't want to see that look on my mother's face, so I stayed away as much as I could without getting in trouble.

I would go down the hill and play with kids I had met when we lived in our house down there. I didn't relate well with most of the kids that lived in the big fancy houses on the hill. I had been born poor, most of them had not.

I think if I had been home more, maybe I would have seen the signs. Noticed the tension growing on my father's face, felt the fear that was growing palpable. I was too busy praying, staying away, and trying to pretend nothing was wrong.

I was a kid, after all. My parents were trying to hide these things from me so I could be a child. So I could have few cares. So I could...

There is nothing that can make what happened next anything but traumatic. There is nothing that will ever get the bitter taste of it out of my mouth. And there is nothing that will ever bring my parents back.

"The cartel," my ghost companion said gently, "they killed them." We were in Sister Dominga's room, she stood in front of the crucifix.

I nodded slowly. My story was heading into deep, dark territory, and I didn't want to tell it anymore. I didn't see how it could do Sister Dominga any good. I didn't see how it would matter. Sister Dominga knew the rough outline of this story, but I hadn't given her much detail, I hadn't told it to anyone.

We all have wounds, things that scar us and change us, that are so integral to us that even speaking of them is an act of intimacy. I felt that if you peeled away the layers of who I was, this is what it would come down to. This act of violence changed my life irrevocably and made me who I am.

She took a step forward and I could see the compassion on her face. I've seen how people look at me when they realize my family was murdered. I've seen that kind of innocent "how can that happen in this world" look of shocked compassion before, and that was not the look this ghost gave me. Her look of compassion was more, "I feel for you because I have experienced similar wounds."

I looked away. I couldn't meet her gaze. I couldn't stand seeing that look of empathy and understanding she was giving me. I couldn't go on.

I left Sister Dominga and flew through the wall out into the dark night. I couldn't stand how I was feeling. I was on the cusp of tragedy in the story I was telling, and bereft of faith in the reality I was living. My life and all its twists and turns no longer made sense.

I expected the bardo to come calling for me, so despondent was I, but it didn't. I picked a direction at random and just started flying. I couldn't stand who I was in the past or the present. I couldn't turn my back on what I was feeling. Movement was all that was left to me.

"Ahh..." Banquo said. "The Basilica of Our Lady of Guadalupe. I guess I shouldn't be surprised."

I had flown above the city until I had seen it, the large round building with the turquoise roof with a cross on the top. My unthinking flight had brought me here. I stopped flying and stared. My mother had taken me here several times, the last just a month or so before their murder.

Banquo had arrived, with a pop, moments later.

"Are you going to go in?" he asked.

I looked at him, thinking he was crazy. The concern

reflected on his face made me worry that I must have looked like a madman or something. His eyes then narrowed as he appraised my condition.

"Perhaps not," he said with a gentle smile.

"What do you believe in?" I asked.

Most people would have probably considered that a strange question, coming out of the blue like it did, but not Banquo. He looked energized, as if something interesting had finally happened. The look of excitement didn't stay on his face long; he was soon floating next to me with his arms crossed over his large belly and his mouth a straight line. "What I believe in," he finally said, going back into teacher mode, "is not important. What you believe in is."

I looked back down on the Basilica. It was a modern structure built in 1974. The roof had the lines of a large tent, with the tent pole off center and the lines gracefully flowing down. When I was a boy, coming here was the most exciting thing, to visit the place that had been built for Guadalupe. The inside of it was so beautiful, so magnificent, I wanted to explore every nook and cranny. Now that I was a ghost, and capable of just such an exploration, I had no desire to go in.

"What do you believe in?" Banquo gently asked. He knew what I was going through. I knew the question was an opening for me to explore it, for me to talk about it.

"I believe it's time to go," I said, as I turned and flew back towards the church and Sister Dominga.

Banquo flew beside me, silently. Below us Mexico City was bathed in predawn light, a few cars on the road, a few people stirring on the streets. Another day for the living getting ready to start.

When we got back to Sister Dominga's room, the other

ghost was there, her hands held above Sister Dominga's body. The compassionate look she gave me made me turn away.

"This is my teacher, Banquo," I said to her. I was surprised that she didn't bolt at the sight of a new ghost. She had the first few times she had seen me. "Banquo, this is Sister Dominga's granddaughter." I was surprised at how sure I sounded when I said that. It felt right, it felt real. I didn't know the story behind it, but I did know she was Sister Dominga's granddaughter.

Banquo's eyebrows raised, but he didn't speak and bowed his head towards her in way of greeting.

"Can you stay?" I asked him. "I have been telling my story to Sister Dominga. It seems to calm her. I... Now..." I sighed. "The story I have to tell now is one I've never told. To anyone. I would appreciate both of you staying, in case I..." I didn't finish the thought, but I was more than half convinced the bardo would finally take me if I continued the story. How could it not?

As a ghost I have never experienced the bardo, but as a boy I did. Banquo calls the bardo "your own personal hell." Well, as a living breathing boy, that is exactly what I experienced.

I moved to the side of Sister Dominga's bed, across from the other ghost. She smiled at me shyly as I put my hands under Sister Dominga's head and heart and let the warmth flow. I could feel the other ghost, it was powerful, the warmth seemed to multiply with both of us doing it.

I looked up at her, her blue eyes capturing me again. They were the softest blue, but seemed so strong. She was shy, that was clear, but below that shyness there was enormous strength. The kind of strength born out of struggle. I think it must have been the way we were connected, both of us letting the warmth flow into Sister Dominga, but I had never experienced someone like this before.

I opened my mouth to say something about it, but she nodded towards me, signaling me to start speaking.

The memories came to me sharp and vivid and I spoke them.

Chapter 13

IN MY MEMORY, THE DAY SEEMS BRIGHT. AS IF SOMEONE turned the sun all the way up. It had rained that morning and the sky was a beautiful blue with not a cloud in sight. It was a fall Sunday afternoon and we had returned back from church. My mother and father seemed happy, and I was sure that God was answering my prayers.

When we got home, I ran upstairs and changed out of my church clothes into play clothes and went out back. In our backyard was a half-done flagstone patio. My father couldn't bring himself to hire someone to do what he used to do, and he hadn't finished it himself. He had been gone so much, and when he was home he didn't seem to have the energy to do anything about it.

So I had started working on it. Many of the stones were too big for me, but I could put in and smooth the base of sand, I could move the smaller rocks, and some of the larger ones I could slowly move. It made me happy to do it, and I could feel myself growing stronger. It was like a puzzle, finding the right rocks for the right spot.

The stones, which had been sitting in the shade, were

cool to the touch and rough. I remember the feel of them on my hands, like sandpaper.

"Very good work," my father said. He had a beer in his hand and was walking on the section that I had built over the last few weeks. His tie was loose, but he hadn't changed out of his church clothes yet.

"Thank you, Papá," I said, my heart swelling.

"Come here, Jesús." He sat heavily on the stone wall that lined our patio. I walked over and he grabbed my hands, his thumbs probing the calluses forming there. "Your hands are growing strong, you have been working hard." My hands disappeared in his, they were so big, but the skin was smoother than I remembered. I also noticed some scarring on his knuckles that I hadn't seen before.

I nodded and swallowed, saying a brief prayer of thanks to God. My father was really noticing me.

"It is good to work with your hands, Jesús, but I want more for you."

I looked up at him, unsure of what he meant. I could smell the yeasty beer on his breath and see the concern in his eyes.

"You are a smart boy, Jesús. You must use your head too. You must study hard and make something of yourself."

"Yes, Papá," I said, my heart pounding in my ears. I wanted nothing more than to be the kind of man my father was before the cartel came. But I couldn't say that to him. Inside, the phone rang.

"You will go to college, you will become a doctor or a lawyer."

"Yes, Papá," I said again, feeling his grip on my hands tighten. It began to hurt, but I didn't make a sound. I didn't understand what my father was talking about, but it was clearly important to him.

"You will have a life that is—"

"Juan, telephone," my mother called, cutting my father off. "It's Francisco. He says it is important."

He blinked and let my hands go. "We will talk of this again. Soon." He got up and went into the house.

I didn't hear what was said, but the change of his tone was clear and frightening. His voice became loud, and then he sounded scared. Through the door to the kitchen I could see his face go hard and then fall as he looked around help-lessly. I felt my knees go weak, my big strong father scared. He hung the phone up and had a whispered conversation with my mother.

She then came out and took my hand. "Come, Jesús, we must pack some clothes."

"But, Mamá, I am working."

She pulled me hard towards the door without saying another word. Her eyes were wide and she was breathing rapidly. They were both so scared; what could they be so scared about?

We rushed through the kitchen, down the hallway and up the stairs. I caught a glimpse of my father, a gun in his hand as he peeked out the curtains from our living room. The gun was a dull black, like the gift Señor Langold had given me for my birthday, but clearly not a toy.

"What... what is happening?" I stammered.

"Hush! Pack some clothes. We are going to go on a nice vacation." She tried to put a smile on her face, but it didn't work. The expression, two parts terror, one part fake hap-piness, made me queasy. She was sweating, and I could smell the fear on her.

She gave me a bag, told me to pack, and left me in my room alone. I stood there for a few moments, feeling my heart pounding in my chest. What was scaring them so? Whatever it was, it had to be bad. Whatever it was, I didn't think packing was going to help.

I dropped the bag and fell to my knees and prayed.

I prayed to Guadalupe and Jesús, I prayed for them to save and protect us. I prayed as hard as I knew how, my mouth moving as I whispered my prayers. It came out as fervent gasps, my lips moving rapidly, my eyes shut tight.

I could hear my mother banging around in the other room—packing, I presume. I could hear the wind hissing through the trees outside. I heard when a car came to a screeching stop in front of our house, followed by slamming car doors and rushing feet.

"¡Escóndanse!" my father hissed up the stairs. He was telling us to hide, a rare lapse to Spanish for him in the house.

I didn't move, I just closed my eyes tighter and prayed harder. My pleas then were only for Guadalupe, only for the mother. I felt she would be more disposed to protect us, to take us into her bosom and hold us tight.

Even then I knew it was the cartel. I knew they had come to kill us. It was why Uncle Francisco had called. And there I was on my knees thinking that prayer could help.

There was a large crash as the front door was kicked in. I heard several shots fired and heard the sounds of bodies dropping. I smelled gunpowder. I feared the worst and my body began shaking as tears flowed down my cheeks. My lips trembled as I continued the most desperate of prayers.

When I heard the heavy footfalls on the stairs, my heart beat so loudly I feared Guadalupe would not be able to hear my whispered prayer, so I said it aloud. "Guadalupe, in your name I pray. Please keep my family safe from harm. It is your..."

I felt his presence in my doorway before he spoke, the hairs on my neck rising and a chill going down my spine. "Guadalupe is not going to save you," he said in Spanish.

I opened my eyes and looked at him. He looked like a monster. He was broad shouldered, like my father, but taller and covered in a layer of fat. His irises were so dark you couldn't see where his pupils started, his eyes seeming like black voids. His face was covered in stubble and half of his right eyebrow was an ugly scar.

I wanted to keep praying. I thought I should keep praying, but I couldn't. I just kneeled there shaking as he lifted his gun and pointed it at me.

Chapter 14

GHOSTLY TEARS FLOWED DOWN MY FACE AS I LOOKED AT Sister Dominga, Banquo, and the other ghost. I saw those tears reflected on both the other ghosts' faces. The warmth had abandoned me and I felt weak and cold. I stepped back from Sister Domingo. I didn't think the retelling of this darkness could do her any good.

"I didn't hide," I said. "I didn't fight back. I couldn't even pray."

"You were a boy," Banquo said.

"How could you do more?" Sister Dominga's granddaughter said.

"I could have hidden," I said, my voice low. "I could have run. If I had..."

"My boy," Banquo said as he walked over to me, his hand touching my shoulder. "You did your best, but this guilt is a poison to you. You must let it out. You *must* let it go."

I stepped away from Banquo's touch. Normally any sensation of touch as a ghost is a thrill and only possible when a ghost has mastered their form, but I didn't want connection right then. I was in too much pain. That moment in my childhood was the moment I first lost my faith. It's hard to explain, but when it happens it's like going from having solid ground underneath you to freefalling in an instant. You have nothing to base your experience of life on.

"Don't stop," the other ghost said. "You need to pass all the way through this. It will help."

Her concern, which was palpable, even though I didn't know her, even though I didn't even know her name, twisted in my mind. It felt invasive. I wondered how sick she was, only interacting with me when it was clear that my childhood was a tragic one.

I wanted to close my eyes, to shut them out of my vision. But since I didn't actually have eyes, shutting the appearance of my eyes did no good. The memory of that moment started coming back to me, and I wanted to shut it out, but I couldn't. It came back, crystal clear, that monster of a man standing before me. My childhood room filled with toy trucks and Legos, bought by the money my father had earned working for the cartel. The walls were painted blue, my mother's choice, with splotches of white applied with a sponge at the top of the wall, looking like fluffy clouds.

The vision of the room became stronger and stronger until I heard a popping sound and I was no longer in Sister Dominga's room. I stood in my childhood room.

I ARRIVED WITH A "POP," SHOCKED AT MY CHANGE IN location. A dim part of me was aware that this was the first time I had done the advanced traveling that Banquo talks about and many ghosts can do. But I had other concerns. As I looked around I first thought I was in the bardo, that I had descended into the memory and was trapped in my own personal hell. But it soon became clear that that wasn't what was going on.

The room, while the same one I lived in as a child, was different. Gone were the blue walls with fluffy clouds along the top. The walls were now yellow and the bed was in a different place and had a frilly bedspread on it. I was in my old childhood room, all right, but time had passed, someone else lived here.

I then became aware of a presence in the doorway. It was large and diffuse, and as I stared at it, it slowly came into focus. It was him, the man from my memory, the man who held a gun pointed at me, telling me my prayers would do no good.

I took a step back. His face haunted me for years. The dark, seemingly iris-less eyes, the snarling lips, the scar across the right eyebrow.

I heard two pops, and Banquo and the other ghost appeared.

Another form appeared, distinct but very transparent. A boy, eight years old, kneeling on the floor, staring up at the large man, tears running down his face, his chin quivering. It was the eight-year-old me.

"What..." I stammered.

"They are not real," Banquo said softly. "It's just your memories playing themselves out.

"How..."

"I don't know, Jesús. Just let it happen. Let the memories flow forth."

I didn't do anything, but the scene began to move.

"Guadalupe is not going to save you," the big man growled. He lazily raised the gun and pointed it at the boy. At me. The boy-me didn't look away; he stared at the man and his gun, his mouth moving as if praying, but no words coming out.

Another form appeared behind the man. It was my mother, her eyes wide, her face contorted in an expression that made her look ugly. Her nostrils were flared, her teeth clenched, her mascara washed down her cheeks with tears. In her hand she held a bronze statue of Guadalupe.

"Don't worry, kid," the man said. "I'll make it quick." He took a half step into the room as my mother brought the statue down upon his head. With a grunt, the big man toppled to the floor, like a marionette whose strings had been cut.

She dropped the statue and rushed over to the child-me and fell to her knees sobbing as she pulled the child-me into her arms.

I remember that embrace. My mother seemed so strong to me then, so powerful. She had knocked out the monstrous man, and it was not lost on me that she had done it with a statue of Guadalupe. I had gotten halfway through a prayer of thanks when I heard it. A snarling groan.

I saw the big man begin to move and watched as my mother and the boy-me froze, silent and listening. My mother looked around frantically for the statue of Guadalupe and saw that it was on the other side of the man. She had dropped it after he had crumpled.

She pulled me to a standing position and said, "¡Rápido, Jesús, corre!" She was telling me to run.

I watched the boy-me as his eyes darted to my mother, to the man now on his hands and knees, cursing loudly, and to the door. The man was between the door and me. The boy-me looked terrified, all thoughts of prayer gone, only one thought left. Survival.

My mother kicked at the man, but he caught her leg and she fell to the floor hard, crying out in pain. The man's face came up, his teeth clenched, his lips curled back, blood flowing freely down the left side of his face.

"¡Corre, Jesús!" my mother screamed as she beat at the man with her fists.

The boy-me ran. I could feel the terror and the guilt I had felt then. I followed the boy-me and looked back just as he did and saw the big man crouched over my mother as his huge fists rained down on her. Her scream kept us frozen for a moment until we could hear her say "¡Corre!" over and over.

The boy-me let out a strangled cry and turned and ran the rest of the way down the stairs and found the bodies. There were three of them. One laying over the threshold of our open front door, another in the living room, and a third draped on the stairs.

"Papá!" the boy-me cried as he kneeled by the body on the stairs, tears flowing down his cheeks. "Papá." The boy-me pushed on the body. It had several holes in the chest and blood was everywhere. The boy-me's hands came back covered in it.

"Papá," he said in English. "Please wake up, please be OK. Please—"

The boy-me's sentence was cut off by the sound of a gunshot upstairs. He turned and looked, his eyes wide, his hands going to his mouth, leaving the stain of his father's blood there. There were the sounds of rough steps and the big man appeared at the top of the stairs.

The left side of his face was covered in blood and he stood there swaying as if dizzy. He raised his gun and began firing at the boy-me.

The boy-me let out a cry and ran from the house. He ran fast, he didn't look back, and once the boy-me was out of sight, all the apparitions of my memory fled. I was left standing on the steps of my boyhood home weeping.

"Come," said Banquo, his hand on my shoulder gently pushing me forward. "It's time to leave this place, my friend."

I could feel the other ghost's hand on my other shoulder. Dimly I was aware of their caring, their concern, of the warmth that flowed from their hands into me. But only dimly. I was, like the boy we had just witnessed, in shock, dazed, confused, and lost.

Los Muchachos
(The Boys)

"While we look not at the things which are seen,
but at the things which are not seen: for the things
which are seen are temporal; but the things which
are not seen are eternal."
2 Corinthians 4:18

Chapter 15

DARKNESS COMES TO US ALL, DOESN'T IT? THIS JUST
seems to be the nature of the existence we are living. That
day as an eight-year-old boy was a terribly dark day. And,
that day as a ghost reliving it was dark too. I don't remember
much of what happened next. But I do know that Banquo
and a ghost whose name I didn't know took care of me,
watched over me, helped me come back to the land of the...

And that was the problem, really. What land was it that
I came back to? It wasn't the land of the living. It wasn't
heaven or hell or even purgatory. It was the land of the
earthbound ghost. So back I came, but what was it that I
was coming back to?

Faith is a tricky thing. It requires that you believe without evidence. What happens when you have evidence of
something your faith doesn't allow for? Do you ignore it,
pretend it isn't there? Do you come up with tortured expla-
nations that desperately try to preserve the shape of your
faith? Do you let go of your faith and live without it? Do you
allow your faith to adapt to the new evidence?

When I came back to myself, my mind was, once again,

full of these thoughts. I looked around and found that I was in Sister Dominga's room. The nun was in her bed, her face peaceful and still. For a moment I thought she had passed, that I had missed the moment I was here for.

Then I noticed her, the other ghost, the granddaughter of Sister Dominga. She had her hands above the nun and I could feel the glow of the warmth that was flowing into Sister Dominga. The ghost looked up at me, her iceberg blue eyes going right through me.

I felt a stab of shame—she had seen and heard so much of my past, seen me run from the ruin of my childhood, knew me in ways that flesh and blood people don't often get to know each other.

It's the Awareness. Free of the flesh, all ghosts are more than a little psychic, and it was clear she was way above normal in this case. With those eyes I swore she could see my soul, my essential self and all its bumps, lumps, and imperfections.

She smiled at me and I felt confused. The smile wasn't one of pity, wasn't what my shame expected. It was a smile of affection. But, how could that be?

"Welcome back, Jesús," she said. She seemed different, almost brighter. Like the shyness she had worn the first few times we had met had been a coat that she had discarded. Something she didn't need anymore.

"What... I... Where is Banquo?" I asked.

"He had to go. He asked me to keep an eye on you."

I nodded and went over and looked out the window. The setting sun was turning the bottom of the clouds pink and orange, the glow making the streets below look safe and warm. I knew they were anything but.

"Can... I..." I stammered, as I came around to the other

side of the bed and looked into those blue eyes again. "Can you tell me your name? I feel like you know me so well and I don't know you at all."

She extended her hand and said, "My name is Lela. Lela May Sykes." When our hands joined in a ghostly handshake, I felt a spike of energy run up my arm and career around my body. I had touched other ghosts before and never felt anything like this.

She let go of my hand before I was ready, but the way I felt then, I don't think I would have ever been ready.

"What happened to me?" I asked.

Lela shrugged. "Banquo said it was the ghostly equivalent of catatonia."

I nodded, putting my hands under Sister Dominga and trying to relax enough to let the warmth flow. I was doing it to help Sister Dominga, I knew that. But I was also doing it because I wanted to be interacting with Lela, doing something—anything—that involved her.

I didn't have faith, but I did have the beginnings of a crush.

"Maybe you should continue your story," she said.

I RAN FROM THE HOUSE AS FAST AS I COULD. I RAN blindly, unthinking, uncaring, just wanting to move. I tripped and fell several times, getting back up right away. I ran into several people as I wound through the streets, heard the shouts or questions of concern, but kept moving. My feet carried me down the big hill we lived on, away from Naucalpan and towards Mexico City proper.

As I ran, I kept smelling blood. The scent of blood put me right back to what had just happened to my parents.

Eventually, exhausted, I found myself panting on my hands and knees drinking out of a puddle of water. My heart pounding in my chest and my saliva thick in my mouth as I stared at my reflection in the puddle. Even the water tasted like blood, and I couldn't drink much of it.

I crouched there panting. As the water of the puddle became calm, I could see my reflection. The right side of my face was covered in drying blood. My right hand had blood on it too. My father's blood. It was what I had been smelling all this time, and what I had just tasted.

The thought made my stomach turn and I vomited. I then found puddle after puddle and began scrubbing off my face and my hands. I did it far longer than I needed to, until my face was raw and sore.

Exhaustion hit me then, like I had just been drugged. I was unsteady on my feet. I found myself in an alley, some cardboard boxes strewn behind what looked like a grocery of some sort. I crushed two boxes, one to sleep on and one to put on top of me. As soon as my eyes closed, I slept.

MY DREAMS WERE DISJOINTED FRAGMENTS. MY FATHER when he had a mustache wearing a white T-shirt, his arms big and strong. My mother at her vanity in the house on the hill sitting and applying makeup for church. Me crouched behind the couch playing invisible while my mother and father discuss the cartel. My father making me speak in English. My mother speaking to me in Spanish whenever my father wasn't around. My uncle Francisco with his thin mustache laughing as he offered me a sip of his tequila. Men with guns chasing me around my room, I try to hide under my bed but I'm too big.

I woke up suddenly, my shoulder hurting from sleeping on the cardboard. The sun was high in the sky and I heard voices from inside the grocery; the back door was open. My thoughts felt thick and my body felt heavy.

I got out from between the cardboard and moved out onto the little street, blinking at the sunlight. I didn't like it. It should be dark and somber, not a bright sunny day. I saw people smiling on the street and I wanted to hit them, make them stop smiling.

I looked around and recognized the neighborhood. I wasn't far from Uncle Francisco's restaurant. He called to try to warn my parents. He knew what was going on. Maybe he could...

I didn't know what he could do, but I did know he was the only family I had left in the country. My father's parents were dead, and my mother's parents were in Spain. I started walking to the restaurant, keeping my head down, afraid someone might recognize me.

When I got there, the purple door of the *La Trainera* (the Drifter) was locked and it had a handwritten sign on it that said, "On Vacation." I was about to leave when I heard some banging inside the building and the muffled sounds of cursing. *La Trainera*, like many restaurants, was buried in the middle of a tight block with apartments above it. Mexico City is an old and crowded city; there is little wasted space.

At first I thought it was my uncle and I almost called out his name, but something about the tone of the voices I heard stopped me short. My heart started beating rapidly and I started sweating. My head swiveled around looking for a place to hide, there was nowhere, just doors to shops and apartments. I heard the sound of the voices approaching the door and I ran down to the next building and jumped into a recessed window. It was a dress shop. I peeked around the edge of the wall so I could just see the sidewalk in front of my uncle's restaurant.

Three men exited. When I saw the one in the lead I almost cried out. He was big, with a scar on his right eyebrow and a bruise and cut on his forehead from where my mother had hit him with the statue of Guadalupe. It was him. The man that killed my parents. The man that had tried to kill me.

"He's not here," one of them said.

"Probably ran back to Spain," the second one added.

"In any case," my parents' murderer said, "he won't be coming back here."

I held my breath, not daring to make a sound. I knew that if they found me they would kill me.

"Do you want take a break?" Lela asked. I wasn't sure if she meant my story or the warmth we were both pumping into Sister Dominga.

"We are almost there," I said, looking into her iceberg blue eyes.

"Where?"

"To the end of this part of my story. It's almost time for that break."

She smiled and nodded, suddenly looking shy, her eyes going to Sister Dominga.

"Is she really your grandmother?" I asked.

"She is," she said.

"I hope you will tell me about it someday."

She looked up at me, and when her eyes met mine, my breath caught. I know, I'm a ghost, I don't breathe, but that is what it felt like. Like I didn't want to move a bit, that I wanted to let the moment stretch out to an eternity, that I didn't want those eyes to ever stop looking at me.

"I will," she said, her eyes going back to Sister Dominga, the moment gone.

I nodded and continued to stare at her. Who was she? Why did I keep feeling these things? My story had gotten so hard to tell, but somehow with Lela here, I could tell it.

WHEN THE MEN GOT INTO AN OLD CADILLAC AND DROVE away, I collapsed against the window of the dress shop and wept. My tears were bitter and my whole body shook. That was the man who had killed my parents—the sight of him made me weak. The smell of him made me sick. The thought of him made me want to die.

I was traumatized, of course. But I didn't know it then. I only knew that I had just lost everything and that man was the cause. The seeds of hate, the kind of hate I had never imagined, were sown in me that day. The kind of hate that would destroy me if it was allowed to bloom.

After about thirty minutes, I dared to crawl out of the recessed window ledge. It doesn't seem like much, but it was an act of great courage. My hands still shook. I slowly moved to the door of my uncle's restaurant, my eyes darting back and forth like something wild. They had left the door unlocked.

I went in and locked the door behind me. I didn't leave for a month.

Chapter 16

LELA MAY SYKES, SHE WAS BORN IN NEW MEXICO AND had died five years ago. A week had gone by and that was about all that I learned about her past. But about her... I had learned plenty. She was wise and gentle, shy and contemplative, and very smart. She was also probably the world's best listener. And she was a person I wanted to spend more time with. A lot more time.

For that week we didn't talk about my past or hers. We also skirted my current big question: faith. We talked about art and science and history. About the world as we each saw it.

I knew I was avoiding my story, avoiding my problem, and I think she knew too. But it was what I needed.

We spent much of our time with Sister Dominga. She remained unconscious, but kept reacting favorably to the warmth we gave her, so we kept doing that much of the day. We would take breaks and talk, and at night I would stay with Sister Dominga and rest, and Lela would leave.

I don't know where she went, but when she was gone

I found my mind kept going to her. Wondering where she was, if she was alone, hoping she would come back.

It seems a bit silly. There I was sitting vigil for someone who had been like a mother to me, struggling with my loss of faith, and I had a full-blown crush. And silly as it may seem, I think it was for the best. That crush gave me something positive to hope for and dwell on. Something both my past and my present couldn't provide.

On a quiet night, a thin sliver of a moon cast a ghostly glow on the floor of Sister Dominga's room through the gap in the curtains. I was standing in the corner watching and resting. Thinking about Lela and all that had happened since I had arrived.

"She likes you too," I heard a voice say.

I was surprised, but it's not like when you have a body. No adrenaline, no involuntary jumping. I looked and saw Yochi at the door to Sister Dominga's room. He must have flown through and I hadn't noticed.

"What?" I asked.

"The girl ghost. She likes you too." He had a grin on his face as if he had told me some great secret or truth.

"I... How... How do you know?"

He shrugged, his shoulders dancing up briefly. "It is as plain to see as the moon in the sky." He stepped forward into the shaft of moonlight, his form seeming to mingle with it.

I nodded and smiled despite myself. Could she really like me? How could she when I was such a mess? What could someone that amazing possibly see in me? And, who was she? Why didn't she talk about her past?

"Come with me," Yochi said, moving towards the door and beckoning.

I looked at Sister Dominga and then back at him. "I... I don't want to leave her."

Yochi paused, turning around and looking at her then me. "She will be fine. There is time left yet."

"YOU HAVE OTHER WORK TO DO HERE," HE SAID AFTER we arrived in the cathedral. He pointed up and smiled his gape-toothed smile.

"The lurkers?" I asked.

He nodded.

"Why me?"

He gave me a Banquo-ish raised-eyebrow look. I didn't like it, but it's hard to argue with Awareness. Yochi knew, and as I relaxed and opened myself up to Awareness, I knew too.

"It's all linked together," I mumbled.

Yochi laughed, the sound of it was loud and unrestrained, as if I had told the funniest joke in the world.

I looked up and saw the flash of movement and heard a distant voice. A chill went up my ghostly spine. What was up there? Why couldn't someone else deal with this?

"She's coming," he said quietly. For a moment I thought he meant a lurker, but then I could feel her gentle yet powerful presence—Lela. Somehow being with Yochi seemed to help me in some ways. It was like when I was with him all the lessons Banquo had taught, all that I had learned, was available to me. I was Aware of Lela even though she wasn't here yet. I could sense the lurkers, their emotions were complex, some joy, but it seemed fake. I could feel people in the neighborhood starting to wake up.

"Tell your story during the day," he said, his voice dreamy. "Play with the lurkers at night."

With a giggle and a "pop" he was gone.

"IS IT TIME?" LELA ASKED.

I smiled at her over Sister Dominga. We had both assumed our regular positions and had summoned the warmth. She knew it was time. She was not a new ghost, surely she was tapped into Awareness. She was probably aware of much more than I was. I am quite sure my face flushed in reaction to my embarrassment when I realized she was probably aware of my growing feelings for her.

She looked away, her cheeks flushing red too. Even though we are ghosts, many of the bodily reactions we had when alive still happen now that we are dead. "You were at your uncle's restaurant."

I nodded slowly. "I was. I hid there, ate the food, and didn't come out, not until I had to." I took a deep breath and let out a sigh (another holdover from having a body). "In many ways, that month was the best of it until Sister Dominga found me."

"Please," she said, her eyes briefly finding mine, "tell me."

UNCLE FRANCISCO'S RESTAURANT WAS A HAVEN. IT WAS stocked with food, had running water and a working toilet. There was even a cot and television in the storage room. Surviving physically was easy. Surviving mentally, though, was not. I was in shock from what had happened to my parents, from seeing their killer come out of the restaurant. I was mentally not at all OK. I barely slept, constantly had nightmares about what had happened, about being found by the big man with the scar, about seeing my father lying on our living room floor dead, about hearing the shot that killed my mother.

I am surprised I survived the first week. That I didn't do something stupid and harm myself. I wasn't suicidal, but I wasn't in my right mind either. There were dangerous things in there, things I could hurt myself with. Knives, fry vats, stoves, and tools. I was having blackouts—I think from the lack of sleep—and could have easily burned the place down while trying to cook a meal.

But slowly it changed. The trauma didn't go away, but it receded back into my mind. I stopped thinking about it all the time. I became numb to it all—except in my dreams. There I would relive it every night, but upon waking I would shove it down and do what I had to do to survive.

Every day I kept hoping Uncle Francisco would show up. That he would be able to protect me and take care of me. I kept hoping, but as the days dragged on, I became convinced that he never would. That he must have fled Mexico back to Spain when the cartel attack happened. He had called the house. He had known.

And one day it all came to an end. It was midmorning, I had no idea what day it was, when I heard a key in the lock of the door. I stood there, a plate of warm beans—I was down to dried beans—I had made for breakfast in my hand. I knew I should run or hide, I was terrified it might be the scarred man coming back to look for Uncle Francisco, but I stood there frozen. Time seemed to slow down, the steam from the beans slowly curling into the air, my heart thumping against my ribs, my head thick and slow. I heard voices speaking in Spanish right outside the door. They were talking about the restaurant. I could smell the beans, my own sweat, and the stale grease from the long inactive fryer vats.

The door opened and a middle-aged *criollo* man stood in the doorway his eyes wide. He had a thin mustache and was dressed in a suit. "What! Who... who are you?" he shouted.

I stood there silent for another two breaths and then screamed. The plate clattered to the ground, shattering, beans slopping over the floor. I ran as fast as I could right into the man. He let out a shout and fell backwards, both of us tumbling onto the sidewalk outside the restaurant.

I blinked at the sunlight. I had kept all the curtains drawn and hadn't seen the sun for weeks. The man pushed me off of him cursing. I looked up and saw another man and a woman. The woman was young and beautiful, the man short and stocky. For a moment, a cruel, cruel moment, I thought they were my parents. I was blinking against the sun and hadn't seen them clearly.

"Mamá? Papá?" I stood, slowly shielding my eyes from the bright sunlight until I could see them clearly. She was not that young, and he was more stout than strong. My heart broke and tears ran down my face. I felt a strong grip on my arm.

"Who are you? What were you doing in there?" the mustachioed man asked. He looked angry, his white suit was dirty from the fall, his mouth puckered like he had eaten something putrid.

Sound came out of my mouth, but no words. I was more animal than human then. I cried and wailed and tried to pull away, but he was too strong.

"The police will have to deal with you," he said.

The thought of this terrified me. The police had ties to the cartel. If the cartel found out a boy had been staying in Uncle Francisco's restaurant, they would guess who I was. They would kill me. What my mother did to save my life would be in vain.

I screamed at the top of my lungs, balled my hand into a fist, and punched the man as hard as I could in the nose. Blood started to stream down his face and he let go of me with his left arm, his right hand slapping me so hard in the face that I fell backwards on the ground and tasted blood.

"You little..." he screamed, coming towards me. He was angry. I knew that he would hurt me. I scrambled to my feet and ran. I looked back once, the sun once again making the other man and woman hard to see, outlined in bright light. I wanted them to be my parents, alive by some holy miracle. I needed them to be my parents, but I knew they weren't.

Just like the night my parents were killed, I ran. I ran as long as I could until I collapsed from exhaustion.

Chapter 17

My first night on lurker patrol I wasn't planning on doing anything. I just went to the cathedral and tried to be Aware. "Awareness of Others" to be specific. In Banquo's threefold lesson of Awareness, I needed to become as Aware as I could of what was going on up there.

The whole thing made me uncomfortable. I used to love this cathedral. Being here brought back memories of my time living here as a boy, but it also brought into sharp relief my current situation and quandary.

When I arrived, I stood in front of the crucifix. The wooden carving showed the agony of Christ. This one depicted the moment when he thought God had abandoned him. In my own way I could relate. I too felt like God had abandoned me. I had stayed strong after my death, dealing with being a ghost, keeping my faith. I had found my killer, I had brought him to justice, but God had not come for me. I had not heard His Call.

"Why?" I asked the crucifix.

The statue remained inert. I wasn't expecting it to start

talking to me, but I guess a part of me hoped that in this sacred space I would get some kind of message.

I floated there, my head level with Christ's about a meter away, staring. This image represented the core of the Catholic faith, my faith. That Christ died on the cross for our sins. That accepting Him and living a righteous life would lead us to Him and heaven.

"Was my life not righteous enough?" I asked quietly. I had sinned, but I had repented too. I had lived a hard life, but I had done my best to make the world a better place with the skills I possessed. What more did He want?

That vague sense of motion caught my attention again. I turned from the crucifix and ignored it for the rest of the night. I positioned myself in the center of the church, lying on my back. Not really "lying," I am a ghost after all, but floating with my form horizontal so I could observe the ceiling.

The wooden arches were graceful, rising high to a pointed peak. The ceiling was a smooth white, forming a slightly curved arch at the top. It wasn't extravagant, but it was beautiful, and comforting. This was as much my church as any.

I let my senses expand and soften as the night slipped past. I could hear the wind whistling outside and the scurry of a mouse or two, but otherwise things were dead quiet. My Awareness didn't glean me much information until midnight came around.

I could feel it coming—all us ghosts can. It is the time we feel the most powerful. This is a fact, observable, unassailable, but not something I have ever felt comfortable with. It seems so... pagan. Midnight is called the witching hour, a time of fear for the righteous, and yet it is the time that I, as a ghost, feel most alive.

As midnight came, the vague sense of movement and the occasional sound I would hear from the ceiling started to clarify.

The movement resolved into what seemed like bodies. From my position I got the sense of a ghostly room forming at the top of the cathedral, and I sensed more than saw the feet of ghosts as they moved about the room. The sounds I heard resolved into voices—I couldn't understand anything, but it was clear they were voices. I also heard what sounded like music.

Yochi was the only ghost that seemed to live in the church. Why just him? I would think a church would be full of ghosts, that they would flock there for comfort, hoping to find a way home.

As my Awareness grew, it made sense. Here were the ghosts, these lurkers. They were up there in what seemed like their own world.

I heard the distinct sound of a door creaking open and then footfalls on wooden stairs, hollow and echoing.

I "stood up" and looked around, but I was alone in the church. There were no stairs here anyway.

The sound became louder and more distinct, and then I saw him.

He was a ghost, his transparency made it obvious. He wore work boots and a worn, blue, collared shirt. He was Mexican and looked a bit scared.

As he approached, the stairs became clear and he became less transparent. The stairs ran along one of the long walls of the church and up to the ceiling where I had become "Aware" of the floor of the lurkers' area.

He stopped when he was several feet above the pews. He looked around, his eyes darting to each corner of the cathedral as if he was afraid of seeing something. He slowly kneeled, his eyes meeting mine.

"Hey," he whispered. "You coming or what?"

Chapter 18

"Where did you go?" Lela asked. "After you left your uncle's restaurant?"

I shrugged.

"You don't know?"

"No," I said. "I really don't. I was in Mexico City, I ranged the whole western side of the city. But I don't know exactly where I ended up. Time passed in this weird slow motion blur. The days were long as I struggled for survival, but they blurred into each other until I wasn't aware of the day or the month, and barely aware of the season."

"How did you survive?" she asked.

I shook my head again and looked down at Sister Dominga. Her face was relaxed, her breathing shallow. All this storytelling, all this Lela focus made me worry I was forgetting why I was here. I was here for Sister Dominga. I was there in case she needed me when she passed. I was there because I had lost my faith...

"I honestly don't remember too much of it. I learned to beg and steal. I learned to take a beating and to give one. I did what I had to do. It's not a time I am proud of, and it's not a time I've ever remembered well."

I couldn't meet her eyes. What I had said was true when I was alive, but now that I'm dead I could remember that time—that improved ghostly memory can be a curse. As I spoke to her, images of that time flashed through my memory: the first real beating I received from a baker over a stale loaf of bread; stealing food from a poor family in a slum—they were only slightly better off than I was, and I felt so guilty; hooking up with a gang of street kids my age, we would work together and break into houses or corner groceries and steal food; the first time I beat someone, a kid a year younger than me I caught stealing some things from my stash hidden in a basement of an old collapsed building.

It was a life I didn't want to remember. A life without love or faith. A life only about survival.

"You did what you had to do," she said quietly.

I looked up and saw moisture in her blue eyes. Had she been "Aware" of the memories that had just flitted by? Did she know I hadn't told her the truth?

"But Sister Dominga found you, right?" she added.

I took a moment, looking back down at Sister Dominga. I gathered the threads of my story. I had lost my faith in God, but right before Sister Dominga found me I had found my faith in something else. In myself. "She did," I finally said. "But not for a while. First I became a Muchacho."

THAT FIRST YEAR ON THE STREET HARDENED ME. I WAS very skinny, but strong and wiry. It had been over a year, and I was ten, but I hadn't marked either of my birthdays, or even known when they were. I hadn't even cared. Life was too hard to worry about such things.

I remember the day things changed for me. January is the coldest month in Mexico City. It was down around four degrees Celsius (40 degrees Fahrenheit) and I was cold. I had been spending the nights on a hill off of Claveles Street huddled under a tree. There were a bunch of small parks on Claveles backing the steep hills I hid in. There were always kids around; no one ever seemed to notice me.

I had recently relocated. Things had gotten bad for me where I had been living and I had moved. The trees offered some shelter, but it wasn't a very good place.

I was skulking by a small *carnicería* (butcher), trying to decide if I dared tried to steal some meat to go with the half a rotten head of lettuce I had found in the park.

"Not a bad hiding place," a voice said in Spanish. "Those trees are thick."

Adrenaline flooded my system and I was in fight or flight. In the beginning it would always be flight, after that first year it became more and more fight. There was a rock along the road and I stooped to grab it before turning to confront the speaker.

He was older than me, around twelve, and he didn't look like a street kid. He had decent, although not new, clothes and didn't have that sunken look in his face that kids like me that begged and stole had. I felt a pang of jealousy imagining that he had a home and a family.

"What?" I asked. I wasn't used to kind voices.

His head bobbed back the way I had come. "Those trees. At least you have shelter, but you don't want to be there for rainy season."

He had a kind-looking face, his posture relaxed, his hands open and away from his body. I relaxed a little.

"Yeah," I said, keeping the rock in my hand and trying to decide if I could eat the wilted lettuce.

"I bet you're hungry," he said. "My name is Rafael, but everyone calls me Rafa. What's your name?"

I looked back up at him. He had held his distance—he was doing everything he could to convey he wasn't a threat. "Juan," I said. I hadn't used the name "Jesús" since the night my parents had died. While it was a common name, I was paranoid the cartel would find me and kill me too. Even in a city of eight million.

Juan was also my father's name. Using it, in some small way, kept my parents' memory alive.

"So, Juan," he said slowly. "I've got an opening on my team. All my boys are fed well. We need kids that are fast on their feet, that can take care of themselves."

"No," I said, walking away from the carnicería and sitting on the low curb. I stripped leaves off the head of lettuce, discarding them until I got to some lettuce that was only old and wilted.

"Mamá, she's making *tortas* for breakfast," he said, squatting down in front of me. "She bakes the bread herself, makes the beans, I think she's got some shredded pork she'll put in it. Her place is warm. You'll be safe, I promise."

The thought of meat made my mouth water, more than the tasteless lettuce I was chewing on would account for. I licked my lips. "Who is this Mamá?" I asked.

"I used to be like you," he said, his eyes leaving mine and going to the forest that was my home. "I was starving until she found me. I am one of her Muchachos now. I am safe and fed now."

Muchachos means "boys," but the way he said it made it sound somehow important. The lettuce had turned to cardboard in my mouth and I stopped chewing, looking at Rafael. The idea of real food that I didn't have to risk a beating for was undeniable.

"Just come, Juan. Come meet Mamá, come meet the other boys. Fill your belly. No obligation. I promise."

I stared at Rafa, he had a gentle smile on his face, one hand outstretched. The smell of rotting garbage, something I was very used to, suddenly became overwhelming and repugnant. I dropped the lettuce I had found and slowly nodded my head.

Chapter 19

"Mamá," Rafael said, "this is Juan." He stood tall and he sounded proud.

He had led me through the early morning streets of Mexico City, to the northeast about ten kilometers, more towards the center of the city. Rafa walked fast and seemed strong. He also seemed to know his way around the city very well. We avoided large streets for the most part.

We had come to an old brick building with boarded windows and graffiti all over it. It looked abandoned. He had led me through a listing, tin-roofed shack leaning on a rough stone wall in front of and below this house, right on the street. We had entered the shack where he had rapped on a door in a complicated pattern. A skinny kid opened the door for us, smiling at Rafa, and we walked through a cool tunnel and climbed up a ladder into a small, dark room. He guided me up the stairs onto the fourth floor into a normal-looking kitchen—except for the boarded windows. The scent of cooking food made my mouth water and my stomach grumble.

"He's smart and fast," Rafa continued. "I've been

watching him for a few weeks now. I think he'd make a great Muchacho."

Mamá was not young, but she was not old either. Her hair was jet black and pulled up into a bun atop her head. She had deep lines cut around her mouth, either from laughing a lot or smiling a lot, I could not tell. She wiped her hands on her beige apron and looked me up and down.

My instinct was to run, but Rafa had coached me about what would happen. As Mamá looked at me, I kept my eyes locked with hers, not looking away. She held my face in her warm hands, I could smell flour on them, she tilted my chin up and gazed into my eyes.

"Your parents?" she asked.

"Dead," I said. "Cartel."

Mamá nodded, her eyes narrowing as she shook her head as if it was the saddest and most common of stories. "How long?" she asked.

I shrugged. "More than a year."

She nodded again. I could feel Rafael beside me; he was standing arrow straight like he was an officer in the army. She let go of my chin and stepped back. I felt the warmth of her hand there even more once she wasn't touching me anymore. I almost lost it, but I took a deep breath and fought back tears. It had been so long since I had been touched in a kind way. I wanted more.

"Can you read?" she asked.

"A little," I said. "I speak English real good, though."

She smiled, her eyes traveling up and down my body. "He's strong," she said, her gaze traveling to Rafa.

"Yes, Mamá, and fast. More than a year on his own, he's done well."

Mamá nodded, a smile creeping onto her face. "Hungry?" she asked.

"Yes, Mamá," I said.

She served Rafa and me fresh-baked tortas stuffed with pulled pork and beans with rice on the side. It was the kind of meal I dreamed about and it felt like heaven to me. The warm gentle touch of a motherly figure, hot fresh food, a roof over my head.

Mamá sat and watched me as I ate. She had a small smile on her face and at first I was afraid I would do something wrong. I took my first bite and looked up at her. I felt guilty, as if the food wasn't mine, as if I had stolen it and gotten caught. She smiled broadly, those lines framing her mouth becoming very deep, and encouraged me with a nod.

She didn't question me while I ate, she just watched. As if she could glean something important about me by how I ate.

When my plate was clean, Mamá took it to the sink. I looked at Rafa and grinned, my smile must have been a kilometer wide. We sat at a rough wooden table with a white cloth over it and two long benches. In the middle of the table was a bowl of ripe fruit. There were apples, tangerines, and pears. The sight of them made me feel hungry even though I had just eaten better than I had in months. The fruit was carefully arranged with a gloriously ripe pear topping it.

I could smell its sweet scent. I could imagine it, silky smooth in my mouth. I hadn't had a pear since before my parents died. Rafa was now at the sink cleaning dishes and Mamá had stepped out of the room. They had so much fruit, what would anyone mind?

I reached out and grabbed the pear. Its flesh yielded slightly to my touch, I knew it was perfect. That it was at the peak of ripeness, that it would be a crime not to eat it. I licked my lips and was pulling it towards my mouth when I felt a vicelike grip on my wrist.

"Put it down," Mamá hissed in my ear. She had come in while I was obsessed with the fruit and I hadn't noticed. Rafa turned from the sink and I saw a look of fear pass over his face before he hid it with a smile. Mamá's face was no longer kind, but scary, those deep lines forming a more convincing frown than smile.

Mamá was stronger than I thought. Her grip hurt. I didn't make a sound, but slowly let the pear go. It bounced onto the table and rolled and fell to the floor. "I thought..." I began.

She let go of my wrist and I rubbed it. She sat on the bench opposite me, the frown gone and the smile back. "I apologize, Juan. You don't know our rules."

Rafa stood back watching, that fake smile still on his face. As if this were the simplest of exchanges. As if there wasn't any danger here. I had lived too long on the street not to know that things might have just turned ugly.

"I'm sorry, Mamá," I said in my most conciliatory tone. "I thought the fruit was for the taking."

Mamá eyes narrowed. She knew I was lying.

"I'm still hungry," I continued. "I never get fruit that good. Please forgive me." I shrunk back into myself, becoming as small as I could. This gesture was one I used when begging. I knew that people often took pity on me when they saw me like that, all skinny and hunched over.

Mamá chuckled and signaled Rafa to sit next to her. "Oh, he's good, Rafa. He's good. I see why you took a shine to him."

I looked from Mamá to Rafa and back to Mamá. They

knew my tricks. I slowly straightened my spine and looked Mamá straight in the eye. "I think I should go now." I was afraid. From experience what was likely to follow was a beating. I was now bluffing with bravado, hoping to escape that beating.

Mamá took a deep breath and let out a sigh. "You don't have to go. No one is going to hurt you. I am sorry for my reaction. You see, we have two rules around this place." She looked to Rafa.

"Rule one," Rafa began. "You can lie to yourself all you like, but you can never lie to Mamá. Rule two. Never take anything from Mamá or the Muchachos without permission."

I nodded slowly. These rules were simple, but would be hard to follow. I had learned to survive by lying and stealing.

"Do you understand, Juan?" she asked.

"Yes, Mamá. No lying, no stealing."

She smiled, her eyes crinkling up. "That's it exactly. What you do out there, I don't care. But in here, among our family, these rules are sacred. These rules keep us together and keep us alive."

In some ways I was relieved. The food had seemed just too good to be true. I didn't trust the carrot until the stick had revealed itself.

"Is there something you'd like to say, Juan?" she asked.

I looked into her eyes. I wasn't sure if she wanted an apology or not. I thought carefully before I said, "Can I please have a piece of fruit, Mamá?"

She smiled broadly. "Of course you can." She then took a fresh pear from the bowl and handed it to me. I looked to the now bruised piece on the floor. "Oh, forget that, child. We have plenty."

I bit into the soft flesh of the pear, its sweet juices rolling down my chin.

"When he's done," Mamá said to Rafael, "show him around. I think he should bunk with you for a while."

I watched as my fate was decided. Part of me wanted to run, didn't trust this place, but with my full stomach and the sweetness of the pear in my mouth, I couldn't say no. And as I thought about it, I didn't think saying no was even an option.

Chapter 20

THE LURKER ON THE GHOSTLY STAIRCASE LOOKED COM-pletely normal for a ghost. His form had sharp edges and was fairly transparent. He crouched down right above the pews and beckoned to me. "Come on," he whispered, his eyes once again searching the church as if he was afraid he would be found. "The door won't be there for long."

I hesitated. I thought of JJ, he would have been up those stairs already, but I had my doubts. I had sensed ghosts were up there, and now I knew they were. But what were they doing and what was that place?

My eyes wandered back to the statue of Jesús on the cross, his face contorted in pain from thinking that God had abandoned him. I turned back to the stranger. "What's up there?"

The fear left his eyes and he smiled. "Heaven, my friend. It's heaven. Come on, we've been watching you. It's time you joined us."

I stood there with my mouth open. Was this some weird form of the Call? Was the way to heaven up a ghostly staircase? I started to fly towards him, but a thought stopped me cold. "What about Sister Dominga?"

His eyes went from me and up and to the side a bit. Right where Sister Dominga's room was. "It's not her time, not quite yet."

I nodded. "But I want to be there for her. I'm... I'm not ready to leave her for good."

His brow furrowed for a moment and then he chuckled. "Oh, I'm sorry," he said. "I think I've given you the wrong impression." He pointed up. "It's not literally heaven. It's just like it for those of us that choose to stay there."

I shook my head trying to clear my thoughts. "I don't know," I began.

The fear came back on his face as his eyes searched the church. "Listen," he whispered, "I can't wait any longer. I'll come down tomorrow evening and see if you are ready." He turned and began ascending the staircase.

"Ready for what?" I asked.

He turned and smiled. "Ready to start living again, my friend."

I watched as he ascended the stairs, opened a door and disappeared. I could still sense the space the lurkers were occupying. I could still hear the occasional murmur of voices and music, but as the time passed it got less and less distinct until a few hours after midnight when it was nothing more than that vague sense of motion again.

I spent the rest of the night wondering at what the man had said. First he had called it heaven and then he had said I could start living again up there. What did that mean?

LELA'S BLUE EYES GOT WIDE WHEN I TOLD HER OF MY encounter with the lurker. We were back at our posts with

Sister Dominga, pumping the warmth in. I had been there a few weeks now, and she had changed. Her face was becoming more and more skeletal as her body consumed itself.

They were feeding her, Sister Helen was dutiful and came in regularly, bathing her, tending to her physical body in the best way she could. Sister Dominga was neat and clean. She was obviously cared for, but she was slowly slipping away.

"Do you know what's wrong with her?" I asked Lela, my thoughts no longer on the lurkers.

Lela nodded, removing her hands from underneath Sister Dominga's body, and held her hand over her abdomen. "The liver is too large, as well as the spleen." Her hands traveled up and down Sister Dominga's body. "Her lymph nodes are all swollen, that's why her neck seems so large while her face seems so thin."

I watched Lela closely as she told me this. Her eyes seemed farther away than usual. She said the words with little emotion, but her face told another story. "The cancer, though, is in her blood, in her lymph, moving throughout her body."

"Leukemia?" I asked.

Lela nodded. "A slow-moving form."

"She's been this way a long time," I said as Lela moved her hands back under Sister Dominga.

"That is partially our doing," she said.

"What?"

"This, what we are doing here. We are slowing the progression of the disease."

I removed my hands and backed up a step. The thought was disturbing to me. Most of my life I had been a person of faith. And for me, that faith ameliorated the fear of death.

Now that I was dead, now that I knew there was an afterlife, I didn't know how I felt about extending the life of someone like Sister Dominga. She was going to die. Nothing was going to stop that. Did I want her to keep living like this?

The smile on Lela's face was compassionate. Her pale blue eyes always made me feel like she could see into me, could see to my soul. She was an accomplished ghost, so I suspected that Awareness helped her perception to match what I felt when I looked at those eyes. She stepped back too, and walked around the bed to me.

"Let's take a break, OK? Sister Helen is on her way anyway."

A few moments later I heard the heavy footfalls of Sister Helen coming up the steps. I nodded and followed Lela out the window.

"So, show me something," Lela said. We had flown to the roof of the convent. It was our usual hangout.

"Like what?" I asked.

She shrugged. "I've never been to Mexico City before. Show me the sights."

I looked down to where Sister Dominga's room was. I felt torn. I was still conflicted about extending her life, but I didn't want to leave her. I didn't want to miss her transition.

"She's not going today," Lela said gently, her hand touching my shoulder. "Open yourself up, you know it too."

The lurker had also told me it wasn't her time yet. I took a deep breath (ghost style) and opened myself up to Awareness. I could feel Sister Dominga, I could feel her pain, her struggle. But her death did not seem imminent.

"What do you want to see?" I asked.

"I don't know much about Mexico City," she said.

I thought briefly. "Well, there is really only one place to start. Chapultepec Castle."

Chapter 21

THE GROUNDS OF CHAPULTEPEC CASTLE ARE EXQUISITE, they were laid out before us as we flew over them. A dark green lake, Lago de Chapultepec, sat in the middle of the property. Large deciduous trees covered the land with manicured gardens and wide brick walking paths lined with vendors' stalls.

The castle itself was built in the 18th century and sits atop a hill overlooking the area. The Aztecs considered the hill sacred. The castle currently holds *Museo Nacional de Historia*, the Nation History Museum.

Also on the grounds are a zoo and various other museums. If you are a tourist in Mexico City, this is one of your first stops. You can spend days here.

I knew Chapultepec well. I had spent my first few months with Mamá and the Muchachos there. The thoughts of them rose up in my mind when we arrived, but I pushed it down. We were taking a day off, I wasn't telling my story, I was having time alone with Lela.

That may seem an odd thought, "time alone." We had

spent days together, but it was all about Sister Dominga or telling my story.

"It's beautiful," she said, her voice quiet. We were hovering in front of the castle itself, with its white and grey stone walls, round towers, and the flag of Mexico flying at the top of it. Below us tourists flowed in and out of the castle, going to visit the museum.

"It's only the beginning," I promised her. "Chapultepec Park is like Mexico's Central Park or the National Mall in Washington, DC."

She nodded, her face beaming. It was a side of her I hadn't seen.

"Shall we?" I said, beckoning her as we flew through the large glass doors on the second floor. Being ghosts, we had unprecedented access and got to tour the entire castle. We flew above the meat folk (a term my friend JJ uses for the living) and visited every room. The ornate dining room with its velvet curtains, high ceilings, and chandelier. The rooms converted to the museum with artifacts from Mexico's history. And finally to the round watchtower that rose above the rest of the building and afforded a fine view of Mexico City sprawling to the east of the castle.

We had encountered quite a few bardo-brained ghosts as we flew through. Some of them appeared to be quite old. We could tell because, although their forms were wispy, we could catch telltale signs of antiquated military uniforms.

It's when we flew through the window of the tower that we encountered a more interesting ghost. He was pacing, looking out the windows. Going to the center of the room and leaning down as if studying something on a table that was no longer there.

He was dressed in an archaic military uniform and,

judging from the stripes on his shoulder, he appeared to be a captain.

My first inclination was to fly back out, and I made a move to do so, but Lela caught my hand and held it, her eyes following the ghost. "Wait," she whispered.

I liked the feeling of her hand in mine. As has been said before, the ghostly sense of touch is just a shadow of what it is like for humans, but it has certain qualities that human touch doesn't. You see, humans "feel" touch so strongly because of their meat bodies. All the sensory nerves, the warmth of the flesh, pressure, texture, that is lost as ghosts, but something is gained. Awareness.

When two ghostly forms come together they can share emotions clearly and easily. It's like a direct connection. I could tell that Lela was excited to see this ghost. She was grateful for time away from what we had been doing. She was happy to be there with me.

While she stared at the captain, I stared at her. She seemed lost enough in the experience to not notice much about what I was feeling.

I had experienced touch as a ghost before, but usually only briefly and not with... with... a woman. This phenomena was new to me, and I was floored by it. I never wanted her to let go.

"Who do you think he is?" she asked. Her eyes briefly meeting mine. "The museum below was great, but right here is the real history. Not words or books, but one of the souls that made that history."

I tore my eyes away from her and studied the pacing figure. He was tall with a lean face and dark brown hair. He had a commanding presence, but was agitated. He seemed to be quite oblivious of us.

"He could be Captain Manuel Agustín Mascaró," I said. "He helped build the castle in the late 1700s. He was accused of building it as a fortress to rebel against the Spanish Crown. He died mysteriously, as the story is told, by poisoning."

Lela nodded eagerly, her eyes still fixed on the ghost. "How do you know all this?"

"I spent a lot of time here. We're almost to that part of the story. I'll be telling it soon."

We watched in silence for several more minutes. Lela intent on the ghost, me completely distracted by her touch.

"Captain," she said finally. She let go of my hand and moved next to the ghost. "Captain Mascaró." The ghost's eyes flickered toward her for just a moment. I watched as Lela quickly transformed herself so she had short hair and wore a military uniform similar to his. In her hand were some parchments with writing on them.

Her transformation was similar to what JJ and I did when looking for my killer and made ourselves look like Tucson police officers. But she did it with such speed and grace that I was in awe.

"I have those reports, Captain Mascaró," she said. "As ordered, sir."

Mascaró stopped and looked her up and down. The table he had seemed to be going to came into form. It was very transparent and dim, but I could see it now. "Very good," he said taking the parchments from Lela and setting it down on the table.

"The general said you would have word to take back," Lela said, her spine straight as she stood at attention.

"Yes, yes, of course," he said. He seemed distracted. "Tell the general that construction proceeds apace. We have had some supply issues with the quarries, but we are getting that ironed out."

"Yes, sir," Lela said, turning away and walking towards me. She morphed back into her normal form, a big smile on her face. The ghostly table disappeared as she did this.

"That was so much fun," she said, her smile wide. "I think that *was* Mascaró. Come on, let's go see if we can find more of these old ghosts. Interact with history itself. This is so exciting. Don't you think?"

She flew out of the window and I followed. I had never seen Lela like this. She was buoyant, effusive. She was bright and happy. I couldn't take my eyes off her and longed for the day when she held my hand again.

Chapter 22

THE BRICKS UNDER ME WERE COLD, BUT THE SUN BEATING on my face was warm. I smelled the dirt and grime that covered me and my fellow Muchacho, Flaco. I shyly gazed up at the tourists, a man and woman, walking by on their way into Chapultepec Castle. They had light skin and were sure to be gringos. I kept my face in the proper configuration: pitiful with the tiniest trace of hope. The man looked away immediately, but my eyes met the woman's. I pursed my lips as if about to plead and then let a shiver run though my body. While the sun was warm, it was February and a cool 7 degrees Celsius (45 Fahrenheit) outside.

She paused, her husband stepping forward several steps before turning back for her. I put my hand to my belly, accentuating just how skinny I was, and shivered again. Flaco kept his head down. I was in training. Flaco was the head *mendigo* (beggar) and had been training me for about a week.

"Come on," the man said in English, grabbing the woman's hand. "They need more than we can give." They both had wedding rings on and they were about thirty. They were here alone, but I guessed that they had young children back home.

I patted my belly again and said in Spanish, "*Comida, por favor.*" I brought my fingers to my mouth miming eating. Next to me, Flaco moaned pitifully and fell into my lap, his eyes fluttering open and briefly connecting with the woman.

"Let's go," the man said, pulling on her.

"No," she whispered, pulling her hand from her husband's.

I patted Flaco on the head and whispered to him to wake up in urgent Spanish. I looked up at the woman again and let a tear roll down my face.

She stepped towards me, her hand in her purse, her eyes moist with tears. "I'm so sorry," she said. "I hope this helps." She dropped a ten-dollar bill into the grimey, straw basket we had in front of us. It only had a few small peso notes in it.

"*Gracias, señora, usted es un ángel,*" I said, my face beaming. I didn't think she would understand every word, but knew she would know I was thanking her and calling her an angel. "*Un ángel,*" I added for emphasis, shaking Flaco who roused himself and called her an angel too.

The husband looked annoyed, but she turned from us beaming, a spring in her step. She would feel good about this all day; she would tell her friends.

When they were out of sight, Flaco grabbed the ten-dollar bill, hid it away in his clothes, and said, "Good job, Juan. Let's find another."

I, OF COURSE, HAD NO IDEA AT THE TIME, BUT MY FIRST few months with the Muchachos, that I spent begging, was my initial training to be a bounty hunter.

You had to study people so you could predict their reactions. You had to get to know the soldiers that walked the ground with their uniforms and their rifles. You had to know which ones you could bribe and how much was enough. You had to be able to size up the tourists—we only ever worked the gringos, foreigners—and know which ones might be open. You had to catch the look in their eye and either reel them in or let them go. If you got too many tourists upset, the soldiers would drag you away, bribe or no.

I didn't like to beg. I had done it, of course, that year I was alone on the street. But I was never very good at it. With Flaco's help, I quickly became adept. There is an art to it, as there is to all things.

Flaco was rail thin and about ten years old. He was so skinny he could just stand and quiver a little and people would throw coins in his basket. But he knew all the tricks, all the ways to manipulate the turistas.

As part of the mendigo squad of the Muchachos, we didn't get breakfast or lunch. Mamá had told me, "You can't just act hungry, you have to *be* hungry." I didn't like it, but it is what I was assigned to do. And it was much better than my life on the street alone.

I didn't actually join the Muchachos. After that meal, after I learned the rules, Rafael gave me the tour of the building, introduced me to the few other boys that were there, and put me to work cleaning.

The next day I was assigned to Flaco's crew and started learning to beg from him.

Flaco was actually bright and intelligent and had a wicked sense of humor. The half-catatonic state he was in for our begging sessions was just an act.

One day as we walked to Chapultepec Castle, I asked

him, "How do you stay so skinny?" I had only been there a week, and even with just one meal a day, I had already started to gain weight.

He opened his mouth and jabbed two fingers towards it, his eyes wide, a wicked grin on his face.

"You throw it up?" I asked.

"Sure thing," he said. "Why not? It makes the gringos go weak." He stopped walking, we were alone on a one-lane street with brick buildings towering on either side of us. He grabbed my arm and turned me towards him. "Besides, this way Mamá loves me. This way I am *El Mejor!*" El Mejor means "the best," it was a term used in the house. For beggars, Flaco was El Mejor. For runners (or *corredores*), Rafa was El Mejor. Each crew at Mamá's had an El Mejor. They were accorded respect, extra food if they wanted it, and usually got their own room.

Flaco's eyes were bloodshot and his grip on my arm was weak, I could have broken it easily. He was giving up a lot for Mamá.

"But... you're not healthy, Flaco."

He shrugged and started walking again. "But I am El Mejor, I am somebody." He walked several paces before adding, "A few days a week I eat a smaller meal and keep it. I don't give all of them back."

My stomach grumbled loudly. I hated missing meals now that I had access to good food.

Flaco stopped me and put his ear to my belly. "What is that, Mr. Stomach?" he asked. He pulled away and spoke to my stomach. "Yes, you should be jealous of Flaco's stomach. Flaco has the best stomach, the strongest stomach, and you should not give your food back and try to be like Flaco."

He pulled away from me, a huge grin on his face and

started trotting down the street, his fist raised. He hummed the theme from the movie *Rocky*—Mamá had a fancy VHS player and a TV. We would all watch movies at night. He waved back and forth, his humming growing louder, the sound bouncing off the brick walls. "¡El mejor mendigo!" he shouted, pumping his fists into the air.

Flaco was happy, actually one of the happiest of the Muchachos. I smiled, laughed, and ran after him. I was too young to realize just how badly Flaco was hurting himself by staying so skinny. And good thing for me that Flaco was right, my stomach could not compete with his. I kept all my food. Flaco didn't.

Chapter 23

FLACO AND I BECAME GOOD FRIENDS. WHILE WE WERE at Chapultepec, it was all business, but on the long walks to and from, we talked. He had this amazing ability to be happy even though the story of his life was no less tragic than mine.

Flaco had been abandoned at birth. He never knew his mother or father. He was one of those babies found in a dumpster. He spent a few years in an orphanage, a few years in foster homes, but nothing ever worked well for him. Flaco wasn't pretty, he had a deep scar on his left cheek and his right eye was droopy—no one ever wanted to adopt him. Flaco wasn't ever very healthy, his asthma and other ailments made taking care of him difficult.

All of this made him a great mendigo. Mamá was the first real mother he had had. He was completely devoted to her. She made sure he had the medicines he needed, never asked him not to eat, and made him feel like he had a place and a purpose.

Through Flaco's eyes I began to love Mamá too. If she

could find a place for him, it stood to reason that she could find a place for me.

"Tonight's the night," I said to Flaco one evening on our walk home. The sky was a dusky orange, the sun just having set. We were skirting an old boarded up building in a bad section of the city.

"What?" he asked.

"The night you fill your belly and keep all your food," I said. I really liked Flaco and made it my mission to try to get him to eat more. "You are so skinny, I think your legs may break. You can't be a good mendigo if you can't walk to the castle."

"You are becoming a good mendigo," Flaco said, ignoring my comment. "Maybe tomorrow you will work alone."

I stopped short. Flaco went several paces down the cracked sidewalk before turning back. "Alone?" I asked. The thought made my knees feel a bit weak. With Flaco it was a game, it was fun. I was worried that I wouldn't be able to do it well on my own.

"It's time," he said, walking back to me. "Did you think you would get to sit with El Mejor forever?"

"I... I..." I stammered.

"If I am a good teacher, then you can do this alone." His face was serious. It was important to him that he taught me well, that he served Mamá well.

"Yeah... You are the best, Flaco."

"Well, isn't this sweet," a voice said. Flaco and I had been busy with our conversation and hadn't noticed the three boys that stood in front of us.

I looked at them. They were a few years older and a lot bigger than us. They looked like they had homes and ate regular meals. I took a step in front of Flaco and said, "What do you want?"

The one in the lead grinned. He was missing one of his front teeth and had a dark, brooding look. "Your money."

I looked around. The street was virtually empty, no traffic, no one close.

Flaco stepped up beside me, his skinny chest thrust forth. "All we have is Mamá's, and you can't have her money."

Rule two. Everything we earned begging was hers. We couldn't spend it, we couldn't lose it, and we couldn't give it away.

The guy in front crossed his arms and laughed. The two boys beside him did too. "Well, my name is Hector, and it's my money now. Hand it over, boys." They each took a step forward.

Flaco held all the money. It had been a pretty good day. We had about one hundred pesos. Not a lot, but enough to feed the Muchachos for a few days.

I had been studying Hector, the way I studied people at Chapultepec, the way Flaco had taught me. He was bigger and stronger and determined to take our money. But I didn't think he was willing to risk too much. I stepped forward right in front of Hector.

"You must not have heard of Mamá and her Muchachos. If you take her money, we will come find you, all of us. We will hunt you down and we will extract our revenge. We will kill you and then feast on your plump thighs." I stepped back and looked at his legs and licked my lips. I had no idea what Mamá would do if they stole the money—to them or us—and I didn't want to find out.

Hector frowned and gulped as if he were trying to swallow

dirt. The other two boys had taken a step back. His eyes grew distant and then he looked Flaco and me up and down. He was deciding what to do…. he was going to take the money anyway.

"Run, Flaco!" I yelled as I rushed Hector, running square into him while my knee came up into his crotch. He was bigger and stronger and I figured I had a better chance at close quarters. He grunted, then cried out and threw me back. I landed hard on the street, the wind knocked out of me.

"Get him!" he growled, speaking to his companions about the fleeing Flaco. "This one is mine."

I heard Flaco's thin cackle as he ran away and two sets of footsteps following him. Flaco was faster than you'd think and knew this area better than anyone. He also had all the money.

I smiled, but not for long. Soon Hector's foot was stomping down towards my face. I rolled out of the way and then got up. He looked angry, but limped awkwardly—I had done some damage.

Hector was bigger than me and older than me and mad. He rushed me, his outstretched arms aiming for my throat, and I sidestepped him. He stumbled and nearly fell. I laughed because what he had done was funny, but mostly because I wanted him to make more mistakes.

I heard shouts in the distance and turned to look. I saw Flaco and his two pursuers as they rounded a corner, headed for Mamá's place. They had gained some on Flaco, but it looked to me like he had a chance.

That was my mistake, of course. Not paying attention to Hector. His fist connected with my face and I went down. I landed hard on the street and tasted blood in my mouth.

He tried to kick me, but I rolled out of the way and got up and faced him.

"Give me your money," he growled.

"I don't have any," I said, stepping to the right, keeping out of his reach.

"I don't believe you," he said, matching my movements.

"If you'll step back a bit, I'll prove it."

He glared at me, but backed up two paces and crossed his arms on his chest.

I spit a mouthful of blood onto the sidewalk and wiped my mouth off. I then pulled open the pockets of my pants and pulled up my shirt. "See, no money."

This seemed to make him madder, his nostrils flared and his fists balled. "Shoes," he said, talking a step forward.

I didn't have anything in my shoes, but I wasn't about to take them off and make myself that much more vulnerable. I sighed, put my foot down on a barren terracotta planter, and leaned down. Instead of pulling my old and dirty sneakers off, I grabbed a handful of dirt and threw it in his face.

He yelled. I ran.

I flew past another abandoned building with boards over the windows and graffiti covering the boards. His footfalls pounded heavily behind me; his cursing fueled my sprint. Around a corner, dodging a drunk, homeless man and out onto another street. Crossing, dodging cars, and into another alley. Past the back door of a restaurant, the smell of cooking meat making my stomach grumble, but all I could taste was my own blood.

My lungs started to burn, but I didn't slow down. I heard his steps a bit farther behind me and his lungs working like bellows. The curses had stopped. I didn't look back—I relied on my ears to tell me where he was and kept my eyes focused on where I was going.

Down another street past a grocery with bins of colorful fruit, the sweet smell of it a temptation. My saliva was thick and I tried to spit more blood out of my mouth as I crossed another street, avoiding cars and people.

Onto another street, jumping over a garbage can, and I saw them. The two boys that had run after Flaco. They were bent over, hands on their legs as they dragged oxygen into their lungs. They looked up and saw me.

My first thought was: Flaco got away! My second thought was: shit!

I tried to rush past, but they grabbed me and held me. Seconds later, Hector was there breathing hard, a smile on his reddened face. I struggled, but it was no use; both of the boys holding me were stronger than I was. Hector punched me in the stomach and I doubled over, barely able to breathe. For the first time all day, I was glad my stomach was empty.

He punched me in the face and then kicked me in the crotch. I cried out, hoping someone would hear me and help. But no one did. The blows fell on me like a monsoon rain, and soon everything went black.

Chapter 24

THE LARGE EMPTY CEILING OF THE CHURCH HOVERED OVER me as I waited for midnight to come. It wasn't a sanctuary anymore, but like some large crouching creature I was afraid would pounce on me. I didn't want to be down here pursuing the mystery of the lurkers, I wanted to be with Lela, flitting about Mexico City, searching for old ghosts and their living history.

Since that first trip to Chapultepec Castle, our days had changed. We would still spend most of it attending to Sister Dominga, but we had begun to take these side trips visiting the old sites of Mexico City, searching out ghosts, trying to talk to them and learn firsthand what their lives were like.

We spent a lot of time in El Centro, the old historic Mexico City, at places like Palacio de Bellas Artes, the Aztec ruins at Templo Mayor, Casa de los Azulejos, and many museums.

We also spent a lot of time at Panteón de Dolores, the huge cemetery Flaco and I spent so much time walking past on our way to and from Chapultepec Castle. This is not the kind of cemetery Americans would understand. It's six hundred acres filled with over 700,000 tombs (a million or more dead laid to rest there). Some tombs are simple, some unbelievably ornate. During *Día de los Muertos*, Day of the Dead, it is one of the biggest parties you'll ever see.

Ghost tourism, you might call what Lela and I were doing.

I had, with great guilt, put off coming back down and dealing with the lurkers. After one of our adventures, after Lela had left to go wherever she went at night, I would sit with Sister Dominga and tell her about it all in great detail. More detail than the stories I was telling of my past. I would tell her everything. How the skin around Lela's eyes crinkled when she laughed. How thrilled I was when she held my hand. How those pale blue eyes that once seemed so distant and foreign were starting to feel like home to me.

Sister Dominga seemed to really like these stories. Her face would always relax, her breathing steady.

When we had first met, I couldn't even get Lela to stay in the same room with me. She was this big enigma. Now she was still an enigma, but thoughts of her were always with me. I was beginning to forget what it was like without her.

The rest of what I have been going through didn't go away. I was still there for Sister Dominga. I still longed to talk about my tattered faith and my ghostly state. But that didn't seem quite so important anymore. My head was full of Lela. There was hardly room for anything else.

The sound of a creaking door disturbed my reverie. I looked up and the stairs were there, the floor above me was becoming more visible. I sensed feet on the floor, I heard snatches of voices, a few notes of music. I heard steps coming down a rickety wooden staircase.

It was the same ghost with his frightened face, his work

boots, and his blue shirt. "Are you ready?" he whispered when he got to the bottom of the steps.

I flew up so I was level with him, but still a few meters away. "What are you scared of?" I asked, looking around, just as he was.

He put his finger to his lips, his eyes getting wider. "Mustn't speak it," he said quietly. "Not here. We can talk about it up there." He pointed to the ceiling.

"What is up there?" I asked. The staircase had become more real as we talked, as midnight came.

A smile cracked his face. "Home," he whispered. "You will like it, my friend. I promise." He took a step up the stairs and beckoned to me. "Come."

I opened myself up to Awareness. I didn't sense danger or deception. I felt joy and a breezy, carefree feeling. I nodded and flew to the bottom step. Banquo and Yochi had told me I had to do this, that this all linked together for me.

When my foot touched the step it became almost real, only slightly transparent. I could feel my foot on the step, almost like when I was alive. It almost felt as if gravity was pushing my form down onto the step.

I looked up to my companion; he had a wide grin on his face. "That's right, my friend. It's different here. It's better."

He slowly climbed the steps, treading carefully, as if he didn't want to make too much noise.

I followed, feeling my "weight" grow as we climbed. The voices and music became louder, it sounded like a party. About halfway up I stopped and inhaled deeply. This wasn't something thought out, but more instinctual. Being a ghost I hadn't had to breathe since I died, or smelled anything either. But there on those steps, as I inhaled, I smelled food.

My companion had stopped and squatted down so our

heads were at the same level. He chuckled and said, "You will love it up here."

"Beans," I said. "I smell beans, and meat, and tortillas."

He rubbed his hands together. "A feast in your honor. Everyone wants to meet you."

I was puzzled and confused, but the smells drew me forth. I hadn't realized just how much I had missed the sense of smell. Even the whisper of gravity I was feeling was a joy. Soon the man and I stood in front of a door. It was a large wooden door scarred with use and age. On the center of it was a symbol. An equilateral triangle pointed down, with an extra horizontal line about a third of the way down from the top.

"Each must enter on his own," he said looking back at me. "I will go first. You follow." He grasped the black metal doorknob and opened the door. The divine smell of food and the sound of laughter wafted out, but I could see only darkness. The door closed after him with a clang.

I stood there after he left. The sensual nature that was in there was calling to me. I looked down, I was high above the floor, the pews and the altars below, the ceiling about eight feet above me as it arched gracefully over.

The stairs underneath me, once nearly solid, were starting to become a bit transparent. What would it mean to enter the door? What was in there? Would I be able to come out when I wanted to? Why did Banquo and Yochi want me to deal with the lurkers? They didn't seem to be harming anyone.

I stood there in indecision as the staircase slowly faded, and the feeling of gravity tugging on my form lessoned.

And what about Lela? I couldn't bear that thought of missing her when she came in the morning.

The door itself began to fade and then the smell of cooking food came upon me again and my stomach grumbled. I didn't have a stomach, how could it do that? I felt saliva entering my mouth, I felt a hunger like I had never experienced before. I took ahold of the cold metal doorknob and pulled.

Light, sound, and smell spilled out of the room and I blinked against the brightness. The man I had followed up the stairs was standing there. It was some kind of foyer, with a brightly tiled floor and coats hung on pegs, just like you might find in restaurants and cantinas all over the world. I took a step forward, my foot pressing solidly on the tile floor.

"I am so hungry," I said.

He just nodded and smiled. The door slammed shut behind me, but I hardly noticed.

Chapter 25

EARLIER, I SAID THAT DURING MY YEAR ALONE ON THE street I had learned to take a beating. But, that's not really right. There is really nothing to learn, as if knowledge or experience can make it better. The only thing you learn is that it is possible to survive a horrible beating. And that does help in the recovery stage—knowing that the pain won't last forever.

"I ran," Flaco said, his voice pitched high. "I ran like the wind. Those older boys with their flabby bellies and fat faces could not keep up with me. I was light as a feather."

I nodded gingerly. I was in my room and Flaco sat on my bed. The room wasn't much. Just two beds, a boarded-up window with a gap at the top to let a breeze in, two cardboard boxes for belongings, and flaking paint on the walls. At that point I had the room to myself.

My lip was split badly and one eye was swollen shut. I had stabbing pains with each breath from the broken ribs. And because of all the bruises, I couldn't get comfortable. There was a bottle of little white pills next to the bed that dulled the pain.

The window had a tiny crack in it that let in just a sliver of sunlight and a tiny breeze. While I lay there, I looked out at the slice of house, part of a tree, and the blue sky. At night we covered all the windows with heavy drapes so no light escaped and our home didn't draw unwanted attention.

"They gave up when we hit the hill up here," Flaco continued. "They are clearly not Muchacho material. I ran through the tunnel and tore up the stairs and found Rafa with a few of the other corredores. I told them what had happened. I told them what you did." Flaco beamed at me. I seemed to have passed some kind of test. Mamá got her money and Flaco didn't get hurt. He treated me differently after that. Before he was El Mejor and I was his student. After, he treated me as an equal.

"We heard you crying out. We found you. Rafa and the boys took care of them, but good. They will steer clear of the Muchachos from now on." Flaco ended with a big smile, showing his missing front tooth.

I tried to smile, but it hurt too much. Despite the pain I was in and my many wounds, I was happy. I felt like I had a family again. People that cared about me. People that I cared about. A place that was mine. A home. Faith was coming back. Faith in my ability to survive. Faith in Mamá and her Muchachos.

That faith didn't last long.

IT TOOK TIME TO RECOVER FROM THE BEATING I HAD taken, but I didn't really mind. I had plenty of food to eat, a roof, and a bed. After a few days, Mamá got me up and put me to work in our building. Technically it was a demotion— the boys that cleaned and did laundry and simple errands, they were called *mozos* (houseboys).

I joined the other three mozos in doing menial tasks. And so as I recovered I had to eat at the mozo table at meal time, not the mendigo table with Flaco. It wasn't a big deal, but it highlighted for me the sharp lines that Mamá drew. Her unbreakable rules about lying and stealing, the strict grouping of us based on our jobs, the regimented way she ran her organization.

As a mozo, when I was almost better, I received a delivery. A small man with a crooked-toothed smile knocked shyly at the door to the tunnel that led into the house. I was on duty, watching the door. He had bloodshot eyes and his breath had a rotting meat smell.

"For Mamá," he said, handing the sack to me. It was heavy, maybe 20 kilos. He also handed me a piece of paper. It was a bill of sale, and on it was listed "cleaning powder."

I told him to wait and hauled the sack up to Mamá, up on the top floor in the kitchen. Halfway up I had to stop and rest, my stamina was not back yet. I found the sack curious. What would Mamá want with 20 kilos of cleaning powder? I carefully untied the sack, remembering exactly how it was tied. I wasn't going to steal, and if it came down to it, I wasn't going to lie, so I wasn't actually breaking any rules. I gasped and my heart began thudding in my chest when I saw what was in the sack. Twenty thick plastic bags with a bright white powder in it. Cocaine. It had to be cocaine.

A sweat broke out all over my body and one word danced around my mind. Cartel. My family died by the hands of one of the cartels, how could I live in a cartel house?

I knew that what Mamá did was unconventional—organizing beggars, Rafa and the runners taking packages from point to point, no questions asked. I knew this was not the kind of orphanage I used to hear about. But somehow in my mind I didn't suspect she was moving drugs.

My legs weak, I slowly sat down on the stairs and wiped the sweat from my brow. I retied the sack, my hands shaking, and took a deep breath. What could I do? Where could I go?

I began the trudge back up the stairs thinking furiously. I knew how to beg now, much better than I did before. Mexico City is a big place. When I was a bit healthier I could strike out on my own, go far away from Mamá and the Muchachos. Find another good place to beg.

I had done my best to calm myself as I made my way up the stairs. Mamá was in the kitchen, kneading dough on one of the tables. Strands of her black hair had escaped the bun and played around her face as her palms pressed into the dough. The kitchen was bright and the smell of yeast hung heavy in the air.

"Are you OK, Juan?" she asked. Wiping her hands on her apron and coming over to me. She squatted down and looked into my eyes, a look of concern on her face.

"Yes, Mamá," I said. "The bag is heavy and I am not back to my full strength." My heart thudded so loudly that I was sure that she could hear it. I was sure that she would know I wasn't telling her the whole truth.

She nodded and slowly stood. She pulled a key from around her neck and unlocked a door on the far side of the kitchen. "Why don't you have a *buñuelo*," she said, indicating the basket on one of the tables. "I'll be a minute putting these away." She took the sack from me and opened the door just enough to slide in and closed it behind her.

I went to the table and took one of the buñuelos. It's a fried piece of dough covered in cinnamon and sugar. One of my favorites, but I could barely taste it. My stomach had soured and I wasn't hungry, but I knew Mamá would think it odd if I didn't eat one.

A few minutes later she came out. I was just finishing my treat and gave her the best smile I could.

"Here," she said, holding out a fat envelope. "Go take that back to the delivery man. Tell him we'll need another batch next week."

I nodded and took the envelope, my knees weak. I didn't know a lot about cocaine, but 20 kilos a week seemed like an enormous amount. Was Mamá the biggest cocaine dealer in the city?

Chapter 26

MUSIC WAS PLAYING ON AN OLD RECORD PLAYER IN THE corner. It was a bit scratchy but was playing old-fashioned Mexican folk music. Several guitars played out a lively tune.

The room was filled with tables made of rough wood. People sat, eating or drinking or playing cards. There was smoke in the air, and although the smell of burning tobacco was heavy, it didn't overpower the smell of food.

There were men, women, and even a few children in the room. Some old, some young, and one sour-looking crone dressed all in black giving me the evil eye. Some dancing, some sitting, some standing in corners having hushed conversations. The dress went from traditional mariachi to peasant. From church clothes to work clothes. There were maybe thirty people in the large room.

"A drink, my friend?" my companion asked. "You can call me Patrón." He guided me to the long bar made of dark polished wood.

"Patrón?" I asked. It was an odd name, a Spanish word that meant landlord or host.

"Yes, my friend. I was first here."

The bartender, an old man with a wrinkled face and long white eyebrows, put two shots of tequila in front of us and shuffled away.

"To the afterlife," he cried, throwing the shot back.

I did the same, letting the liquid burn its way down my throat and warm my stomach. Things were real here. Not as real as when I had been alive, but much more real than the ghostly norm. I felt gravity. I could smell. I could feel.

"What is this place?" I asked him.

He laughed, signaling the bartender to pour us two more. "You don't have nearly enough tequila in you for that question."

We drank two more shots, and then he said, "But first, my friend, tell me your name."

"Jesús," I said.

The smile melted off of Patrón's face. Suddenly the Cantina was silent. I looked around and all eyes, young and old, were on me. The only sound was the tick-tock of a large grandfather clock in one corner. The time was 12:15.

He looked me up and down, his lips a thin line. "The Jesús that grew up here, that took the surname of one of the sisters?"

"That's right," I said. I could feel the alcohol starting to do its work at the same time that fear crept into my belly. "My name is Jesús Manuel Rivera Dominga."

Behind me a woman sucked in air sharply and I heard a few mumbles.

"I did not know that," Patrón said. "You must leave. Now."

The room was silent again, the tick-tock of the clock abnormally loud.

"Why?" I asked. "What's wrong?"

He put his hand on my shoulder and began guiding me to the door. "You must never come back. I... we..."

I stopped and looked at his face. He was scared of me for some reason.

"But..." I began.

The pressure he exerted on me became greater and I stumbled forward. I didn't want to leave. I liked smelling and feeling, and I was desperate to eat something. I twisted around and ran farther into the room. I grabbed a piece of steak off of someone's plate and shoved in my mouth. Saliva rushed into my mouth as I chewed on the juicy meat. I closed my eyes in ecstasy and sighed.

I hadn't realized how much I had missed eating and tasting and smelling. I was ashamed of my actions, but I couldn't help it.

A strong hand clamped onto my bicep, and I was pulled towards the door.

I opened my eyes and saw Patrón. "This is so good," I said as I continued to chew. "Why can't I stay?"

As we approached the door, it swung open revealing the ghostly staircase and the wall of the church. The closer we got, the duller my sense of taste became.

"Don't try to come back," Patrón said as he shoved me out the door. It slammed and I stood there staring at the triangular symbol burned into the old brown wood.

I stayed there for the longest time as both the stairs and the doorway faded. I could no longer taste or smell, and as the staircase faded, so did my sense of gravity.

Soon I was hovering at the top of the church. I would occasionally sense motion from where I knew the Cantina was. I would occasionally hear a snatch of conversation. But it was no longer substantial. It was no longer real to me.

A sadness descended on me. The people in the Cantina had so much more of a life than I had out here. I longed for it.

"IT'S NOT REAL, YOU KNOW," BANQUO SAID.

I was still hovering at the top of the cathedral like some pitiful dog desperate to be let into the house. It was morning, sunlight streaming in the stained glass windows. A janitor was sweeping the floor of the cathedral, the swish-swish of his broom my only companion until Banquo popped in.

I nodded and said, "Maya."

"Exactly," Banquo agreed.

Maya is a Sanskrit word that means "that which is not, but appears real." I had learned about it when we hunted for my killer up in Tucson. I had found a burned down home with the ghosts of the family that had perished in the fire still going about their business. They had created an illusion together of their life, of what it once was, and continued to act it out. When I knocked on their door it was somewhat substantial. Not as substantial as the door I hovered in front of had been, but more than the ghostly norm.

"I don't care if it is maya," I said. "I want to smell and taste and feel food in my belly." I looked at Banquo. He knew something of my history, he knew how much I had been hungry as a child after my parents were murdered.

Surprisingly, Banquo did not try to drag me away or distract me, he just slowly nodded his head. "This is the choice we have all faced," he said quietly, as if conveying a secret. "To live in the world as it exists or to hide away in a world that is more to our liking, but not real."

We both hovered there for some time looking at each

other, the swish-swish of the broom scratching out a lazy rhythm. After a time, I looked away from him and back to where the door had been. I was ashamed, but I couldn't deny the attraction of the Cantina and its unreal-reality.

"I'll check on you in a little while," Banquo said as he flew away through the wall of the cathedral.

The janitor had finished, I was left in utter silence, except for the almost-heard snatches of sound that came from the Cantina.

I floated there wondering at Banquo's behavior. Why didn't he fight harder to pull me away? Why didn't he bring up Sister Dominga and what I was here for? Why didn't he bring up Lela and what I was experiencing there?

Below me I heard the great wooden door to the cathedral open up with a creak and then heard the soft shuffling of feet. A woman, old and stooped, with grey hair dressed all in black slowly made her way up the aisle between the pews. She stopped before the crucifix and crossed herself. She then slid into the front pew, pulled down the kneeler, knelt, and began mumbling a prayer.

I couldn't hear her exact words, but I became Aware of her intent. She was praying for her son who had been killed recently, a victim of drug violence. She had long suspected he was involved with one of the cartels, and she now fervently prayed for his soul. That his sins be forgiven. That he be welcomed into heaven.

I felt complex emotions stir in me. She was truly grieving the death of her son, truly fearing for his eternal state. She was devout. She had faith. She made me angry.

With one last look at where the Cantina door had been, I flew down to her. I wanted to hear what she was saying.

"I beseech you, Guadalupe," she said, "take my son to

your bosom. Forgive him his sins. He fell to temptation like all of us, but in his heart he was a good man. He wanted to be a righteous man, but…" Tears flowed down her cheeks and she took a deep breath. "It is I that failed him. I, his mother, that should have better bestowed your teachings. If anyone is at fault, it is me." She opened her eyes and stared up at the crucifix. "Punish me, Lord, but please allow my son into your kingdom."

She sniffed and shakily rose to her feet, wiping her tears away with a white handkerchief. She slowly walked over and lit a candle before turning and leaving the church.

After the door creaked shut, I suddenly felt all alone. I was jealous of the woman's faith and also disgusted by it. Her son could be a ghost like me. Maybe there was no heaven, maybe we cease to exist when we aren't ghosts anymore.

The thoughts that ran through my head felt dangerous. They were sacrilegious, they were unthinkable. What would my mother think? What would Sister Dominga think?

Despite my desire to go back to where the Cantina door had been, I could no longer stay in the church. My thoughts and doubts were impure and did not belong here. I flew out the front door and found the old woman crouched on the steps of the church. Her body heaved as tears ran down her face. "Please," she said over and over, begging for her son's salvation.

I stopped and let myself become more Aware of her. Not just her words, but her feelings. She doubted. Deep in her heart, she doubted that her prayers had any effect, she doubted that the righteous life she had tried to live did any good. So many times she had been disappointed. Images floated past and I knew that she had lost her first son in childbirth; that her husband had abused her; that she had struggled all her life just for enough food to eat. And all this time she had prayed, she had gone to Mass every Sunday, she had confessed and done penance. And all of that hadn't stopped the terrible things that happened to her and her family. It didn't seem to have made a difference.

She wiped her face again with the handkerchief and blew her nose. She slowly rose to her feet, took a deep breath, and squaring her shoulders, walked resolutely away from the church.

I knew she would be back in the morning.

Chapter 27

"FLACO," I SAID, MY VOICE A LOW HISS. "WE NEED TO talk."

We had just left Mamá's house for the first time since the beating. I was sore and slow, but well enough. After I had found the cocaine, I had done my best to keep my mouth shut and get better so I could get out of the house.

"You feeling OK, Juan?" he asked, a look of concern on his face. He stopped and took me by the shoulder. I could see Mamá's grubby, grey, boarded-up, brick building behind us. I had been dying to talk to him, but didn't dare do so under Mamá's roof.

"Yes. Fine. Do..." I licked my lips and studied Flaco's thin face. He was pale and drawn with dark circles under his eyes. This wasn't unusual, but it seemed to be more so. I had been so preoccupied with my own recovery that I hadn't taken a close look at him in a while. "How long since you kept your food, Flaco?"

He shrugged and let go of me and walked away.

"Flaco, you have to keep your food more."

"I am El Mejor of the mendigos. I am Mamá's favorite mendigo."

I stopped in my tracks. I had so wanted to talk to someone. Flaco was my friend. I had thought Flaco would understand. But he starved himself to be a better beggar for Mamá. Would he even care what she did? What would happen if I told him of my worries and he told Mamá?

I caught up with him, deciding to take a different tack. "Do you know what Rafa and the corredores do?"

"Why do you ask?" Flaco said without turning or slowing down.

"I've gotten a little fat during my time as mozo. I was thinking someday I might become a corredor. But I realized I don't really know what they do."

Flaco glanced back at me, a frown on his face. He thought being Mamá's mendigo was the highest calling, and he was probably insulted I was saying I might want to be a corredor.

"I have realized," I began dramatically, "that I don't have Flaco's stomach. Although I think mendigo is best, my flabby belly liked being a mozo, liked eating and always keeping its food."

He glanced back again, but this time he had a smile on his face. "Silly stomach, doesn't know what is good for it. Poor Juan is slave to his weak, weak stomach."

We walked along in silence. Down the streets, over the pedestrian bridge, past the tombs of Panteón de Dolores until we got into the lovely paths and beautiful trees of Chapultepec.

"The corredores run," Flaco said. "You know that."

"Yes, but what do they run? Where do they go?"

Flaco shrugged. "They run where Mamá says. They take

what Mamá gives. They bring back what they should. They don't lie, they don't steal, they don't look in the packages."

Sweat sprang to my forehead. The first two rules I was familiar with, the last, "don't look in the packages" I was not. I had looked in the package. I knew. Did any of the other boys?

I BEGAN TO OBSESS ON FLACO'S HEALTH. IN PART, BECAUSE someone needed to, and also because if I wasn't obsessing about his health, I was obsessing about what Mamá really did and that she was part of a cartel, as were all of her Muchachos. As was I.

And I think I would have left, except for Flaco.

"Hello," I said to the shaved ice vendor. She was round with a broad smile and good teeth. It was because of those two things that I chose her. I had been studying the vendors that line one of the brick pathways that Flaco and I walked to and from Chapultepec Castle on.

"Let me see your money," she said. She wasn't smiling. She saw us every day. She knew who we were. She knew what we did.

"No money," I said, holding out my empty, filthy hands. "But..." I looked around conspiratorially. It was almost quitting time, but I had left Flaco at the castle entrance telling him I needed to find a toilet. "You've seen my friend, Flaco, haven't you?"

She nodded, her lip moving into a frown. On her face, it didn't really belong, like an umbrella on a sunny day.

"He's starving himself so that he can be a better beggar."

The lady shrugged, but I could see a trace of concern in her brown eyes.

"Every dollar, every peso we make we have to give to Mamá. It is the rule." I had decided that for what I wanted to do, only the truth would work. I did, though, use everything I knew about begging to make her feel compassion for us.

"Look, kid. I'm sorry. No money, no ice."

I sighed and nodded my head, letting my eyes mist up just a bit. I turned to go, took a step away, and turned back. "Look. You seem like a nice person. Let me tell you what my plan is. Can I do that?"

She nodded slowly. It was dusk, the end of the tourist day. She and the rest of the vendors would be closing up shop soon.

"If you give me one of these, I can get Flaco to eat it. It will melt, so we can't take it back to Mamá. That way..." my voice cracked and I took a deep breath. I was embellishing a bit, but the emotion was there, that wasn't faked. "That way he will actually get some calories in him."

"It's just sugar. This is not very good food."

I stepped closer to her colorful cart, looking her squarely in the eyes. "Every night he eats with the rest of us. But then... then he gives his food back. He won't keep it anymore. This, he can't save this for Mamá. This he can't give back. It may not be good food, but at least it is food."

She blinked several times and then looked away towards the castle entrance. "If I give it to you, every kid that stops by will expect me to give them away too."

I shook my head vigorously. "I will work for it. Haul trash away. Clean. Anything you like." I put a hopeful smile on my face and then let if fall away. "Please. I am so very worried about him."

She sent me away and wouldn't hear another word. I wasn't really that disappointed, I didn't expect it to be easy.

But, I didn't stop working on it either. I was determined to do something for Flaco. Anything.

AT TIMES, LIFE WITH MAMÁ AND THE MUCHACHOS SEEMED to be too good to be true. We had food, shelter, and work. We weren't just children being cared for, but were a vital part of our community. We all did our share, we all benefited from what we did. We were a family.

That made me nervous. After I had gotten into the rhythm of things, learned to be a mendigo, had bonded with Flaco, I began to worry. Except for the cocaine, it seemed too good to be true.

One day at dinner I looked around and noticed that the mendigo David wasn't at our table. David was not El Mejor, like Flaco, but he was close. He led two other boys working the *Basílica de Nuestra Señora de Guadalupe* (Basilica of Our Lady of Guadalupe). The Basilica is one of the most popular pilgrimage spots for Catholics worldwide, second only to Rome. It's a good place to be a mendigo. I was glad, though, that I was with Flaco at Chapultepec. I would have felt guilty begging in front of the most sacred place of Guadalupe.

"Where is David?" I whispered to Flaco. He was seated at the head of the table, the seat opposite him at the other end of the table was David's and was empty.

He nodded his head slowly and bit down on his lower lip. "He was mugged on the way home," Flaco said, his voice hushed as he looked around.

"Is he all right?" I asked. "Was he hurt badly?"

"No, but he won't be back."

"Why?"

"Rule number two," Flaco whispered. The room was busy with talking boys, the mozos bringing plates to the table. That night it was heaping dishes of rice and chicken with vegetables. When the dishes were set down in the middle of the table, all hands stayed were they were. The food had not been given to us. No one took without permission.

"He did not take it," I hissed after the mozos had left. I leaned close to Flaco so I could hear his reply. "I don't understand."

Flaco shrugged. "Losing is the same as taking. That money was Mamá's. He broke rule number two. He is no longer a Muchacho. He is banished."

I felt a lump in my throat and the smell of the rice and chicken no longer made my mouth water.

"Eat up, my Muchachos," Mamá said as she looked over us all and she wiped her hands on her apron.

I took a helping when it was passed around, but didn't start eating immediately. At first the idea bothered me. David had done nothing wrong, he had been attacked, and yet he was now banished.

And then, in some strange way, I found it comforting. This place had its own harsh, unbendable rules. It wasn't too good to be true. It was just like the world as I had come to know it.

I smiled and dug into my meal, sure that I would never lose Mamá's money.

Chapter 28

"I DON'T KNOW WHAT I'M DOING," I SAID TO LELA. HER iceberg blue eyes were more penetrating than usual.

She had found me on the stairs of the church. I hadn't moved since the grieving old lady had left. I felt an affinity to her. She had spent her life praying and still had been beset by tragedy after tragedy. My life hadn't been anything approaching pure, but I had tried, and I didn't understand this afterlife. I didn't know why I was still here.

"You are holding vigil at the deathbed of someone you dearly love," she said, with the smallest of smiles. "You are telling her, and me, your story."

The street that runs in front of the church, *Calle General José Morán*, isn't remarkable in any way. It's just two lanes wide with some room for parking on the other side of the street. Directly across from the church is a furniture store, on the corner is a restaurant. On the other side of the furniture store is a little neighborhood market. Just up the street are apartment buildings.

I spent years kicking around this neighborhood. I knew the owners of each business. I knew who lived in each house. I knew their stories and the sorrows. I knew their faces and their names. This place was my home for many years, and now it felt foreign and strange, like I didn't belong.

I didn't belong in the church. I didn't belong in the neighborhood I grew up in. I suddenly felt a longing to be back in Tucson with JJ. I had grown comfortable there, and as I looked over the neighborhood with Lela, it became clear to me that by staying in Tucson I had been avoiding coming back here. I had been hoping to not come back here.

JJ goes on and on about how dangerous it is to revisit your meat-life once you are dead. I understand that now. Coming here hadn't offered me any clarity on my situation. It had just made it worse.

"You can't leave me hanging," Lela said.

I shook my head, trying to bring myself back to the present. "What?" I asked

"Flaco is starving himself to death. You are trying to get some shaved ice to help him in some small way." She was silent for a few seconds. I think she was waiting for me to say something, but when I didn't, she continued. "You left us hanging there."

I looked at her closely. She had that small smile on her face, and I was dimly Aware of a need she was radiating. A need for my story, it seemed. "You like stories," I said.

She shrugged. "Doesn't everyone?"

As I focused on her and looked away from the neighborhood, I started to feel a bit more like myself. I started to become a bit more Aware. "But for you, it's more than just that." Her smiled faded and she shyly looked away. "You haven't told me anything about your own story yet. I want to know more about you."

She met my eyes briefly and pursed her lips. "How about we finish your story first," she said.

I nodded. Not because I really agreed, but because I didn't know what else to do. I was here to sit vigil with Sister Dominga. I was supposed to do something with the lurkers. I was enjoying Lela's company. The rest was too much. I couldn't do anything about it.

As MIDNIGHT APPROACHED I FLOATED OUTSIDE, STARING at the large wooden doors to the church. The street was quiet with just a few hungry dogs slinking around looking for food. Lela was gone, Sister Dominga was still in a coma, still the same, and I longed to smell and touch and taste with the lurkers.

I wasn't in the church, because I didn't want to confront the crucifix of my holy namesake and I knew I was not welcome with the lurkers. They would not open their door to me, let me enter their land of maya. *That which appears real, but is not.* Illusion.

With Mamá and the Muchachos I had certainly been laboring under an illusion. She and her gang of boys were not what they appeared to be. As I stood there staring at the door, wanting to enter another illusion, I wondered what other illusions I was laboring under. Was my faith and religion an illusion? Something that appeared real, but was not. Was the balance I had briefly found in Tucson with JJ and Banquo an illusion? Was what I was feeling towards Lela an illusion? How could I tell the difference?

I was about to leave when a mangy old dog trotted up the steps and started sniffing around. He was medium sized and had flat greasy brown fur and a chunk out of his right ear. I felt for him. In many ways I had been him—struggling for survival on the streets of Mexico City. He foraged, begged, and looked for a better home, just like I did. And when he found a better home he eyed it with great distrust until enough time had passed. This was my mistake with Mamá. I was too hungry, too lonely, too tired of being on my own to look things over carefully soon enough.

Hey, boy," I said, "did you try behind the market?"

The dog stopped sniffing and cocked its head.

"The market," I continued. "It's right over there. You must know about it. You're not going to find any food here." The dog's tail swept back and forth in the smallest of wags.

So the dog could sense me somehow. I didn't really think about it or analyze it. Now, as I look back, it's not that surprising. Animals have much better sense than we do, and aren't loaded up with the preconceived notions that we are. I was attracted to the dog because I understood his position in life.

"Come on, boy," I said loudly as I flew down the steps to the street, beckoning the dog forth. "Over here. Behind the market."

He didn't come right away, but he did cock his head again and look my way. It only lasted a moment and he went back to sniffing around the door of the church, and a few moments later he headed off.

I stood there, frustrated. I was helping to ease Sister Dominga's pain, but I worried about extending her life (such as it was). I longed to be with the lurkers—even though I knew it wasn't good for me or the right thing to do—and couldn't even do that. I wanted to find a way to understand what it was I was going through with me being a Catholic ghost who never hears the Call, but I was making no progress on that mystery either.

I saw a deep red flickering on the edges of my form as I felt frustration turn to anger. I was blocked at every turn, unable to act, barely able to react. Not even the bardo came calling for me. I was stuck, mired in my afterlife.

I let out a shout and looked up to the sky. The moonless night was awash of dark grey with a few tiny pinpricks of light, the lights from the city overwhelming all but the brightest of stars.

The dog, from halfway up the block, yipped and ran away.

I wanted to hit something or someone. I wanted to do something... anything.

I racked my mind for something that would provide what I needed. The Cantina door.

I flew around to the side of the church, high up on the wall, just where the staircase and the door should be. I didn't want to even see a glimpse of Jesús on the cross staring back at me.

I flew through the stone wall and found myself in front of the door. It was nearly midnight and the door was solid. Old aged wood with that odd triangular symbol. I could dimly hear music and voices.

I balled my fist and struck the door, making a satisfying thunk. I felt my hand contact the wood, I felt the roughness of it and a hint of warmth. The whisper of sound that I could hear dimmed briefly. I balled my fist and hit it harder, the thunk getting louder, the sensation of my hand striking wood stronger.

I smiled and balled the other fist. And started alternating them hitting the door as hard as I could. I didn't speak, I didn't plead for them to let me in. I just banged on the door over and over as hard as I could, venting the frustration that had built up.

After a while, I realized there was no more sound coming from the lurkers' Cantina. It was dead quiet, only the bass thumps of my fists on the door could be heard. I then noticed that no matter how hard I hit the door, my hands didn't hurt. They did, though, begin to go a bit diffuse. This effort was not painful, but it was costing me something. I had to focus on my hands to keep them solid.

Wordlessly I kept it up for nearly two hours, until the door began to fade and access to the Cantina would not be possible much longer.

I would have kept beating on the door, but it opened. Patrón stood there, his face tight with dark circles under his eyes.

"What the hell do you want?" he asked.

Chapter 29

DEALING WITH MY SHAVED ICE VENDOR—ALMA, I SOON learned was her name—was kind of my graduate course in begging. She was no *gringa*, no *turista* she knew exactly who I was and what I did.

As the days passed, it was plain to anyone who looked that Flaco was not doing well. Unfortunately, as he got worse and worse, his proceeds from his begging got better and better.

Every day I would excuse myself and leave Flaco up at the castle begging. Every day I would come see Alma. She was a large woman with those hard, observant eyes.

"Today?" I asked. It had been about ten days since I first asked. "I will be your friend forever if you help Flaco."

"Why the hell doesn't this Mamá of yours stop him from vomiting his food? There's a word for that you know, bulimic."

I shrugged. I had my theories on why Mamá did what she did (because she was part of the cartel and the cartel was evil as was everyone in it—my young mind's logic on this was simple, ignoring that Flaco and I were also in the cartel). "She has tried," I said.

"Well, not hard enough. You boys should be in a proper orphanage."

I didn't like the idea of an orphanage. Some of the Muchachos had been in them, and the stories they told were not pretty. And while this line of conversation was not helpful, I knew she was involved now.

"Please," I said. "That will take too long, Flaco needs help today."

She nodded slowly, the look of worry on her face made me sad. I had only used the truth on her—maybe Flaco was worse off than I thought. "Come back on your way out."

"Thank you, *Tía*," I said as I ran back to Flaco. Tía means "aunt." When I looked back I could see the smile lighting up her face. *The mark should feel good about what they're doing.* Only I knew in this case, she wasn't a mark. She was my only hope for Flaco.

TÍA ALMA WAS GOOD TO HER WORD. ON OUR WAY OUT, I left Flaco briefly and Alma handed me some shaved ice. It was cold in its paper cup, with blue and red staining the ice.

"Look, Flaco," I said proudly as I handed it to him.

He looked up at me, his eyes sunk into his head, his complexion pale. "Where did you get this?" he asked.

I shrugged and said, "I made a friend. Hurry, you should eat it before it melts."

The vendors were starting to close up their carts, the sun just having gone down. A few gringos wandered about, but it was mostly us locals.

He shook his head and handed it back to me. "Flaco has the strongest stomach. It never gets lonely."

I took a small bite of it. "Oh my God, Flaco. You've got to try this. I think the red is cherry and the blue is blueberry." I took another small bite. While my stomach was screaming for some food, I didn't really want to eat it. I was trying to entice Flaco. "No, no. I think the red is raspberry and the blue is watermelon."

His eyebrows furrowed briefly. "You are being silly, Juan. Watermelon is not blue."

"Well, it tastes like watermelon. I swear."

Flaco reached for the cone, but then pulled his hand away.

"It's just water, Flaco. It won't make your stomach weak."

He nodded slowly and took the cone. He licked it timidly, like a cat seeing if their food is acceptable. "The blue is plum not watermelon."

We traded off the shaved ice as we walked home. I would take as little of it as I could, trying to get Flaco to eat as much as possible.

I was so happy. I was doing something for Flaco. It wasn't enough.

I WASN'T A MENDIGO MUCH LONGER. FLACO TEASED ME and said it was because I was so fat. He called me *gordo*, Spanish for fat, it is a common term of endearment for chubby people. Which was funny, I was hardly fat, but I did look that way next to him.

Sunday dinner was a big deal for the Muchachos. Mamá cooked more food than we could eat, and we often got to watch a movie.

About a month after I got Alma to give Flaco shaved ice every evening, it happened. I was sitting next to Flaco at the mendigo table. The room was loud with laughter, happy laughter, and the raucous talk of boys. The smell of meat and bread filled the air. It was a happy moment. Flaco didn't look well, but he did look a tiny bit better. I was telling him stupid jokes to try to get him to stay at the table. He had eaten a good meal and I didn't want him to get up. I knew if he left the table, he would be "giving back" his meal.

"Today is a special day," Mamá said. She had been busy at the kitchen counter, none of us paying attention to her. But when she spoke, the room quickly became quiet. "A very special day."

She turned and was holding a cake. It had yellow frosting and burning candles on top. We ate well at Mamá's house, but this kind of thing was very unusual. "Today we honor one of our own," she continued. She walked to the mendigo table and stood between me and Flaco. My heart skipped a beat. I was so sure she was going to do something to get Flaco to eat properly. That she had finally noticed what he was doing to himself. That she would finally stop him.

When she set the cake down in front of me, my heart sank and my face fell. Mamá saw the change in my demeanor, her smile briefly replaced with a frown. But it was only a moment, and soon we were both smiling again. My smile was put on. I hoped that hers was not.

"Juan here has acquitted himself very well as a mendigo. He has learned much from our Flaco. But as we have all noticed, he is getting a bit too fat to be a proper mendigo." There was laughter and shouts of "gordo!" "So, it is time for our brave Juan, who recently proved himself a true Muchacho in defending Flaco." She was referring to that alley where I was almost beaten to death by Hector and his boys. It didn't feel brave. I was just trying to protect Flaco.

"So come with me, Juan," she said, taking my hand. Rafael had come around and taken the cake. I expected her to lead me to the *guía* table. It was the next step up. Flaco had been teaching me about Chapultepec in anticipation of me becoming a guide for the *turistas*.

But that is not what happened. She led me to the table of the corredores. Rafa was smiling broadly and everyone was clapping. The corredores were the highest rank a Muchacho could achieve. I knew it to be an honor. I also knew what they did—ran drugs. I kept the smile on my face and didn't let it waver. Flaco had taught me well to present the proper emotion for the situation. I did it all day while begging. Happiness was not an emotion I was used to faking, but the principal was the same.

Mamá spoke more, but I was only half listening. Rafa and the rest of the corredores took turns shaking my hand and slapping me on the back. They called me brother. They told me how great it would be. But all I could think about was Flaco. Who was going to take care of Flaco?

Chapter 30

THE SMELLS AND TASTES WERE INTOXICATING. TAMALES with pork surrounded by sweet masa. A hot bowl of menudo. Spicy chorizo. Soft tortillas. Smooth refried beans. Ice-cold beer.

Patrón watched every move I made.

I stuffed the food into my mouth ungracefully, as if I had been starving for a year. And in many ways I had. I inhaled the scents of each bite deeply, shoved the food into my mouth and chewed as fast as I could, a groan often stealing past my lips. I then swallowed, with a sip of that beer that never seemed to grow warm, and started all over.

As my belly began to fill, I began to slow down and look around me. When Patrón had brought me in, I had seen nothing but the table full of food sitting there as if it had been waiting for me. But now, I could see things were different.

The Cantina was empty with chairs askew or on the floor and one table broken, slivers of wood littering the floor. The bright green wall had an ugly crack in it, adobe flecking off. And Patrón himself, he did not look well.

He was pale and a cut ran down from the outside edge of his right eye to his jaw. It was moist and red and dripped blood occasionally. Each time it dripped, he would take a clean handkerchief out of his pocket and dab the blood up.

"What happened?" I asked, indicating the wall and his face with my tortilla filled with beans.

"You," he said, his face bland.

I blinked, looked around again, and put my tortilla down, clearing my mouth with some more beer. "Where is everyone?" I asked.

"Hiding," he said. "From you. They are very afraid."

I thought back to Patrón's cautiousness when we first met in the chapel, to the pain and passion I had put into banging on the door to this place. Could I have done this? Had they been right to fear me? "How did I do this?"

He shrugged.

"Why didn't you just let me in? Why did you kick me out last time when you learned my name?"

"Your coming was foretold. What you see here was foretold."

"Foretold?" I asked. I felt dumb, what he was saying didn't make any sense. "Who foretold it?"

"Gloria did. You may have noticed her the first time you were here, an old lady dressed in black. When she was alive she had the gift of sight. Now that she is dead... well, she sees many things clearly. She said you would bring destruction."

I slid my chair back, it scraped noisily on the wooden floor, and I got up. I didn't want to be distracted by the food. I walked to the crack in the wall and looked at it. It was a jagged, lightning bolt shape, about five centimeters at its widest. But something wasn't right, the crack was the darkest of blacks. I could see nothing inside of it.

I was about to put my index finger in the crack to see if I could feel anything when Patrón said, "I wouldn't do that."

I turned back to him. He was dabbing at his wound again. It too was jagged like a lightning bolt. "Who are you?" I asked. "This crack looks just like your cut."

He nodded, his face clenching like he was in pain. "I was the first, I told you that. This place *is* me." Patrón looked like he was in his thirties, but I noticed then that his eyes looked much older.

"You and the others," I said, "you have created this place. Together."

"Yes. We will it to be and it is."

"And this crack? Your cut?"

"Your will was to break in, and you did."

"But you let me in," I said, feeling guilt settle on me, dark and heavy.

He smiled. "We haven't had enough tequila for this discussion." He signaled me over to the bar and poured us two shots.

The liquor was dark, well aged. It went down smooth, bringing warmth to my stomach. I sighed and he poured us another which we both drank.

"I let you in," he said, "because if you had broken down the door, the damage would have been much worse."

"I am sorry. I..." I faltered. I wanted to explain, but didn't really understand it myself. "I am going through a lot. I wanted to feel something."

He nodded and poured us a third shot. We drank it and I began to feel the effects of the alcohol. It wasn't as intense as when I had been alive, but it was orders of magnitude more intense than anything I had felt as a ghost. I liked it.

"How long have you been here?" I asked.

He shrugged and asked, "What year is it?"

"Two thousand eleven."

He snorted. "That would be fifty-seven years then. I died in 1954."

"That's a long time to be in this Cantina," I said looking around.

"Time is different here. I know I've been here a long time, but it doesn't feel like that long."

I thought back to Banquo and Yochi. They had tasked me to "do something" about the lurkers, helped me understand that it was "all linked together." But what was that something? Get them to leave their well-appointed maya-land? Help them all move on? Have a tequila with them?

"But why are you here?" I finally asked. "Why haven't you moved on?"

Patrón laughed and poured us more drinks. "I don't know if we have had enough tequila for that conversation, but I will try."

Chapter 31

"Spit it out, Juan," Mamá said, her face hard and cold. The party was over, the rest of the boys were watching a movie. It was Mamá, Rafa, and me in the messy kitchen.

I took a deep breath. I couldn't lie to her, it would be breaking one of the cardinal rules. The rumor was she would know each and every lie you told. And if you lied, even a tiny lie, you would no longer be a Muchacho. There were ex-muchachos, but no one would talk about them or what happened to them. After the brief whispered conversation I had with Flaco about David, he refused to speak his name again.

"I am worried about Flaco," I said. It was the truth, but I didn't elaborate.

Rafa smiled and slapped me on the back. "Flaco is El Mejor. He knows exactly what he is doing. He's the best Mendigo we've ever had."

I ignored Rafa and looked at Mamá. "He's getting thinner and weaker. He hardly ever keeps his food now. I'm afraid he will..." I just let it trail off. Flaco was like the brother I never had. I wished I could get him, and myself, out of this place.

Mamá sat next to me and took my hand in hers. I was struck at how warm they were. How could her hands be so warm? She was using desperate boys to make money for the cartel. Shouldn't her hands be cold like a witch's? Shouldn't the concern in her face look less real than it did?

"Rafa, we must listen to Juan," she said, looking at Rafael, her warm hands squeezing mine. "He spends his days with Flaco. He knows him better than we do. He is corredor now, his words rise louder among the Muchachos."

Rafa nodded solemnly.

She looked back to me. "Juan, I am most grateful you have brought this to my attention. I will deal with it. This is my burden and you should not worry yourself about it one more second."

Was she really being tender or was it the kind of acting Flaco had taught me? I didn't see a way to do anything more, so I shoved down my worry and did my best to forget about it. Just like when my parents had died, I turned my back on that part of my life, only the nightmares reminding me. So right then and there I turned my back on my life as a mendigo. I had to. To survive.

To this day I regret that decision. I wish I had more courage. Not for me, but for Flaco.

MY LIFE AS A CORREDOR WAS INTERESTING. RAFA TAUGHT me the ins and outs of the city, or at least of our territory. He showed me the shortcuts and the areas to avoid. He built on what Flaco had taught me about reading people and taught me to run when I could and to fight when I had to.

I was so physically active I lost the extra few pounds I had gained, even though I got to eat twice a day and ate as much as I could. At the end of my days I was exhausted and had little time for my friend Flaco.

I took Mamá at her word, that she would tend to Flaco. But, I knew she wasn't, or if she was doing anything it wasn't effective. He wasn't gaining weight and his face became so gaunt that his once infectious smile was hard to look at.

I didn't do anything about it either. I didn't think I could. On a warm September day three months after I had become a corredor, everything changed.

"Come quick," a mendigo named Oscar said. He was skinny, like all mendigo, with a long neck and scraggly hair. "It's Flaco." I had just gotten back, exhausted from another run. Oscar had been waiting by the entrance for me.

My fatigue forgotten, I flew up the steps after Oscar. He led me to Flaco's room. My friend was in his bed, his face pale, his eyes full of pain. Some of the other boys hovered around watching, and Mamá sat on the edge of his bed stroking his forehead, speaking to him softly.

I hesitated, seeing her show him tenderness. What were we to her? Did she care or were we just tools? I was young then, it was hard for me to conceive that we were both. She loved us and she was using us. When she looked at me, there were tears in her eyes.

"Don't you boys have something to do," she said sharply, wiping at her cheeks and sniffing loudly. "Juan and I have things to discuss." She signaled me over and I elbowed my way through the crowd, but no one else left.

She rose, putting her hand on my shoulder, and her face hardened. "Out!" she shouted, her hand gripping my shoulder hard enough to be painful. The room quickly emptied. She pulled me down and we both sat on the edge of the bed. The bed was small, but Flaco was so skinny there was room for us too.

"Hey, man," I whispered to Flaco.

He nodded, his head barely moving as if it suddenly was a huge weight. "Hey." His voice was thin, really just a whisper.

"I'm going to talk to Juan for a minute," Mamá said to Flaco. "And then I'll send him back in."

Mamá pulled me up and I almost fell, my legs were so weak. We corredores do literally run a lot, but my recent run was not enough to explain what I was experiencing. She guided me out of the room and shut the door behind us. I followed her down the hall and into the empty kitchen.

"I tried," she said, a catch in her voice. "I tried to get him to eat. He promised he would. But... It's too late now." Her head hung low and she slumped against the cheap laminate countertop.

"But..." I began. "Can't we... Doctor. What about a doctor?"

"He was here. He drew blood and rushed the results. Flaco went too far, his organs are shutting down. He doesn't have long." Tears flowed freely down her cheeks in silent rivulets.

Gripping the counter, I slowly sunk to the dirty plywood floor. The feel of it, cheap and harsh, was in some small measure comforting. I took a deep breath and wrapped my arms around my knees.

If only I had said something earlier. If only I had taken better care of Flaco. If only—

"You mustn't blame yourself," Mamá said. She was squatting next to me, her warm hand on my cheek. "This is *my* fault. He, all of you, are *my* responsibility."

I looked into her eyes, confused. I had begun to think of her as an uncaring person, one who used children to do the work of the cartel. One who did it for money and no other reason.

But from where I am now, I think those words were some of her purest. She did love us, and we loved her. She thought she was doing right by us—giving us a home when we had none, a place to sleep, food to eat, work to do. As an adult, I believe she felt that running drugs was justified by the benefit we all received.

But I was a child. I was confused. I let her take me into her arms and I cried. I let go of my doubts of her and embraced her as the only mother I had.

After a time she pushed me away, handing me a towel to blow my nose on. "Enough of that. You must be strong, Juan. You are a brother to Flaco, he loves you. He needs you. And while he does, you will be mozo. You will sit with him. You will tend to him."

I nodded. The thought of watching my brother die terrified me, but the thought of not being with Flaco was even worse.

"Can you do that?" she asked.

I nodded, and she guided me back to Flaco's room and told me what I had to do.

Chapter 32

As midnight approached I stood staring at the door to the Cantina, studying the rough brown wood. It appeared old as if it had spent a century or two in the weather with a rough texture, like mini canyons running through the old wood.

Patrón had told me his story. He had come to the church after he died, not understanding he was a ghost. He found several other ghosts and they spent several years together. He was as lost and confused as I was. Why hadn't God taken him home? Why wasn't he in heaven?

One day they were floating up in the ceiling of the church and he started talking about this cantina he used to love. As he spoke it, it became the ghostliest of realities around them. The rest of them started to talk about it and see it and soon it became more and more real.

At first it had been difficult to maintain, but after time they got better, and more and more ghosts that wandered into the church, looking for answers, ended up with them.

"Here we feel. Here we seem real. Here we are safe," he had concluded, his voice slurred from the tequila.

I licked my lips wanting to feel the burn of tequila again, but I felt guilty. This was maya, this wasn't real, this wasn't my answer. In fact, it was my question. Everyone here had the same question I did—why am I still here? But they had given up. They had retreated into the illusion of a life. I wouldn't do that.

I ran my fingers over the roughness of the door and sighed. I could feel it. Beyond the numb touch that skilled ghosts can manage. It felt rough, like a splinter might fleck off and pierce my flesh.

It had been a week since Patrón told me his story. And each night I had come up here. Each night I had resolved not to go in. Each night I eventually opened the door and Patrón and I ate and drank and felt.

Tonight would be different. Tonight I would turn my back on it. Tonight I would be strong enough.

With a sigh, I opened door.

SISTER DOMINGA WAS STARTING TO REMIND ME OF FLACO. Her skull seemed to be pressing against the flesh of her face, as she lost more and more weight. What was she still doing here?

"Are you OK?" Lela asked.

I nodded. Things had been tenser between us since I started going to the Cantina. I had told her about my first visit there, where they had kicked me out, but not all the times since.

The sun was shining in the window to Sister Dominga's room, but it somehow seemed dim. It wasn't bright like the Cantina and it was too damn quiet. I missed the songs playing on the old phonograph, I missed the laughter of the ghosts, I missed the taste of food and the coolness of beer.

"You don't want to tell me," she stated.

I shrugged. I was too guilty to tell her. From time to time I thought of asking her to join me, but I knew she wouldn't. She wasn't weak like I was.

"If you don't want to talk, then we won't talk." I was grateful when those eyes of hers left me and went to Sister Dominga. Our little outings to explore the old sites of Mexico, to find "living history" in the form of ancient ghosts, had stopped. I had offered, but she turned me down without saying why.

This, what was happening between us over Sister Dominga, was why. The Cantina was why. Maya was why.

A FEW MORE DAYS OF THE SAME. TIME WITH LELA AND Sister Dominga. Time with Patrón and the ghosts of the Cantina. Things with Lela were tense, my time at the Cantina, while enjoyable, laid on a burden of guilt.

"I'm going to go," Lela said. Her voice was steady, but her eyes looked moist. She stood in front of the window, the yellow light of dawn shining through her. She was more transparent than usual.

"What?" I asked. The sun was just coming up and I had just arrived at Sister Dominga's room, the memory of food and taste and smell was thick around me like a haze of fog.

"This is no good for any of us." She took a step towards the bed and stopped, her iceberg blue eyes making me feel weak. "You are barely here. I thought we were..." She paused and then sighed. "This is not good for Grandmother anymore." She looked at Sister Dominga, her thin face tight with pain.

"But..." I began, but could not think of how to defend myself. She was right, I was barely there.

"I will know when her time is close. I will come back then." Our eyes met briefly, and then with a "pop" she was gone.

Chapter 33

"HERE, MY FRIEND," I SAID TO FLACO. ALMOST TWO weeks had passed, and I was his nursemaid. Flaco opened his mouth and I dripped a drop of fentanyl into his mouth and he let out a guttural sigh. Fentanyl is like morphine, but much more potent. The doctor had recommended it and Mamá had gotten it. Flaco loved it.

"Now some water," I said holding the straw to his mouth. He sucked a little in, but mostly to please me. He only wanted the fentanyl now. He barely spoke, his infectious smile never appearing.

"You've proved it, my friend," I told him as his lids fluttered closed. "Flaco is El Mejor of the mendigos of all time. Flaco has the strongest stomach in the world." With the barest flicker of his lips, a sad hint of a smile, he fell asleep.

I did my best for him, but it wasn't enough. I was holding his hand when he took his last breath.

WE HAD A MEMORIAL FOR FLACO, THE TABLES PUSHED together, all the boys one family. Not corredores and mendigos and mozos, just the Muchachos. Mamá spoke,

Rafa spoke, and they tried to get me to speak, but I couldn't. I was living in this fog, I could barely function. Flaco, my Flaco, had died.

I felt a grief sharper than I had felt since my parents died. In addition, I felt guilt like a lead weight pressing down on my chest. I wanted to run away, but I still did not have the courage to leave Mamá. As much as I hated that we were part of the cartel, this was my family now. This was my home. Even without Flaco.

I stumbled through another week as mozo until Rafa told me it was time to make a delivery.

"Sorry to put you out there," he said as apology. "But we're extra busy and need you." He told me the address and had me repeat it back to him. He put the carrying bag on me, the strap on my right shoulder, the bulk of it against my left hip. I patted it with my hand, something dense and soft was in there. It felt like two kilos of cocaine.

He walked with me to the entrance of our hideaway. "You are corredor," he said. "You know what do."

Rafa did not come out with me, and I stood alone in the sunshine blinking rapidly. I had not been outside in weeks; the sun seemed foreign, dangerous. I scraped my foot against the dirt with my worn tennis shoes.

Flaco believed in Mamá and the Muchachos. Flaco had loved this place. *I can do this*, I thought. *For Flaco, I can do this.*

With a grunt I took off running. I was corredor. I had a mission and a home and a family.

As we look back, the days that marked great change in our lives seem special. As if the air was hushed and rarified, as if everything was brighter. As if it should have been obvious that the world was about to change.

My memory of the day that my parents died is like that. Why didn't I know a storm was about to hit? The day Rafael found me scrounging for lettuce was a bit like that. And this day that I set off running in the early morning before the heat got too bad, was like that too.

But I had no idea what was about to happen. I was still numb from grief, just doing the best that I could.

CORREDORES RAN BECAUSE WE HAD TO. THE CITY WAS full of dangers; keeping in motion reduced them. We ran, too, to get the job done faster.

My breath came fast and deep, my mouth developing the stale taste of fatigue. The package was gone, I had delivered it to a dapperly dressed criollo at the back of a kitchen, the smell of grease and rotting vegetables wafting over us. He had taken the bag, looked in it briefly and handed me a sealed envelope.

As we did the exchange, I studied his face. He had known the correct response to my query.

"How far to Guatemala?" I had asked.

"Too far, little bird," he had answered, a thin smile forming around the cigarette that he smoked.

A simple exchange that let me know he was the intended recipient of the package. His face I studied as a precaution. I wasn't allowed to open the envelope. I wasn't supposed to know what was really happening. So, I studied his face so I could describe him to Mamá if there were a problem.

He had narrow eyes shaded towards mocha. His hair was a very dark brown like the coat of a seal. He was in his forties and had crow's feet settling in around his eyes as lines creased his forehead.

"Thank you, little man," he said as I stuffed the envelope into my *bolculta*. "Bolculta" is a made-up word that combines "bolsa" and "oculta." It means "hidden pouch."

Each corredor had a similar set of shirts. The undershirt, just a modified T-shirt, had a pouch sewn into the back. And then we wore a button shirt over that to hide the bolculta.

As I ran back, I could feel the envelope against the small of my back. I felt the sweat that pooled there. The shirt was tight, so it held the envelope securely to my body.

Corredores never take the same route. Rafael's words of instruction rang through my head as I ran. I wound my way past the edge of an open market. The shouts of haggling striking my ears and the smells of roasting meat making my stomach grumble.

Corredores avoid the police. I saw some soldiers up ahead and took a sharp right through a small park, jumping over some garbage and a sleeping homeless man.

Corredores never stop running. And while this wasn't strictly true, it was the spirit of it. A moving target was much harder to catch. But I was out of shape from my time as a mozo. My feet hurt, my lungs burned, and my spit was thick as paste.

I exited the park and crossed a street. I came to an old cobbled road that ran up a hill. I snorted. I just didn't have it in me. My run slowed to a jog, and as the street got steeper I slowed to a walk.

Corredores always know whose territory they are in. I looked around at the adobe houses as I climbed the hill, my breath coming in ragged gasps. I was less than a mile from our base, but I wasn't sure about this neighborhood. I knew this road would get me closer, but I couldn't remember who laid claim to it.

Just like my body wasn't at its full potential, neither was my mind. Thoughts of Flaco kept floating by. His smile, so easy and quick. His thin, curious fingers. His bright brown eyes. His unending pride at being El Mejor.

Corredores use all their senses. I could hear the honking of horns and the shouts from the market below. I smelled sweet musk rose blooming in one of the gardens I passed. I heard the scrape of a foot against the dirt close by.

Corredores never show their fear. I felt it, though, but didn't change my course or pace. I listened carefully. There it was again. I stopped, taking deep, slow breaths. I pretended to tie my shoe. I moved my head to the side, letting my peripheral vision take in the street behind me. I didn't sense any movement, it seemed to be empty. The owners of these fine homes would either be working or inside hiding from the day's heat. It was approaching eleven a.m., and while Mexico City has a rather mild climate—it was about twenty-five degrees Celsius (eighty Fahrenheit), the sky was cloudless and the sun unrelenting.

I stood up and walked, cresting the hill and coming to a larger cross street. I took it heading towards the west, past houses that quickly went from nice to normal to run down. I would be in Muchacho territory soon. While the mendigos and corredores ranged widely over the city, we did have an area that we considered ours. That other gangs (I guess that's what we were, but I didn't think of it that way then) tended to respect.

I heard the scraping a few more times, but didn't turn back around. I was being followed. My goal was to get to our home turf before the chase began. I knew it best. If I had looked back, if I had seen my pursuer, the chase would have started, and I had just gotten my breath back.

I wound my way past a boarded-up theater and turned up a very narrow street, not much more than a driveway. One step in, I started running. I was hopeful that if my pursuer couldn't see me running then I could get a bit ahead.

Up a narrow street, across a big street, dodging cars over to another small street where I cut through a warehouse with trucks parked in the yard. There was a dumpster there and the smell of garbage was strong, but I knew there were some edible things nearby. That year on my own, my nose had gotten good. I didn't smell garbage as a single scent. I smelled the rotting vegetables, some of them very far gone, but I also got a whiff of overripe bananas that were probably still good. Yes, I was hungry, which was why my mind was distracting me right then.

I went out the back entrance of the warehouse down a long driveway and out onto another street and I headed west, slowing to a walk, not wanting to draw attention to myself. I took the next street north. Almost there. Past the barber and the bakery, the smell of baking bread making my stomach grumble. As a corredor I got more to eat, but given how active we were, it was never enough.

A Corredor always stays focused on his goal. I shouldn't have, but I looked back. I wanted to know if I had lost my pursuer. There were men smoking in front of the barber and people going in and out of the bakery. An old Volkswagen Beetle chugged down the street and a few people walked on the sidewalk. I glanced ahead, making sure I wasn't about to run into anything, and looked back again. I saw a boy, maybe thirteen, rounding the corner about fifty meters behind me, his head swiveling back and forth. Our eyes met, he grinned, his eyes becoming narrow slits. I stopped. Didn't I know him? My mind couldn't come up with it, but my body knew. Adrenaline dumped into my bloodstream and my pulse quickened.

He started running, the grin on his face widening, like a wolf sighting its prey.

I turned to run, but it was too late. Hector grabbed me. Just a glance made it clear it was him. Those missing front teeth, that fetid breath, that strong, plump body. He had a scar on his cheek I hadn't seen before. My guess is that Rafa did it to him after our first encounter.

He jerked me into the garage of an old apartment building, the door bent and permanently cracked open. The garage was right next to a small purple shrine to Jesús Christ that took up half a parking space on the street. It was a simple arch made of stone backed with tile that showed him laying hands on the sick and needy. Fresh flowers were in vases, and while the tile was worn, the work was lovely and the shrine well tended. The image stuck with me.

Corredores must do their job, their lives depend on it. Hector wasn't alone either. He had another boy with him, and their blows started raining on me as soon as we were clear from sight. Fists and feet came at me relentlessly. I tried to defend myself, but one of Hector's first shots was to my jaw, making my head ring. I tasted blood and felt fear. I went down, my face hitting the grimy cement. I heard the sharp retort of my ribs cracking. They were out for revenge. They were going to kill me.

Chapter 34

"Search him," Hector said. I was barely conscious, my body a constellation of pain. But despite it all, I felt this thin thread of joy. As the rough hands patted my body and rolled me over onto my stomach, I tried to follow the joy, find out what it was.

"Found something," one of the other boys said. The boy following me had caught up and all three of them had beaten me senseless. "It's some kind of pocket, against his back." He had found my bolculta.

That was Mamá's money. I had to take it to her. I tried to speak, but only a wheeze and a groan came out. Mamá would be so mad at me for losing her money.

"Oh my..." the third boy said. "This... oh my..."

"Let me see," Hector said, his voice loud, but I could hear a quaver of fear in it. I heard him leafing through bills.

"Put it back," the second boy said. "That is too much, they will come for us. They will..."

"Shut up," Hector hissed. "Look at him, they will come for us anyway." There was silence, and then Hector chuckled, the sound of it like a stuttering engine. "But with this much we can get out of here, and fast. They'll never find us. We'll live like kings."

I tried to speak again, thinking how I had just lost my place with the Muchachos by being caught. For Hector it was a lot of money, but I know now, not nearly as much as he thought. It was probably the most money he had seen by far. It might get them out of town, it might let them survive for a time. But it wasn't enough to get him past the reach of the cartel.

They kept talking, but I wasn't listening anymore. That little trill of joy was back, like a beautiful note of music reaching through the cacophony of my pain and grief. It called to me, and in my mind I tried to follow it, I tried to find that joy.

It was evasive and I had to concentrate on it. The world receded and I couldn't hear Hector and his boys anymore. I couldn't feel the press of the stinking cement against my bruised and bloodied cheek. I couldn't smell the rotting garbage or my own blood. I couldn't feel cool cement beneath my body.

All I knew was this elusive sense of joy. What was it? What did it mean? I was like a boy chasing a butterfly, its erratic path eluding me. And like a carefree little boy I gave it all my attention, ignoring the ugliness around me.

I didn't give up. I caught up with that sense of joy. I found out what it was, what it meant, and the feeling of joy expanded around me, cocooned me, protected me. It whispered its secret in my ear.

It's your turn now, Jesús. You will see your parents soon. You will see Flaco soon. It's your turn to die, Jesús.

And I was happy, I was ready, I wanted to die.

I had a smile on my face as consciousness fled my beaten and bleeding body.

"Juan. Wake up, Juan."

I groaned. I didn't want to wake up. It brought only agony. I felt sharp pain with each breath. But the voice was insistent. It kept saying that name that wasn't really my name.

"Jesús," I mumbled, trying to correct the voice.

"What? Juan, who did this to you? What happened?" I felt hands reaching back to my bolculta. "Juan, who took the money? Who took Mamá's money?" I could hear the fear in the voice. He didn't understand the joy I knew. Death was coming for me. Death would release me of all these worries.

"Going..." I began to say, but my voice was garbled. I spit out blood and opened my eyes a crack. I couldn't quite focus, but what I could see combined with the voice told me it was Rafael in front of me. I almost laughed, but the pain in my mouth stopped me. The boy had the name of an angel, a healing angel. "Going home now, Rafa," I managed to say.

I heard whispers from the three other Muchachos that were with Rafa. They were afraid. "It's, OK. I am ready," I added, trying to ease their worry. I wanted to tell them more, that I was desperate to see my parents. That I hated life without Flaco. That my mother taught me to believe that death was not the end.

"Who did this?" Rafa asked. "Please, Juan. I need to know."

He held my shoulders tightly, too tightly. It hurt, but among the sea of my pains it was a small thing.

"Hector," I said and immediately regretted it. Rafael

swore and stood up, talking rapidly with the other Mucha-chos. Just as Hector had been after blood with me, Rafa and the rest of them would be after blood with Hector. It would be another gang war, like the one that claimed my family, only perpetrated by boys. Their acts would damn them.

"No," I said, but my voice was not much more than a whisper—no one took notice. I tried to prop myself up, but I didn't have the strength. "No," I said again.

"We will avenge you, Juan." Rafa said, his face so close to mine, I could feel his breath on my bruised cheek. "We will uphold the honor of the Muchachos. We will make them pay."

Avenge me? I thought back to David, the Mendigo who came back without his take, having been mugged on his way home. He was banished. He was no longer a Muchacho.

Rule two. Never take anything from Mamá or the Mucha-chos without permission.

Losing was the same as taking. I had lost Mamá's money. That was the same as taking it. Rafael was going to aban-don me. That thread of joy gone, I felt fear flood over me. Who was I if I was not a Muchacho? Despite all my conflicts about what we did, this was my home. This was all I had.

As Rafa and the other three boys strode purposely out of the garage, I tried to speak, I tried to move, managing to get myself propped up on one arm. "Wait," I said, the word sounding so pitiful to me. I tried to stand, but my arms shook from the effort of propping myself up. I collapsed back to the dirty cement and cried. I could see the edge of that purple shrine to Jesús through the bent garage door and I laughed.

I had failed Mamá. I had failed the Muchachos.

And what did it matter to them? They would find another

boy on the street to take my place. Another pitiful boy digging through garbage, happy to find the scant calories that rotten lettuce could supply. I would soon be replaced—no one would miss me.

This time when the darkness came for me, I feared it. How long since I had been to Mass? How long since I had even been in a church? How many times had I sinned to survive since my parents were murdered? How would I be judged?

"Please..." I mumbled as tears ran down my bloody face to the cement. I was speaking to Rafa and the boys as they quickly walked away. I was speaking to Jesús in his purple shrine. "Please, just one more chance."

I collapsed to the sidewalk knowing I was going to die.

Chapter 35

AFTER LELA LEFT, I STOOD THERE A FEW FEET FROM Sister Dominga's bed the whole day. I didn't approach, I didn't flow the warmth into her. I just stood there. I didn't even leave when Sister Helen came and attended to her.

Sister Dominga was in pain and restless. I saw it, but couldn't do anything about it.

I wanted tequila, and I hated that I wanted it.

"Oh my.... Oh my...." Sister Helen intoned as she bustled around Sister Dominga. Changing her soiled beddings. Cleaning her body. Feeding her a thin broth. "The lord may be slow, but he will be here for you soon."

That seemed to wake me up from my ghostly catatonia. I moved closer to Sister Helen, her round face was showing the strain of all this. Her eyes were hooded; it didn't look like she was getting much sleep. I knew Sister Helen. She was six or seven years older than me. She had come to the church as a new sister right before I came there. She had been shy and skinny and I thought her to be so pretty. Now she was plump and round and haggard looking.

This death Sister Dominga was having seemed cruel. It

seemed unnecessary for it to take so long. And my efforts to ease her pain had probably made it take longer.

What good was I to her? What good was I to anyone? What did I expect to do when she died? What if she was a ghost? What good could I do to help her? Just share my doubt, my lack of faith.

It hit me then, like a slap to the face. I wasn't there for her. I was there for me. I had been hoping that Sister Dominga would be a ghost, that she would be able to help me find my faith like she had once before.

My realization of selfishness turned to shame. Shame deep and dark like a bottomless well that I was falling into. Lela must have seen it, this is why she left, not just my preoccupation with the Cantina, but my selfishness drove her away.

All of this time had been about me. Sister Dominga had raised me better than that.

Sister Helen was just about done and was rolling Sister Dominga's frail body onto her right side a bit and propping her up with pillows. She was trying to prevent more bedsores from developing.

With one sharp cry of "No!" I flew out the window and around to the church and through the doors. Down through the aisle towards the crucifix.

I stopped short. The old, stooped woman that came praying for her son's soul was there. Her wrinkled lips mumbled the same prayer. She asked for her to be punished, but for her son to be saved. She asked that her son be allowed into heaven even though he had fallen to temptation. She prayed earnestly, but in her heart she doubted. Her faith was an act of courage that shamed me further.

She looked up to the crucifix. The statue of Jesús in his

own moment of doubt when he thought God had forsaken him.

A thought flittered through my mind, *I haven't had enough tequila for this,* and I felt even more guilty.

I looked up to where the Cantina was. It wasn't close to midnight, the door would not be accessible. But I needed in. I had to go in. I couldn't stand this world and its reality. It was too damn real. I wanted less reality. I wanted maya.

I flew straight up to the ceiling of the cathedral. All I could think about was the scratchy sound of the phono-graph. The laughter of the ghosts there. The smell of enchi-ladas. The smile on Patrón's face as he poured us tequila...

And then I was there.

"Here you go, my friend," Patrón said, handing me a glass of amber liquid.

I looked at the ghosts, they were in a circle around me. They had gentle smiles on their faces. A few nodded towards me. Each had a shot glass with tequila in it.

"To Jesús!" Patrón cried, lifting his glass to his lips. I noticed that his face was healed, not even a trace of a scar from the wound he got when I was beating on the door.

"To Jesús!" was echoed around the room and everyone drank.

I didn't drink though. I was too confused.

"How... how did I get here?" I asked.

Patrón chuckled. It was a deep rumble, like distant thunder. "Only guests come in through the door. You are one of us now."

La Cantina

"For we are saved by hope: but hope that is seen
is not hope: for what a man seeth, why doth he yet
hope for?"
Romans 8:24

Chapter 36

DEPRESSION ISN'T SOMETHING I AM THAT FAMILIAR WITH. I was a happy child with loving parents—until their deaths. After that I was too busy struggling for survival for depression—it was a luxury I couldn't afford. After my life on the streets and with the Muchachos came my time with Sister Dominga, who wouldn't tolerate a moment of me feeling sorry for myself. And then came my apprenticeship with Quinn and a career as a bounty hunter—too busy and too dangerous for depression.

So as my life in the Cantina fell into a routine, I really didn't know what was happening to me.

A huge party had followed my arrival, and then Patrón had taken me to my room.

"I have a room?" I had asked standing in front of the plain wooden door. It had a brass plate on it with my name engraved in it.

He nodded. "Everyone does."

I stood staring at the brass knob. I could see tiny, distorted images of Patrón and me reflected like some kind of funhouse mirror. I was more than a little drunk and my belly felt full to the bursting. Both of these things, though, could be overcome easily. Maya feels real, but it's not. So you can sober up quickly if you want to, or decide not to be uncomfortably full. I did neither.

"I thought you were afraid of me. What about Gloria's predictions?"

Patrón shrugged, but his smile had faded. "Gloria is not always right, her visions not always clear. I think you've already done all the damage you are going to do. Besides you are here now by your own choice. That is what binds you here. Nothing else."

I nodded, looking back at the door. "What's in there?" I asked.

"Whatever you want it to be. This is *your* room. You decide. You control. Big or small. Lavish or simple." He placed his hand on my shoulder and I looked at him. He had a mischievous glint in his eyes. "And only you can open the door. No one can enter without your permission."

He had me place my hand on the bright brass knob and imagine as clearly as I could what I wanted my room to look like. He then left me there. I stood for the longest time trying to decide. What kind of room did I really want? The room that stood out most in my memory was my various childhood rooms, especially the one when we lived at the big house on the hill. I felt so important having so much space.

But, I wasn't a child anymore. My bedrooms as an adult had been a place I had rarely been. When I had died I had been renting a small room from a widow who lived within walking distance of Chapultepec Castle.

A room for myself. It didn't really seem right. I was a ghost now, right? Why did I need a room?

I eventually felt silly just standing there in that long

hallway with door after door with shiny brass knobs. Other Cantina residents would pass me, smiling or saying a hello, sometimes singly, sometimes in couples.

I eventually decided on four walls and a bed, nothing else. A plain, spartan room.

Since that night when I came to become one of them at the Cantina. I spent a lot of time in that room. Mostly sleeping. Sometimes staring at the rough, beige adobe walls. Usually depressed.

I had failed Sister Dominga—only really being there for myself. I had lost Lela. I was a ghost who believed in a God and a heaven that was beyond my reach.

Chapter 37

How much food and tequila can you drink? How many games of poker or lotería (a game similar to bingo that uses cards that are reminiscent of the tarot) can you play? How many conversations can you have? How much dancing to the sounds of a scratchy phonograph? In the Cantina you can do these things forever. It is a constant party with residents rotating in and out as it suits them.

"Buñuelos, my friends," I said, my second day there. I had a large basket of the cinnamon coated, brown balls of fried dough. It was tradition that new residents bring in their own favorite dishes. Patrón had showed me the kitchen. A simple room with cabinets, ovens, refrigerators, and freezers. Each had a brass handle of some sort. Cooking was simple. Hold the knob, imagine what you want vividly, and then open. For the buñuelos I used the oven, although strictly speaking they would have come out of a fryer, and there you have it. Food, fresh and delicious.

There were about forty souls in the Cantina. More than usual, most of the Cantina's population. Everyone was still curious about me and getting to know me.

I passed them out to the young ladies dressed in bright skirts who usually started out sharing a table together, but by the end of the night, once the tequila had flowed, often ended up paired up with some of the younger men.

"Thank you, Jesús," Valeria said. She had long, silky, black hair and a heart-shaped face. She leaned over the basket examining the treats, giving me a fine (and I am sure intentional) view of her ample cleavage. There were, clearly, other physical delights to be experienced in the Cantina. "Can you save a dance for me later?"

"Umm..." I began. "I don't really dance." I quickly moved on to another table.

Later that night, when Patrón and I stood at the bar with a few of the other men, he nodded his head towards the table of ladies and said, "They are not all as young as they look."

"No?"

"No. And they were not all that pretty when they were alive either."

"But," a short bald man named Mario said, "who cares? They are young now. They are lovely now." He tipped his glass in their direction and shot the tequila back. He then shouted, "Time to dance!" and sidled over to their table, his arms raised over his head, his feet sliding over the floor with surprising grace.

I smiled at Patrón and poured us both another drink.

Later that night (if it was night, I had no idea, that is just how it felt), Valeria and I talked for some time. The Cantina was nearly empty and I was feeling very drunk.

"I don't know what I believe in anymore," I said, sloshing some of the beer I was drinking onto the table. "Is there a God? And if so, why is he such a cruel bastard?" I put my hand to my lips and giggled. I was very drunk. "I shouldn't talk like that. I've always been such a good Catholic boy. Trying to do the right thing, even when I was on the streets, even when I was working for the cartel—unwittingly, I might add."

Valeria nodded and smiled. Her lips where full and a bright red, the white cloth covering her breasts just the perfect weight—it left the right amount to the imagination. I don't think she cared at all about what I was talking about, but she was a good listener.

"And why don't women want you to drink tequila. Can I ask you that? My mother hated when my father drank, I bet you—"

"I don't mind," she said with a sweet smile, cutting me off. "Should I get you more, Jesús?"

"No. I am too drunk for tequila, but not too drunk for beer. She... she thought I was distant. She didn't like me coming up here for meals and a few drinks. She... she..." I looked around the Cantina, my sodden mind hoping to see Lela, as if she would just stop by.

Valeria smiled again and filled my beer glass from a pitcher on the table. She was round and feminine and classically beautiful. Lela was thin and wiry and had those eyes... I did miss those eyes. Valeria was not the kind of woman that ever paid much attention to me. I was short and stocky, like my father. I was not beautiful. I was not anything special.

"You are such a good listener," I told her.

"I like listening to your stories," she said. "A bounty hunter. That is so... so... important."

I snorted. It was dirty, dangerous, hard work. I never really thought of it as important. It was just what I did.

Several beers later, there were only a few other people

left in the Cantina. The party had finally died down, most residents going back to their rooms, singly or in couples, or in a few cases, in threes or fours.

"I'd love to see your room, Jesús," she said, her smile making me feel somehow important. Lela had the eyes. Valeria had the smile.

"My room?" I asked. I didn't quite understand. I was very drunk.

"Yes, I would like to see your room." Her eyes narrowed and she nodded slowly. It meant what you think it means, but I wasn't in a space to understand it.

"No," I said, shaking my head. "My room is nothing. I couldn't decide, so it is nothing. Why would you want to see my plain four walls and my little bed?"

"A little bed is all we will need," she said leaning forward, displaying her cleavage.

I finally understood. "Oh... Oh... I... Oh my."

She just sat there beaming that smile at me while I stammered, stuttered, and blushed.

"You are so beautiful, Valeria. I am so flattered. It's just... I... Lela." I stood up suddenly, the room spinning about me, my chair clattering to the ground, the smell of souring beer and tequila suddenly making me feel sick.

I'm not a prude, despite my Catholic upbringing. Nor was I, in the right circumstance, against casual sex. But Valeria's offer brought something into sharp relief for me. Lela. I couldn't be with Valeria because of Lela.

"I'm sorry," I mumbled and left, stumbling down the long hallway to my room.

I SLOWLY TURNED, LOOKING AT THE FOUR PLAIN ADOBE walls of my Cantina room. I felt my heart thumping in my chest and my throat was tight. I was a bit dizzy from all the tequila and my belly was full from all the eating.

My heart thumping in my chest.

I blinked rapidly and put my hand in front of my eyes. I could feel the faintest touch of soft lashes brushing against my skin.

"What?"

At first I thought Valeria had done something, that something had happened to me. And as I look back now, I know something had happened to me: I had become one of the Cantina ghosts. I had been there long enough for my sense of a physical self to get vivid. I was used to feeling the tequila. I was used to smelling and tasting and feeling my belly full. I was used to feeling the pull of gravity on my body. But I was not used to having a body that felt *real*.

I opened my mouth and stuck my fingers in, like a baby. Teeth, tongue, my fingers came out moist with saliva and my hands tasted of cinnamon from the buñuelos I had served. I pulled up my long-sleeved black shirt and gasped.

There was a chest under there. I pulled on one of my chest hairs and felt a pluck of pain. A strangled gasp of laughter burst forth.

I sat on my bed and pulled off my brown cowboy boot. Underneath it was a dirty white sock, and underneath that were five toes. I pulled on each one, laughing again. And then a thought occurred to me and I stood straight up, dropping the boot to the floor with a clunk.

I had felt something hearing Valeria's offer, seeing her sensuous lips. But surely...

I unbuttoned my jeans and looked. It was there. I was whole. I was a man.

A wave of dizziness crashed against me and I slumped to my bed. One boot off, my pants undone, my head spinning. What was this place?

Chapter 38

I'VE THOUGHT LONG AND HARD ABOUT THE CANTINA. About what I experienced and felt in the realm of maya. I know it wasn't "real," but it felt *real*. So very real.

And I think it's like what happens to the living sometimes when they give things up. Take sugar, for example. If you truly give it up and start to live on the substitutes, you begin to experience Sweet'N Low as the same thing as sugar. You don't know any better at that point. The substitute begins to feel real.

I think maya is like that. I had been dead for a full year. Long enough to begin to forget what it was truly like to have a body with all its aches and pains, all its quirks and aspects, all its feelings. So what I experienced in the Cantina, while not real, seemed very real to me.

In some ways it was like Sweet'N Low and all those other sugar substitutes: it was overly sweet and a little bit off.

No aches and pains. No quirks or oddities. Just feeling and desire. It was too sweet. Just a shadow of reality, but so much more than the wisp of a shadow that a ghost experiences. It was entirely intoxicating.

Sitting on my bed, I marveled and laughed and gasped at this "real but not real" body I had. My chest was broad—not as broad as my father's—and strong. There were muscles under there and I could pinch the skin covering them. My skin felt warm as I put my hand to my throat feeling for a pulse.

I couldn't find it.

I panicked for a moment and pressed three fingers in to where my jugular should be. I felt warmth, a vague sense of something beneath, and the tube of my esophagus, but no pulse.

I then looked at my bare foot. I remember there being a trace work of blue veins there. I couldn't find them. My foot was smoother, more prefect than it should be. No calluses or rough skin. It was perfectly clean.

My laughter stopped cold and I felt my chest constrict. I longed for the burn of tequila sliding down my throat. The un-reality of this reality had become clear.

I quickly put my sock and boot back on followed by my long-sleeved black shirt. I didn't want to be reminded of it. It was like I was some character out of a science fiction story who had thought he was a man and just discovered he was a robot. That the illusion of his humanity didn't run very deep.

Fully dressed, I ripped open the door to my room and ran down the long hallway. It was quiet and I was glad no one else was there. I didn't know exactly what I wanted, besides escape.

I stumbled into the nearly deserted Cantina. There was one couple in a corner, their heads close together as they whispered to each other. I heard a low laughter and worried that they might be laughing at me.

I ran through to the small foyer. On the walls were pegs that had dozens of coats hung on them. As if people were coming and going all the time. As if this were a real cantina.

I put my hand against the warm roughness of the door. It felt real, that Sweet'N Low real. I quickly ran my hand up and down it, daring a splinter to flake off, to pierce my "skin," to cause me to bleed. But it didn't. In fact, it didn't hurt at all, and my hand didn't even warm up as it should have from the friction.

I stepped back and stared at the door. I knew on the other side of it was the real world. A world that, as a ghost, did not feel real, but was.

I looked back in the Cantina. I could see the couple, their heads together, his hand gently caressing her back. Another snatch of laughter gently floating in.

Why was I here? I struggled to remember.

Lela had left. I couldn't bear to watch Sister Dominga die anymore. The faith of the old lady in the church had, even in the presence of her doubt, deeply shamed me.

That's what was beyond that big door.

I turned back and walked into the Cantina. I hadn't had enough tequila yet to go back through that door.

THE CANTINA WAS EMPTY, JUST ME SULKING AT THE BAR, when I smelled her. The remaining couple had finally left. The scent was the combination of something light and floral—like lilacs—with something heavy and musky—like patchouli. The scent was sensual and intoxicating. It was full of promises, dark and mysterious.

I heard the swish of fabric, felt the smallest tickle of air on my cheek from her passing. I turned and looked. Valeria.

She was dressed plainly in a brown skirt and a white blouse, the makeup around her eyes restrained, the red of her lips not quite as dark. I am sure the intent was to make her less attractive, but it had the opposite effect on me. She looked more real, and that I found attractive.

She held her hand up, palm forward. "I thought we might talk, just talk." She moved behind the bar, opened one of the brass handled cabinets under there, and pulled out a steaming carafe of coffee, cream in a tiny ceramic creamer, and two big black mugs.

She stayed behind the bar, the dark polished wood separating us, and poured. The scent of coffee overwhelmed her sweet, sensual smell, and I inhaled deeply. God, how I miss coffee.

"Cream?" she asked.

I nodded and she poured some in, the white mingling with the inky black. She stirred it with a silver spoon and pushed the mug over to me.

I held the warm mug in my hand, appreciating the heat. I took a small sip, the roasted bitterness of it putting a smile on my face, and forcing a sigh from my lips.

"Thank you," I said.

She nodded. "I'm sorry I came on too strong. You are new, and we don't get new around here very often."

I looked up from my coffee and nodded. She was beautiful, there was no doubt about that, but she was no longer a siren. Just a woman.

"And I've spread the word to the rest of the girls. They'll take it easy on you."

"Thanks."

"I know it's hard, this adjustment. But, we need you."

"Need me?" I asked.

She nodded, taking a sip of her coffee. "This place. It's always been more real than the outside world." Her head tilted towards the big wooden door. "But it hasn't always been *this* real."

I blinked, not quite understanding, and took another sip of the coffee. Just like the tequila, it had an analogous effect as its land-of-the-living counterpart. I felt myself wake up, my senses sharpen. "I don't think I follow."

She nodded and started slowly pacing behind the bar. "One ghost, alone, can't do much, really. You can fly and pop around and such, but that's about it." I grinned as she spoke. She obviously had never heard of JJ Lynch. "Two ghosts together, if they try real hard, can create something a little more real. They can touch—kind of. But take three ghosts or ten ghosts or twenty ghosts... Well, then you can create something. Create a world. All your energies together. All for the same purpose. All with the same goal. And..." She trailed off, her hands gesturing towards the rest of the Cantina. Her knuckles rapping on the wood of the bar.

"All of this is what we have created together. The more of us, the more real. We need you."

I bit my lip and looked down. They *needed* me, but what for? To spend eternity hiding from reality? Was that something I wanted to contribute to? But, did I have the courage to face reality anymore?

When I looked up, she was smiling, her eyes searching mine. "Gloria was right to fear you. You don't know what you want."

"And you do?" I asked. It came out rather harsher than I intended. She had hit a nerve and I was feeling defensive.

She laughed, the sound of it ringing in the empty room. "What I want, Jesús, is to eat, and dance, and live my life."

She twirled around in the cramped space behind the bar, her skirt rising and brushing against the wall. Her laughter died suddenly and the room seemed too quiet, too small. "But I can't really live, can I?" She leaned close, the moisture of her breath caressing my cheek. "I am dead, so are you. We have to make the best of it, don't we?"

Chapter 39

VALERIA AND I STARTED MEETING FOR COFFEE WHEN THE Cantina was empty. She was smart and perceptive and a very good listener. She had that thousand-watt smile, not to mention that scent of hers, all sweet and musky.

When the Cantina got busy, I would have drinks with Patrón until I felt good and drunk. I would then eat and socialize with a few of the other residents for a while. But before the party got too crazy, I would go back to my plain four walls. I would sleep as much as I could and sulk when I couldn't.

No fading here like back at the graveyard, but something more like sleep. Vague dreams, waking up groggy with heavy limbs. The Sweet'N Low version of sleeping, but still much more than I had experienced as a ghost before the Cantina.

As I said earlier, I was depressed. Caught between the real world of being a ghost and the maya world of feeling real.

"How did you end up here?" I asked Valeria one morning.

She did a half-laugh, her smile carving out dimples in her cheeks. "Just like everyone else," she said.

"Can you please elaborate?"

She shrugged, and I was distracted by the movement of her flesh underneath her blouse. I am sure it wasn't meant to be sensual—she was just shrugging—but in my maya-real state, my body responded to the feminine flow of her body.

"I lived a long life," she began. "I witnessed the Mexican Revolution. I had children and grandchildren, and even one great-grandchild." She paused, dramatically, a dimple-rich smile on her lips.

"You were old," I said. It was what she was waiting for. "You don't look old."

Her laughter rang out and she spun around behind the bar. "I don't feel old." When she stopped spinning she leaned a bit closer. "For that I am grateful."

"So you died?"

She nodded. "Peacefully, in my sleep, surrounded by family. My death was as good as it gets."

"But you're a ghost?" I was puzzled. Those of us left behind, as it were, generally have unfinished business.

"Yeah. Confused me too. This was in 1983. So finding myself a ghost, what did I do?" I shrugged in answer. "I marched down to my church, figuring the answers would be there."

"And?"

She snorted. "No answers, just Patrón and the Cantina. It was smaller then—in size and in number of souls—a far cry from what it is today. But..." She trailed off and smiled shyly. "But I could eat and dance and feel more real. I could feel young again."

"And each soul helps make this place more real," I said. It wasn't a question, I understood how it worked now.

She smiled that smile at me and I felt warm.

"I... Can I..." I stammered, my cheeks flushing red. "I think I'd like to see you as you are." She looked puzzled, so I forged on. "I mean, as you were when you died. The real you."

Her face darkened, deep lines briefly appearing between her eyebrows. And then just as quickly the playful smile was back. "I don't think we know each other nearly well enough, Jesús. You'd have to come to my room if you wanted to see the 'real' me."

TEQUILA, COFFEE, AND VALERIA. THAT BECAME MY LIFE in the Cantina. That and all the time spent sleeping and staring at the walls in my room. I think it would have been easier if that had been enough. In fact, it was, for a while, in this something-is-missing kind of way. That all ended the day Banquo showed up.

I was lying in my plain room, staring at the roughly textured adobe walls, wondering why I refused to do something with the place. Put a picture up. Add a window that overlooked a beautiful scene. Add one of those magic cabinets with the brass knobs so I could eat or drink in here. Anything. Something.

I lay there, my mind bouncing around endlessly and uselessly until I heard a knock on my door.

I bolted upright. That had never happened.

"Come in," I said.

"You know I can't do that," a muffled male voice replied.

I nodded. Of course. My room. My door. Only I could open it. As I walked to the door, I thought it must be Patrón. Maybe something special had happened. Maybe something new. When I opened the door, my jaw dropped and I stared at him.

"Hello, Jesús," Banquo said. He had a smile on his face and a cigar in his mouth. Tendrils of thin grey smoke winding up around his head. The sharp smell of the burning tobacco made me long for tequila. Smoking and drinking just go together.

"Can I come in?" he asked.

I nodded mutely and stepped back and then closed the door after he came in. He looked around briefly before his eyes landed on me. I felt a bit weak in the knees. What the hell was Banquo doing here? And why was he partaking?

"You don't look good," he said.

I shrugged. Still at a loss for words.

"Do you mind?" he asked, gesturing towards my narrow bed. I nodded and he sat down with a sigh and a smile. "It is wonderful to really feel, isn't it?"

"Yeah," I said.

"And dangerous, too."

"Umm-hmm." I didn't want to have a conversation with Banquo. I didn't want to hear that what I was doing was wrong. How I should be stronger. How I could do better. How I was leaving those that needed me in the lurch.

Banquo took a deep draw of the cigar and slowly exhaled, that uncharacteristic smile staying on his face. "God, how I miss this." I stared at the burning cigar in his hand as he blew on the end of it and watched it glow red with a sizzling hiss. "It was my vice, you know. Cigars. What was yours?"

"Tequila."

He nodded. "I prefer vodka, Russian if I can get it."

"I'm sure Patrón can come up with some for you."

Banquo chuckled. "Oh, believe me. He was pulling out

all the stops. He said they thought we could pull off an annex to the Cantina—a replica of Shakespeare's Old Globe Theater. He would really like me to stay, to join his merry band of souls. Add to the strength of the maya."

Banquo was passionate about all things Shakespeare. When he was alive he had been a professor of English Literature and even his name, "Banquo," came from Shakespeare. He was a bit of a mystery to us—none of us knew his real name or much about his past—but his love for Shakespeare was never in question.

"And?" I asked. On one hand I was hoping he was considering it, I would feel less weak that way. On the other hand, if he was here, it would be an eternal reminder of what I am missing by being here.

He took another long drag of the cigar, and puffed it out in circular rings. "It's tempting, believe me. And I dare not stay too long. But, no. My place is not here."

I nodded, feeling both relieved and guilty.

Banquo lapsed into silence as he happily smoked his cigar.

"Why are you here?" I finally asked.

"Oh. Right," he said, as if the experience of being here had chased it from his head. "Sister Dominga's time has nearly arrived. I thought you should know."

I stood there blinking. She was why I had come. She whose faith seemed indomitable. She who saved my soul and my body. "How... how long have I been gone?"

"About three weeks."

I gulped. It felt like maybe a week. "And Lela?" I asked.

The smile left his face, the cigar dangling loosely in his hand. "She's quite angry and quite worried. If you decide to leave, you've got some fences to mend there, my boy."

I wanted to leave, I was sure of that. But I didn't know if I had the strength.

"How... how do I leave?"

Banquo shrugged. "Patrón knows, but I doubt he'll tell you. The door isn't going to work, that's only for guests. You're one of them now, part of this shared maya." He blew on the end of the cigar again, delighted by the sizzle of it. "Do you want my best guess?"

"Yes, please."

"I think it's like leaving the bardo. There you've got to find something more important to you than your suffering. Here? I think you've got to find something more important to you than your addiction."

Chapter 40

ADDICTION. AFTER BANQUO LEFT, THE WORD REVERBER-
ated in my head. I know, it's obvious. All the drinking and
eating and sex that goes on in the Cantina is everyone
indulging their addictions. The sensual biological addictions
we all lost when we died.

We were all addicts.

I was an addict.

The realization was sobering. It was the equivalent of
a living alcoholic spending his days with the drink of his
choice instead of taking care of his family and his life.

Sister Dominga was my family, and I was dimly aware
then that I had wanted Lela to be in my life.

I paced my little room after Banquo left. Back and forth.
Back and forth. I felt my anger rising. Anger at myself. Anger
at Patrón—he was the dealer here, the one who stood to
gain from my addiction.

But did I have the strength to leave?

I opened my door and listened. I could hear the sounds
of laughter and music echoing down the hallway. The party

in the Cantina was in full swing. I closed the door and paced some more. How could I get Patrón to tell me the way out?

Only guests come in through the door, he had said. So, I doubted the door was the way out. But what if it was? Sister Dominga's time was nearly here. I had to try.

I opened the door and walked down the long hallway to the Cantina. Valeria and a group of women were dancing, with the men standing around and clapping. The phonograph was playing a lively mariachi song. Patrón stood at the bar, pouring drinks. The tables were loaded with food, and the smell of melted cheese and enchilada sauce made my mouth water.

I walked through, ignoring everyone and keeping my head down. I entered the foyer and stared at the big wooden door. I didn't see a door handle. Patrón had always let let me out when I came to visit. If he had used a knob, I hadn't seen it.

"You can't leave that way." I turned and saw Patrón standing behind me, his arms crossed.

I thought back to the long hallway, each soul had their own room, their own door. A door only they could open and close. "This is your door, isn't it?"

He nodded.

"And the Cantina is your room."

He nodded again. "Actually, this whole place. Everyone contributes, of course, but since I was the first, it's all linked to me."

"How do I get out?"

A smile crept onto his face. It was wide and showed too many teeth. "You don't."

A felt a cold sweat blossoming on the back of my neck. "What?"

"So you should just make the best of it," he said. "I know you and Valeria have been spending time together. She's a good woman, just roll with it."

"I'm going to leave," I said. Trouble was, I could hear the sound of the crowd, I longed for the taste of tequila, I thought I caught a whiff of Valeria's sweet and musky scent. I didn't know if I was strong enough.

Patrón shrugged his shoulders and turned to go.

"I almost beat this door down from the outside before. What's to stop me from doing it now?"

My host chuckled and turned around. The Cantina was suddenly quiet and I saw a wall of bodies looking over Patrón's shoulder.

"We'll stop you, Jesús," he said. "Whatever it takes."

He took a step forward followed by five other men, all of them bigger than me. I didn't have a chance.

VALERIA LED ME BY THE HAND DOWN THE LONG HALLWAY that leads to everyone's rooms. I had spent what felt like a long time in my room. Patrón and his goons had unceremoniously marched me to my room and stood there until I had opened the door and gone in.

Her hand in mine was warm and soft, her sweet, musky scent potent, but I was in no mood for it. I was a prisoner. I wanted to leave.

And believe me, I had tried. I had beaten on the walls. I had tried many times to get to the door. I had screamed and shouted and made a general nuisance of myself. All to no avail.

In all the craziness, I had verified that pain was pretty much missing from the world of the Cantina. I could hit the wall of my room as hard as I could and barely feel it. It was only a whisper of pain, not pain itself. All sense of feeling here was not quite real, but pain... it wasn't there.

Somehow this hardened my resolve to leave. I know it may sound strange, but pain is part of life. The lack of pain here made it clear that the Cantina was not a real life.

"Almost there," Valeria said. We were traveling down the hallway past the wooden doors on both sides with brass nameplates and brass doorknobs. The names went alphabetical, from A to Z. We had started at J and were coming to the end of the hallway. I had never been down it this far.

Before we got to the end, she said, "Close your eyes." She seemed to be much more cheerful than the situation warranted.

I sighed and crossed my arms.

"Please," she said softly, her eyes narrowing and darting back and forth. She was scared. "For me."

I nodded and closed my eyes. She got behind me and gently guided me down the hallway and around the corner.

"OK, open now."

Two doors were directly in front of me at the end of the hallway. They were double doors, actually. The left one had a nameplate that said Valeria, the right one said Jesús. The doors led to the same room.

"What?" I asked, looking around. The hallway had ended in a T. We had taken a right turn and come to these doors. I looked around and saw the other end of the T led to a big door that said Patrón.

"It's an honor," Valeria said. "This is how much he wants you to stay." She paused and took my hand, that thousand-watt smile of hers warming me again. "*I* want you to stay."

I shook my head, pulled my hand from hers, and walked back down the hallway.

"Please!" she said. She rounded the corner, but stayed at the end of the long hallway.

I began to run, the doors flying by until I came to the Js. Juan, Jose, Jaime. I stopped short looking at the doors again. There was no "Jesús," my old room was gone.

I marched back down to Valeria, the fear on her face was blatant now, her arms wrapped around her chest. "Where is my room?"

"It's over here," she said quietly, indicating the double doors she had showed me.

"What's going on?" I asked.

"We want you to stay. We need you to stay. Just come see." She took my hand again and tugged me towards the door. "I think you'll like it."

I let her pull me forth. She let go of my hand and placed her hand on the brass knob of the door on her side. I didn't move.

"We have to open the doors together, just this first time."

I sighed and put my hand on the knob of the door with my name.

"On the count of three," she said. "One... Two... Three."

The double doors swung out and I saw what was inside. It was unbelievable.

Chapter 41

"Isn't it exquisite?" Valeria asked as she twirled in the middle of the large room. She was dressed plainly, not in her party outfit. I liked her better this way, and I think she knew it.

Under her feet were hand-painted tiles with a flower-like pattern in blue, orange, and red. Tears sprang to my eyes. The work was impeccable—it was the kind of work my father had done. The center of the room was filled with three leather couches arranged in a U, with a few small tables and cabinets. Behind the couches were windows and a glass-paned door. Through the glass I could see sun shining and a beautiful garden. There were two doors leaving this room, one to the left and one to the right.

"Let's close our doors," she said, running lightly on her bare feet to her door and closing it. "We will have privacy this way."

I nodded and closed my door. When I turned back around, Valeria had a bottle of tequila and was pouring it into two crystal glasses. She handed me one. "To us," she said.

I walked over to the low table in the center of the U of couches and put my drink down. "No alcohol. Tell me what the hell is going on."

"No one leaves," she said, knocking back the tequila. "No one has ever left." She poured herself another one. "Patrón wants you to be happy. I want you to be happy." She moved close and rested her hand on my chest. It felt warm and comforting. The touch of a beautiful woman. A life of ease and wealth. I can't say I wasn't tempted.

"We can make a life here. You and I," she said. "This life can be whatever you want. We can make it whatever you want it to be. I can be whomever you want me to be."

I blinked. Her voice had lowered as she said the last sentence, reminding me strongly of Lela. And I pictured Lela in this room with me. Living a life with me. I knew, right then, that Valeria would make herself look like Lela if I only asked it.

"I have to go," I told her.

Her nostrils flared and her eyes clouded up. "But you can't," she whispered. Her hand slid from my chest as she stepped back.

"I will find a way. If it takes a year, I will find a way."

Valeria swallowed hard and nodded. "I hope she's worth it." She drank her drink and poured herself another one.

I can't tell you how badly I wanted a drink. Just one drink. "Why don't you come with me?" I asked.

She set her glass down with a clang as she sank into the couch. I watched the amber liquid slosh to and fro. She sat there hunched on the couch, her head falling into her hands.

I sat next to her and touched her shoulder. "None of this is real. Please, come with me. Help me find a way."

She looked up, and tears stained her face, her dark mascara running in tiny rivulets down her cheeks. "I... I... It's so much, so good. How could I turn my back?"

It occurred to me then what Valeria's addiction was. It wasn't alcohol or dancing or sex. It was youth. She had lived a very long life and knew what it was like to be old. Here she could look young and act young.

"Let me see you," I said, my voice hushed. "Let me see the real you."

"No!" she said, pushing me away as she rose from the couch. She stood, hugging herself as if she were cold.

"You said if I came to your room you would show me. This is your room."

Her mouth opened and her brows furrowed. "He gives you this," she said, her voice high and strained. "He gives you me. And all you want is to see me as an old, broken woman. As the Valeria after time had had her way with her. As the Valeria that was weak and useless. As the Valeria I swore no one would ever see again."

I sat there studying her, using my lessons in Awareness. She was much more scared than mad.

"Please," I said quietly.

"I don't understand. Who are you? Everyone wants me this way." Her hand swept up and down her voluptuous body. "Why do you want me old and shriveled?"

I paused as tears stung my eyes and nodded slowly. "What I want, what I am desperate for, is something real. Something true." I took a deep breath and let it out in a slow hiss. "I should have never come here, and truth be told, I don't have a single clue on how to leave. But if I don't get some reality soon... I... I don't know what will happen to me."

I was living in a dream and I knew it. That changed

everything. The almost reality of the maya was no longer comforting. It was hurtful. My addiction to tequila and food was no longer distracting. And yet I still didn't know if I had the courage to find a way to leave. I wanted that "one" drink, that "one" more meal. I wanted to take the young Valeria in my arms and rip the clothing from her beautiful body. I wanted these things. But I wanted reality just a little bit more.

She stood there silently studying me. Her shoulders hunched, she looked weak and vulnerable—but still attractive. In that youthful body of hers she couldn't be anything but attractive.

"I'll make you a deal," she said slowly. "If you will give this some time, just a little time. Have a meal, have a drink, sit and talk with me. I will show you."

I pursed my lips and nodded. "As long as you look like you did when you died the whole time." I knew I was asking a lot, but I felt I needed it. I liked Valeria and I thought my fondness was not just about her looks. I needed to really know.

"Very well," she said, her voice suddenly sounding gravelly.

I watched as her youth slowly faded right before my eyes.

Chapter 42

I THINK I MAY SOUND CRAZY HERE, BUT I LIKED VALERIA better as a crone than a vixen. I was more relaxed around her and she seemed, after some initial embarrassment, more at ease too.

The old Valeria was stooped, her shoulders thrown forward, her back in a perpetual curve. Deep lines, almost trenches, were carved through her face, and her once luxurious hair was thin and bone white. After the transformation, she quickly tied it back and smiled. She had several teeth missing.

She had been very old when she died. "Thank you," I said when she was done.

She nodded, but wouldn't meet my eye. She rose up, her back never straightening out, and went to some of the cabinets and pulled out plate after plate of food. Broiled shrimp and boiled lobster, filet mignon, an enchilada casserole topped with goat's cheese, and tequila. It was a sumptuous meal.

She laid all of it out on the coffee table in front the leather couch and sat back down. "Eat," she said. "Drink. You promised." Her voice was rough and cracked as she spoke, reminding me of the old phonograph that played in the Cantina. She kept looking down and wouldn't meet my eye.

I gently put my hand under her chin and lifted her head. She kept looking back and forth, but eventually she looked me in the eye. I saw her shame and felt bad for having asked this of her. Her brown eyes where still there, but now as cloudy as a monsoon afternoon.

"You are still beautiful," I said.

She pulled away and looked at her hands folded in her lap. She didn't believe me.

"Eat," she whispered. She was desperate for this to work, for me to stay. For a moment I almost gave in. For her.

I sighed and got up, going to one of the cabinets.

"You promised," she said.

"I did, and I will keep my promise." I closed my eyes and held the brass knob on the cabinet and then opened it up. I pulled out a plate of fruit and bread and a bottle of water. I slid some of the more sumptuous dishes to the side and set the fruit and the water down. I tore a piece of the bread off of the loaf and popped it into my mouth. "See," I said to her. "Eating."

She frowned deeply, the lines around her mouth echoing the shape of her lips, reminding me of the topography of the Grand Canyon. The river was the deepest line, but that same line would be echoed in the strata of the rock around the river.

Thinking of the Grand Canyon made me wonder about my friend JJ. Where he was. What he was doing. Was he OK? I closed my eyes, enjoying the fact that you can actually do that here, and opened myself up to Awareness. I got a brief impression of confusion and paranoia. I heard the echo of steps on pavement; he was afraid. JJ was not OK.

I held my eyes shut and tried to calm myself. I couldn't do anything for JJ. I wasn't even sure I could do anything for myself. When I opened my eyes, Valeria was staring at me. She looked away as soon as my eyes found hers.

"Don't do that," I whispered.

"I am old. How can you look at me?"

"What sin is there in age?" I asked. I died when I was forty-one. I could have done with a bit more age myself.

When she looked back at me, there were tears in her eyes. "Here I don't have to be old. I can be young and dance every night. Every man looks at me with desire. Every woman with jealousy."

"This is not real."

She snorted. "I don't care."

I nodded. Who was I to force her to face reality? I hadn't been doing a very good job of it myself.

I took another bite of the bread. Compared to what I had been eating, it was bland and uninteresting. Before I had known of this place, being able to taste or to chew like this would have been a revelation. Now it didn't seem like much. How fast we become numb. We always want more.

"That young body of yours. Is that how you really looked in your youth?"

She shrugged. "More or less. Perhaps here my skin is a bit smoother, my breasts a bit..." she trailed off into a smile. "More or less."

"You must have had many men seeking your hand when you were young."

"I did. I was born in 1902 and was coming of age at the

end of the revolution. It was a heady time and many a man came calling."

She proceeded to tell me stories from her youth. She relaxed and started eating. She picked at the fruit and ate some of the shrimp, but didn't drink any of the tequila. I told her a little about my own youth and the situation I was in before I came to the Cantina.

It was a lovely time. It didn't matter to me that she looked old; actually, it made it easier. I found her laughing more and telling me things of substance, things that mattered to her. The young Valeria had not been like that. The old Valeria is someone I could talk to for days.

The sumptuous food and the tequila called to me. I wanted to lose myself in it. And in some ways I wanted the young Valeria back and to lose myself in her beauty. But there were things in the real world I needed to attend to. Sister Dominga. Lela. Maybe JJ.

I knew if I continued having this pleasant conversation with Valeria I would slide back. I would have "just one" drink and would be lost again. I would ask her to show me her youth again. I would tell her I would stay with her.

"Thank you," I said, standing and brushing crumbs of the bread I had eaten from my jeans.

"What... Where..." she stammered.

"I am leaving, Valeria. I don't know how, but I am. You could come with me."

She was silent for a long time. Her eyes distant, lost somewhere to the past. She rose with a sigh and stepped up to me. She still had that same scent, lilacs and patchouli. Her stoop made her seem shorter, but the smile on her face still dazzled. She placed her hand. all boney and marked with age spots, on my chest. "I could be yours," she said.

"Just yours. All yours. Any way you want. Old, young, any way."

I felt my heart thumping in my chest. Could I give it up? A beautiful young woman to sleep and play with, an old wise woman to talk to. The best food, the best tequila. As much as I wanted. As often as I wanted.

It would be so easy.

I grabbed her and pulled her into a tight embrace. I smelled deeply of her scent, sweet and musky. My body trembled and I knew what I was addicted to.

While Valeria was addicted to her youth, I was addicted to my denial.

It had saved my life after my parents were murdered. I had shoved that pain down as deeply as I could and survived. It had saved me with Mamá and the Muchachos. I had shoved my knowing of the cartel deep so I could survive, so I could help my friend Flaco. I had done it again after I died. I had been with my friend JJ. I had shoved down my confusion on finding myself a ghost, on not being judged immediately upon my death as my church told me I would.

These things I had done to survive. Turning my back on reality. I had to.

But I couldn't do it any longer. I couldn't stay in the maya with Valeria, forgetting my past, ignoring my friends. It was time to face reality.

Tears were flowing down my cheeks as I kissed her on the top of her head. I saw her hair was jet-black again and I felt the allure of her young flesh pressing against mine. She was doing everything she could to get me to stay. Some dim part of me was flattered.

"Old or young, you are beautiful. Will you please remember that?" My voice came out strangled.

I felt her head nodding against my chest, but she didn't speak.

I remembered Banquo's words:

I think it's like leaving the bardo. There you've got to find something more important to you than your suffering. Here? I think you've got to find something more important to you than your addiction.

And I knew how to leave. It was simple, but it wasn't easy. I was most of the way there already. As I thought it, Valeria's flesh felt less substantial and my body felt light. The gravity that I had come to take for granted was diminishing. I opened my eyes and the room began to look transparent.

"Come with me," I said.

I felt her head shake against my chest, but again she did not speak.

The room and Valeria slowly faded and soon I found myself floating at the top of the cathedral. I was alone. I couldn't smell or taste or feel anything. *What have I done?*

I took a deep ghostly breath. It felt so weak and insubstantial compared to the maya, but it was all I had. I took another and another. I focused on my form, making it as tight and solid as I could. It was nothing, really. Like smoke in the shape my body had once been in. A cheap illusion, but real.

I laughed, and it didn't sound right. The sound didn't bounce off the ceiling above me, because I wasn't making a real sound, just a ghostly one.

In the Cantina, things had seemed real, but weren't. Here things didn't seem real, but were.

It would have been so much easier to stay with Valeria.

I flew out of the church into the night, the moon full

above me. I flew around to Sister Dominga's room and flew in.

What I saw made me wish to go back to the Cantina and to never leave.

Lela stood there, ghostly tears running down her face as she said, "Please, Grandmother. Please. Come back to us, please." Sister Dominga's body was in the bed, even more skeletal than when I had last seen her. And there was a third presence, a spirit hovering over Sister Dominga's body. A gape-jawed, wide-eyed, wispy mess of a ghost. It was clearly Sister Dominga's spirit, and she was clearly in the bardo.

Part 4

Sister Dominga

"And now these three remain: faith, hope and
love. But the greatest of these is love"
1 Corinthians 13:13

Chapter 43

IN THAT GARAGE IN MEXICO CITY IN SIGHT OF THAT PURPLE shrine to Jesús Christ after Rafa and the other Muchachos had left me for dead, something woke me from what I was sure was my end. I felt strong arms lift me, and even though it made my pain worse, I liked it. How long had it been since I had been held? Mamá was not like that; she had touched me, but rarely. The Muchachos were not like that.

"Mercy," I heard a voice whisper. It was a woman's voice, rough and strong.

For a moment I thought I was dead, that I was in the loving arms of my maker, that I was finally going to be taken home, that I would see my parents and Flaco. That thought fled, chased away by my guilt. Would I even be welcomed into heaven after all that I had done? Did I even believe anymore?

The woman grunted and I felt her lift me into the air. I groaned in pain. She was strong, this woman. I struggled against the darkness and managed to open my eyes a slit and look at her. My eyes would not focus, so I could not see her clearly. She had a broad, determined face with brown eyes. Her hair was covered with a simple white coif on her head and she smelled of Castile soap.

She took a step, a slight jolt running through my battered body. I let out a cry of pain. "I've got you, child," she said, looking down on me. Part of me rebelled at being called a child. I was a Muchacho. I was eleven years old, almost twelve—I hadn't been a child since my parents were murdered three years ago. And another part of me liked it—I had no idea how starved for affection I had been. "It was a miracle I heard you groan as I walked by. Hold on, child. I know a doctor. He is not far."

I could hear the strain in her voice. Strong as she was, I was not a light burden.

I closed my eyes, the lids so heavy and the sun above too bright. As the woman carried me forth, she whispered "mercy" with each step.

Mercy, mercy, mercy. We exited the garage.

Mercy, mercy, mercy. She carried me past the bakery, its smells making me nauseous instead of the usual response of hunger. I felt a drop of sweat drip from her face to mine.

Mercy, mercy, mercy. Onto a busier street. I could hear the cars honking and smell the exhaust. Each step she took a strain for her and agony for me.

Mercy, mercy, mercy. It seemed to go on forever. Strong arms, jolting walk, unrelenting pain. I began to wish for the darkness even if it brought with it judgment for my sins.

Mercy, mercy, mercy. And then we were there. I heard her shout for the doctor and heard surprised voices. I managed to open my eyes again and saw her face. We were inside and I could see her more clearly. She had brown eyes set wide and a prominent nose. Sweat covered her face and she was breathing heavily, the smell of sweat starting to overpower the smell of soap.

"Who... who are you?" I managed, my voice thin and weak.

She looked down on me and smiled. "I am Sister Dominga."

THE GRAVESTONE WAS SMALL AND SIMPLE. *SISTER LUCIANA Sofia Dominga. 1938 - 2011.* Every time I looked at it, I felt guilty. But I couldn't look away either. I was afraid if I did, I would march back to the Cantina and never leave. Maybe if I did, Patrón would take me back, Valeria would take me back.

The graveyard wasn't much. It sits along the road to Oaxtepec in Milpa Alta, which is the southernmost borough of Mexico City, and by far the most rural. Out here there is land, and space, and rolling hills. The graveyard sits on a few acres of land filled with the dead, weeds and uncut grass, some cactus, and one large oak tree, all encircled with a simple wooden fence.

Rain was falling, it was late in the rainy season and water was spitting forth in dramatic fits and bursts. Being a ghost, the rain didn't bother me, and this distinction just depressed me further.

Her moan distracted me. I looked up from the gravestone and saw Sister Dominga. She was still attached to her body, her ghostly form half submerged in the ground, her mouth wide with the terror of the bardo. I looked away and back to the gravestone, rivulets of water tracing erratic paths down the polished stone.

If I had been alive, I would have put something else on

there besides her name and those dates to say something about her life, to say something about what she meant to me. Maybe "Beloved by Many."

I sighed and started pacing around her ghostly form and her grave. It had been several weeks since she had died. When I had come into her room and saw her bardoed, Lela had stopped her crying and given me a look. The kind of look I hoped to never see on her face. The grief was there, but a hardness crept in and then she frowned and shook her head and with a "pop" she was gone.

It seemed clear to me that she thought this was my mess. I was off drinking tequila and spending time with Valeria, hiding away in maya-land when Sister Dominga died. I should have been there. I might have been able to do something. I needed to fix this.

And I had tried, I had tried desperately. When Sister Helen found her body and began wailing, I tried to wake Sister Dominga up. When Father Finnegan came in and started saying last rites, I tried to wake her up. When they took her body to the mortuary and prepared it for burial, I tried to reach her. It wasn't until the casket was lowered into the ground, the sisters and priests gathered around, some crying, some silent, that I stopped trying.

I didn't know what to do. I didn't know how to reach her.

During that time, I sensed Lela now and then. She was close, she was paying attention, but she wouldn't come out. I tried talking to her, pleading with her, but it was just like when I first came here, she wouldn't communicate.

I've been wishing Banquo would come visit, but he hasn't. He must be off doing something important. He would know what to do.

No Banquo, no Lela, just me and the bardoed ghost of Sister Dominga.

Well, that's not exactly true. There are other moaning bardoed ghosts here and a few regular ghosts that seem to live here. But they are shy and won't talk to me either.

I've rarely felt so alone.

As I paced round and round her grave, focusing on keeping my form sharp, making my steps look realistic, I began to speak.

"Mercy... mercy... mercy..."

Just like when Sister Dominga had found me beaten and dying in that alley. Each time my right foot came down I said it. *Mercy.*

My memories of her and what she did for me are so clear. She saved my life and my soul. If there is anything admirable about who I am today, I owe it to her.

Mercy. Mercy. Mercy.

I don't understand why I'm a ghost, why she's a ghost. But I have to help her. I have to find a way.

I looked up from my pacing to the ghost of the woman I loved so much. Her mouth was closed and her face a bit relaxed. It's clear she's still not having a good time, but it is an improvement.

"Do you need to hear this part of the story?" I asked her.

She didn't answer, of course, but I could feel it. She needed to hear it. And I could feel Lela, she was somewhere close. Maybe my story will draw her out again.

Chapter 44

"EAT," SISTER DOMINGA SAID, HOLDING A SPOON OF THIN broth to my lips. She had a flat face with her mouth formed into a thin line and thick, black eyebrows like caterpillars resting on her forehead. Her clothing was simple, a white coif over her head and a simple white habit. All the white contrasted sharply with her brown skin and eyes.

I turned away, locking my mouth shut. I was tired of the bland food. I'd lost a lot of weight in my recovery and was beginning to look like Flaco. I choked at the thought of him and felt tears stinging my eyes.

"You'll have to talk to me someday," she said, setting the bowl of soup on the little wooden stand next to my bed. The room was tiny, with the bed, a dresser, a honey pot under the bed to relieve myself in, and a crucifix on the wall. The window was open and I could smell cooking meat wafting in from outside.

"You eat this," she said, nodding towards the soup, "you talk to me. Tell me your name. Tell me where your parents are, tell me where you live and..." She nodded again, this time to the open window and the world outside. She left and I heard a lock click on the door.

I waited for a few minutes after she left before slowly getting up. My right arm was in a cast, my ribs taped. The bruises that covered my body ached with every movement. I hobbled to the window and gazed out, searching for landmarks. This was not an area of Mexico City I was familiar with. Despite Rafael abandoning me in that alley, I longed to be back with the Muchachos and Mamá.

The air was warm and I caught the faint whiff of hyacinth roses—spring had come. I sighed and slowly moved back to the bed and sat on the edge. The bowl of brown broth had a piece of bread next to it. I gingerly ate both. My lip was still swollen and it hurt to eat. My fingers found the bandaged wound on my side where the chest tube had been. It hadn't been out long and was starting to itch.

The nun, Sister Dominga, had taken me to the doctor and then the hospital several weeks ago when she found me. I don't remember much. Just her strong arms and the way she said "mercy" with every step. And there were a lot of steps to get me there. I was in and out of consciousness. Every time I would awaken I would see that broad face of hers with her thick eyebrows and hear her say "mercy." As time passed, the strain of her carrying me became clear. Her brow was pinched by the effort and covered in sweat.

I didn't like her. I didn't trust her. She was a nun, a Catholic nun. I had not been to church since my parents were murdered. I had not prayed since they were ripped from my life. What this woman represented was repugnant to me. Any god that would let my parents be slaughtered like that was not a god I wanted to have anything to do with.

It was more complicated than that, of course. I also

missed Mass. I couldn't think of my mother without thinking of daily visits to the church in our old neighborhood. Of
her warm hand holding mine, her beautiful, smiling face,
her rose water scent.

Tears began to flow down my cheeks again as I sopped
up the remains of the soup with the last of the bread. I
hadn't allowed myself to think of her very much in years.
But I was trapped here in this Catholic orphanage—I had
nothing else to do.

Sister Dominga was nothing like my mother. Where my
mother was lithe and beautiful, Sister Dominga was big and
ugly. My mother had doted on me, Sister Dominga was strict
and unrelenting. She reminded me more of Mamá than my
mother, but she had saved me, she was caring for me. And
as much as I hated to admit it, I needed her.

She came back several hours later, with another bowl
of brown broth and another hunk of bland bread. She
didn't try to feed me, she just set it on the little stand next
to the bed, whispering "mercy" with each step. When she
leaned down I could smell the castile soap she must use.
She turned, saying "mercy" with each step toward the door.

She was almost to the door when I asked, "Why do you
say that?"

"Say what?" she asked. She turned around and stood at
the foot of my bed, her lips in a straight line.

"'Mercy.' Why do you say that with each step you take?"

She smiled then, suddenly not looking so ugly. I know,
it is not an appropriate thing to say, but Sister Dominga
was not gifted with a pretty face. She was ugly unless she
smiled. And then... I don't know how to explain it, but her
face didn't seem so flat, her cheeks rose up and danced with

her eyes which had a sparkle in them. She seemed like an entirely different person.

I smiled back despite the pain, I couldn't help it. Her smile was like that.

"Will you tell me your name if I answer your question?" she asked.

I nodded.

"I am praying." I didn't understand and it must have shown on my face. She stepped around to the side of my bed and sat on the edge of it. "For me, prayer is the most important thing I can do. It brings me closer to God. It opens me up to His will. It keeps my heart open."

I nodded slowly. I kind of understood; it was something my mother would have loved to do. It would have delighted her to pray with every step.

"Why 'mercy?'" I asked.

"It's something we all need. It's something this world can't get enough of. So I pray for it with each step I take."

I felt my eyes well up, but I held the tears back. If there was anything in this world that I needed then, it was mercy. Sister Dominga had shown mercy when she rescued me and took me in. I wasn't ready for her religion, but I needed her mercy like the desert needs rain.

If she knew what I was thinking, she would have corrected me. It wasn't her mercy I needed, but God's. But I wasn't ready for that.

"Your turn," she said, the smile gone from her face. I missed it.

"My name is Jesús," I said. I didn't tell her Juan like I had Mamá. I didn't even think about it. The truth slipped past my lips like a thief.

"Of course it is," she said, the smile returning to her face, bigger this time.

"I'm scared," I said, allowing the tears to flow.

"I know you are, but you are safe here. You are in God's house. He will protect you."

My tears stopped and I wiped my nose on my shirt sleeve. I felt a cold anger in my belly and my face must have shown it, because Sister Dominga suddenly stood.

"I don't believe in God anymore," I told her.

Sister Dominga silently stared at me for a moment and then slowly backed out of the room.

"WHAT ARE YOU GOING TO DO WITH ME?" I ASKED SISTER Dominga. Several days had passed, she brought me soup and bread four times a day, but we hadn't spoken again. I feared my declaration of not believing in God had put my stay in jeopardy. In some ways that was fine with me, but I knew I wasn't ready to be out on the streets again.

"I'll answer your question if you answer mine," she said, her face stony. I nodded. "I'm not sure what we are going to do with you. I think that's largely up to you. We have a small orphanage that is part of our church. You are a bit old, we normally only take in children under five, but it might work for you to stay."

I bit my lip, both prospects—staying or going—scared me. In my mind, I heard Flaco laughing at me. He was disappointed that I seemed to have forgotten everything he taught me. I was a beggar here and not using the skills I had acquired. But I couldn't. She was a nun, and despite my distaste for Catholicism, my training with it ran deep. I couldn't lie to her.

"Now your turn," she said gravely. "Why don't you believe in God?"

I slowly shook my head and tried to adjust my aching body into a position that didn't hurt. "It's a long story," I said.

She shrugged. "I've got time. Start at the beginning, Jesús, and don't leave anything out."

I studied her face, thinking she could have given Flaco and his begging skills a run for his money. She was completely inscrutable. I had no idea what she was thinking, what she wanted to hear from me, what would be best for my situation.

"My parents were murdered by the cartel," I finally said. "I lived on my own on the streets for over a year before being recruited by Mamá who runs a group of boys that beg for her and do drug deliveries."

She blinked, her face still a blank mask, but her eyes softening. "What had happened to you when I found you?"

"Rival gang of boys that had it in for me," I said, keeping my face calm, stating the facts as flatly as I could.

She stared into my eyes for the longest time until her strong hands took one of my hands and gently squeezed it. "Life can be so hard, can't it? Making it so difficult to understand His ways, His purpose for us."

I wanted to pull my hand away, but I was so starved for touch. Her speaking of God made me very uncomfortable.

Her mask fell away and there were tears in her eyes. For Sister Dominga this was a major display. "Listen to me, Jesús. You are safe here. I will talk to Father Finnegan about you staying on. He can't turn away a boy named Jesús."

She seemed so sure about it, but I was doubtful. My

name was Jesús, but I didn't believe in God. How could there be a place for me here?

Chapter 45

IN THE CENTER OF THE GRAVEYARD, NOT TOO FAR FROM Sister Dominga's grave, grew a lone tree. It had dark, almost black bark with leathery green leaves and was about twenty meters high. On the ground were some rotting acorns marking it as an oak.

As I paced around Sister Dominga and told my story, I kept looking at the tree. It had this noble air to it, as if it were holding court over the graveyard. I kept thinking of Lela every time I looked at it. Like her, the tree was silent, strong, and mysterious.

I walked over, letting my sense of Awareness expand. There were other ghosts here, not just the bardo-brains. As I paced and talked, I had seen them creeping closer, peaking around the gravestones, listening, hungry for the story I was telling.

In Tucson, in that graveyard, storytelling is central to our community, and in many ways, central to our health. This graveyard lacked that. This graveyard needed it.

"Hello," I said, addressing the graveyard when I got to the tree. "My name is Jesús Manuel Rivera Dominga. I was born and raised in Mexico City. I used to be a bounty hunter. I died in Tucson, Arizona. I am here because someone who was a mother to me needs me."

I paused. Giving a speech wasn't my kind of thing, but I felt I needed to do something for the ghosts here. They needed Banquo, but what they had was me. Besides, I couldn't spend all my time gazing into my past. It was just too hard.

"You don't need to be afraid of me. I will not hurt you." As I spoke I could feel and then begin to see the ghosts peeking out. From behind a rock or shrub or a gravestone. A few heads rising from the ground.

"I have a story to tell about my life. About this woman that saved my life. We all have these kinds of stories, and it is good for us to share them. I will be sharing mine. I hope you will share yours."

I placed a ghostly hand against the bark of the tree. I couldn't feel it, of course, but I imagined what it would feel like. Rough bark, cool to the touch. "That goes for you too, Lela," I whispered. "I know you are in there. I wish we could talk."

And she was in that tree. I could feel her, but I didn't do more. I didn't try to reach in and touch her—that would have just made things worse. "For now," I whispered, "please accept my apologies. I am sorry I disappeared for so long."

When I turned from the tree, a ghost was standing in front of me. She was stooped with age and had long silver hair pulled back in a ponytail. "We don't want to hear your story," she hissed, pointing a bony finger at me. "You disturb our rest with your constant talking. You think only of yourself."

I stood there stunned. I shouldn't have been surprised,

I guess. On my long walk to Mexico City, I had encountered many ghosts and discovered that our graveyard in Tucson was not the norm. There were many different ways of being a ghost.

"Forgive me," I said. "I am sorry if my story disturbs your rest, but it helps ease her suffering, and I can't turn my back on that."

"Of course you can't," she hissed and turned from me.

I heard Sister Dominga moan and went back to her. She seemed to be in agony, I had been away from her for too long. I resumed my pacing and continued my story.

THE CROWDED ROOM SMELLED OF MUSTY BOOKS AND aftershave, both a fondness of the man behind the desk, Father Finnegan. He had curly red hair and white skin with bright blue eyes. A gringo. An Irishman.

His office was dark, illuminated only by the sunlight streaming in the small window. It was full of bookshelves overflowing with a chaotic jumble of books. He sat behind a large wooden desk, his blue eyes appraising me.

I knew this for what it was. An audition.

"Sister Dominga, she tells me you want stay," he said, his Spanish awkward, his heavy accent making it even harder to understand him.

I had told the sister that, but probably not in the way she thought. I wanted to stay because I had nowhere else to go. My body was still healing and I couldn't imagine being out on the streets like this.

"Yes, Father," I said.

"You are old for our orphanage. You know?"

I nodded. They typically took much younger children, under five. I was eleven.

"Older kids, often a problem for us," he added. "We adopt out the young ones. No one will adopt you."

I nodded and looked down at my hands, the right one still sticking out of the cast on my arm. He didn't want to keep me, I could tell, even through his horrible Spanish. What could I offer him? What could I do?

"I speak English, you know," I said to him in English. "My father, he taught me well from the time I started talking myself."

A smile cracked his freckled face, his ruddy cheeks rising, making his eyes seem small. "Oh thank God!" he said in English, his Irish accent still making him hard to understand. "No one around here does. I so miss the mother tongue. I was born in Berlin, you know, and can speak German, but my parents spoke English at home, being from Ireland and on mission as they were. Spanish, though, I didn't start learning it until last year when I came here. I—" He stopped speaking suddenly, as if embarrassed about going on so long. He took a deep breath. "I'm sorry, son, this is about you, please..."

I smiled shyly and nodded. "I could help you with your Spanish, Father."

"You could at that, boy. You could at that. But..." he trailed off, the lips thinning and those intense blue eyes of his boring into me.

"I am a hard worker. I could help. I just need a chance."

"You must never lie to me, Jesús," he said, his tone low and gravelly. "Never."

I nodded my assent.

"Tell me now, what was your worst sin when you were out on the streets?"

My stomach clenched and I felt a cold sweat spring to my forehead. My worst sin? I am sure from his perspective there were so many, but I was just trying to survive. "Is this a confession, Father?"

He shook his head. "This is an interview. You do need to go to confession, but right now I am trying to get to know you. What was your worst sin?"

I swallowed hard and thought. "Not leaving," I said, letting the tears out. I could have stopped them, but this was an interview. I needed his sympathy.

"What, son? I don't understand."

"One day I received a bag from this man at our building. I looked in. I saw the cocaine. I knew then that it was the cartel running the place. It may not have been the same cartel that murdered my parents, but they are all the same." Despite myself the tears were gone and I was spitting the words out in anger. "I stayed knowing this. I stayed partially because I had friends, one that needed looking after, but mostly because I was weak. I was afraid."

At the end when I said "afraid," my voice cracked and the tears began to flow again. I felt so guilty for being a part of what had destroyed my family. I felt so weak for not leaving, not running far, far away. And then I felt Father Finnegan's strong arms around me and I couldn't stop crying.

I just knew they wouldn't want a boy like me. I wasn't good enough. I wasn't strong enough.

Chapter 46

"WAKE UP, JESÚS," SISTER DOMINGA SAID THE NEXT morning as she threw the curtains open to the little room I was sleeping in. My eyes were puffy from crying and my body still ached, but I was healing. Slowly.

I groaned and pulled the cover over my eyes with my good arm. My stomach grumbled and my bladder was full, but I didn't want to get up. I didn't want to face the day. I didn't want Sister Dominga to tell me I couldn't stay.

"Now," she said, her voice not loud but insistent. She yanked the covers off of me, the cool morning air chilling my skin.

I sat up rubbing at my eyes with my left hand. The sun had just come up, it was early. "What? Why?" I asked.

"Moving day, Jesús. You are well enough to be of use around here."

"Use? Around here?"

She nodded. "I don't know what you said to Father Finnegan, but he has approved you for a trial run. You have five minutes to get dressed, or when I come back in here, I'll dress you myself."

She left so quickly I could feel the air from her passing, smelling all soapy and clean. She said "mercy" with each step as she left. I couldn't imagine what I had done, how crying like a baby had earned me a spot here. I must have sat there for a full two minutes pondering it, until the thought of Sister Dominga dressing me woke me up from my stupor. I dressed quickly despite the cast on my arm.

I stood there ready when Sister Dominga came back in. "Time to meet your kids," she said before turning and marching down the hallway.

My kids? What was she talking about?

SIX BOYS AND FOUR GIRLS, RANGING FROM TWO TO TEN. My kids.

Sister Dominga introduced them one by one. They all sat around a large table in the orphanage's kitchen. I had thought the room I had been recovering in was in the orphanage. It was not. It was part of the nun's cloister— which was embarrassing to discover.

There was also Sister Helen, a young nun with a thin face and bright eyes. She bustled about cooking, carrying dishes, attending to the children. She was thin as a twig and was constantly in motion.

Sister Dominga clapped her hands twice and said, "Listen up, everyone." The room got quiet except for the youngest, Ena, a two-year-old girl in a highchair, tended to by Danielle, a pretty ten-year-old girl with a scar on her cheek. It was clear that everyone here was used to doing what Sister Dominga asked.

I felt a wave of dizziness. It reminded me so much of Mamá in her kitchen.

"This is Jesús, he will be staying with us and helping us out. He is older than all of you and you will listen to him. Is that clear?"

There were nods and yeses.

"Jesús, spend the day with them, see how things work around here. After dinner, Sister Helen will tell you how to find me. I want your recommendations on what kind of improvements we can make." She turned and walked out, the swirl of her white robes stirring the air.

I stood there looking at these ten children, struggling to remember their names—Paco, David, Danielle, Ena, Gabrielle—wondering what I could possibly do here.

THE CHURCH WAS EMPTY SAVE FOR SISTER DOMINGA kneeling at one of the pews, the faint scent of incense hung in the air.

It wasn't as big or as ornate as the church my mother used to take me to, but it was beautiful. My breath caught and I could hear my heart beating. I hadn't been in a church since the last time my mother took me. My mouth open, I gawked. Tall, rectangular stained glass windows depicting angels, Jesús Christ, and Guadalupe. Rows of pews in worn, dark wood. A large altar up front made from rough stone. And the crucifix.

On it Christ hung, his lips parted in pain, his eyes looking up. I reflexively crossed myself, my right hand going to my forehead, heart, left shoulder, right shoulder, and did a half kneel.

My cheeks flushed hot as anger descended on me. Why had she wanted to meet me here? This place that so reminded me of my mother, of what I had lost, of what was wrong with my life. I quickly turned to go, the sound of my foot scraping on the stone floor reverberating around the empty church.

"Please," Sister Dominga said quietly, "come."

I turned and Sister Dominga was now sitting in the pew, her hand beckoning to me. I took a deep breath and slowly made my way to her. She patted the pew next to her and I sat heavily on the hard wood.

"This place disturbs you," she said. It wasn't a question.

My cheeks flushed again. "Yes."

"What happened to your parents seems like a horrible injustice," she said.

I nodded.

"And what about what happened to Him?" she asked, her gaze going to the life-sized crucifix. "Even He suffered horribly."

I looked at the crucifix, but could not keep my gaze there. The pain on his face made me look away. "What is wrong with him?" I asked.

Sister Dominga was quiet for several breaths. "This depicts his moment of doubt. When he thought God had abandoned him, when he cried out 'My God, my God, why hast thou forsaken me?'"

I stared at her as she gazed at the crucifix. I didn't know what to say.

"All of this He did for us, but this moment especially. At some point don't we all feel forsaken?"

I nodded slowly. I had spent years feeling that way.

"But God never did forsake Him, you know."

I nodded again, but didn't speak.

"Come," she said, standing and grabbing my hand. "Let us talk somewhere else about matters more mundane."

I was only too glad to go. Once again, I loved the feel of my hand in hers, the simple pleasure of a parental touch. I was afraid they would not find me worthy and I would be forsaken. Again.

Chapter 47

A LOOSE CIRCLE OF GHOSTS HAD FORMED AROUND ME AS I paced and talked. About seven now. A girl, about six years old, who reminded me of Danielle from the orphanage. A man, stooped and old. The boney-fingered woman who told me she didn't want to hear my story, and several others. I looked to the tree, but no Lela yet.

"Did they find you worthy?" the little girl asked, her brow furrowed deeply. "Because if they didn't, that would be a terrible story."

I smiled and took a step towards her and squatted down. "I can't tell you that. Not yet."

"Why?" she asked.

"It would ruin the story. I have to tell it in the order it happened so that you understand what I was feeling."

"Is she in the story?" the girl asked, pointing at the ghost of Sister Dominga. I looked back, her jaw was slack and her form slowly swayed above her fresh grave.

"Yes. She is Sister Dominga. She saved my life."

The girl giggled, putting her hand to her mouth. "Then why are you dead?" she asked.

I smiled. "You are a smart girl. And that is a very good question." I scooted forward so I was only several feet away from her and extended my hand. "My name is Jesús, what is your name?"

She stared at my hand as if it were a knife or a gun—something dangerous. "We are ghosts, we can't shake hands."

"Yes we can. Tell me your name and I'll show you how." I felt the other ghosts move in closer.

Her eyes wide, she said, "Pasha. My name is Pasha and I died of coughing."

I smiled and nodded. At least one thing was the same here. "My name is Jesús and I died by an icepick to the eye." I then carefully modulated my hand to match hers and gently shook it.

Her eyes went wide as she stared at my hand, and then her eyes met mine and a huge smile spread on her face revealing a missing front tooth. I let go of her hand and she was silent for just a moment. She then clapped her hands together and started running around the graveyard crying "I felt something" over and over again.

The circle of ghosts around me was tight, and one by one they came up to me, introduced themselves, and wanted me to shake their hands. Each of them had a reaction, but none like Pasha.

The boney fingered old woman was last. She looked me up and down slowly, her eyes narrow, before saying, "My name is Esmeralda. I died in 1986 of a broken heart."

I carefully took her hand and slowly shook it. Her eyes widened and she blinked rapidly. I felt sorry for her and wondered what my afterlife would have been like if Banquo hadn't been there to teach me.

I turned to go back to Sister Dominga, to resume my story, when I saw another ghost.

She extended her hand to me and said, "My name is Lela. I died when I slipped and fell off a cliff on the Navajo reservation in northwestern New Mexico."

I took her hand and shook it. Her form was impeccable so I could "feel" more with her than with the others. I wanted to apologize, to tell her what had happened, to beg for her forgiveness. But a look in those cool blue eyes of hers stopped me. She had presented herself to me this way for a reason.

I nodded and said, "Nice to meet you, Lela. My name is Jesús. I died when the murderer I had captured stuck me in the eye with an ice pick."

"That must have hurt," she said with a shy smile.

"Enough," Pasha said loudly. "I want him to shake my hand again. Can you teach me how to do the trick? I want to shake everyone's hand!"

Lela laughed and let go of my hand. "I know how to do it too," she said. "Why don't Jesús and I teach all of you how to do it."

"Yes!" Pasha cried. "But I want Jesús to teach me."

I caught Lela's eye and she smiled. It was a small thing, and I knew I had so far to go yet. With her, with Sister Dominga, with the questions that plagued me. But it gave me hope that there would be a way out of this mess I had gotten myself into.

THE ORPHANAGE KITCHEN WAS EMPTY, JUST SISTER Dominga and I sitting at the long wooden table. I ran my finger across the wood feeling its roughness, avoiding her eyes.

Right then I wished that I was whole and grown. I didn't want to be dependent on anyone for anything. I wanted to be able to make my own choices. It's probably the kind of wish most eleven-year-olds have. But maybe more for me. I was tired of having to conform myself to someone else's expectations to survive. Little did I know what it is really like to be an adult.

"What are your recommendations?" Sister Dominga asked. Her tone was even.

"Umm... I... You know I only spent a day with them."

She nodded. "Yes, but you are a sharp boy. You know how this world works."

I studied her face like I used to do when Flaco and I worked Chapultepec Castle, but there was nothing there. No clue as to what she wanted. I wanted to stay, I knew I needed her to do that, but I didn't know what to do. I sighed. It probably wouldn't have helped anyway. I didn't seem to be able to lie to her. Maybe because she saved my life, probably because she was a nun.

"Paco and David need to resolve their differences." Sister Dominga nodded, but didn't comment. "They both want to be El Mejor, but they both can't be. They got a little rough with each other, but Sister Helen kept breaking them up. She needs to let them sort it out."

Sister Dominga nodded, her eyes not wavering one bit, her face not betraying any reaction. "Anything else?"

I patted the table. "Everyone eats like savages. It is chaos. Easy to fix, though. No one gets to eat until Sister Helen gives the word and then each one takes their turn."

A small smile flickered on her lips. "And how do you propose we get that to happen."

"Tell them the new rules. If they do not obey, then they don't eat."

"We have to feed them," Sister Dominga said.

"Well then, Sister Helen can make up their plate for them and that is all they get."

"What else?"

I paused, wishing she would give me some feedback. It felt strange telling a nun the things Mamá would do. "The older ones need more chores, more things to do to help out. Everyone should contribute to the best of their ability."

She nodded, her hand rubbing at her chin. "Tell me about this place you used to live. This Mamá."

I suddenly felt hot. How had she known I was using things I had learned while there? "We worked hard every day. We ate and laughed at night. Sometimes we got to watch movies." I shrugged. "There is not much to tell. I was a mendigo for her and then a corredor. All boys, everyone works, you can stay while you are useful and until your voice changes."

"How did you end up there?"

"One of the corredores found me on the street. Took me to meet Mamá. She fed me, I didn't leave."

Sister Dominga was silent for a long time, her eyes staring at the small crucifix on the wall. I fidgeted in my chair, trying to get my finger under my cast and scratch the itch that always seemed to be there. Finally, she pushed back her chair and rose.

"I'll talk to Sister Helen about your recommendations," she said as she swept towards the door. Before leaving, she turned back and added, "Make sure Paco and David don't really get hurt."

With that she left me alone. She was going to take my

advice? I felt proud and scared at the same time. Proud that she had thought my opinion worth listening to, scared that my advice would turn out wrong.

"SISTER DOMINGA TELLS ME THAT YOU DON'T BELIEVE IN God," Father Finnegan said from behind his big desk.

My days had gotten very busy. I slept in a large room with the rest of the orphanage boys. It was my job to get them up and to breakfast. After that we all had to attend Mass. We then had schooling, several nuns taught us. Lunch, more class until the early afternoon, and the chores. After dinner, several nights a week, I spent time with Father Finnegan teaching him Spanish.

No one had ever told me I was going to be able to stay. I just never left.

I cleared my throat, pretending to study the books on his shelves. I figured they were all dry religious doctrines, not anything interesting, most of them probably beyond me, and most probably not in Spanish. I knew how to read, but there had been no school since my parents died.

"Is it true?" Father Finnegan asked.

I nodded, avoiding his eyes and shifting in the hard wooden chair I sat in. I was afraid that this would be it. I didn't believe in God. I would have to go.

"Look at me, boy," he said. "This is important." I reluctantly looked into his blue eyes. "I want to make sure you understand something. Are you listening to me, Jesús?"

"Yes, Father," I said.

"God doesn't need you to believe in Him. In fact, your belief or lack thereof makes no difference whatsoever."

I really looked at him then. His face was serious, no hint of humor. I didn't understand what he was getting at.

"Does the sun need you to believe it will rise in the east every morning?" he asked.

"No, Father. Of course not."

"It's like that with God. Your faith is for you, not for Him."

I shook my head. "I don't understand."

He smiled gently. "Let me put it another way. You not believing in God doesn't hurt Him, it only hurts you."

"God doesn't care if I believe?" I asked.

Father Finnegan chuckled. "Of course he does. He wants the best for all of his children."

"I... I..." I stammered.

He stood up, his chair scraping noisily on the wooden floor. He walked around his desk and stood over me, his aftershave filling my nose. "But I don't think you've told me the truth about your feelings around God."

"What?" My heart raced, here it was.

"No. I think you do believe in God. I think you have the potential for a great faith."

Father Finnegan had been speaking to me in English and I was afraid I had missed something. "I don't understand."

He nodded and smiled. "Exactly. You don't understand why your parents had to die. Why you had to get mixed up with the cartel. Why you have had to struggle so hard in your young life."

I nodded, tears forming. I poked at my eyes, embarrassed by them.

"What you are, Jesús, is angry. Angry at God for all the hardship you have suffered."

I bit my lip and nodded.

"And you couldn't be angry at God if you didn't believe in Him."

Chapter 48

"ARE YOU ANGRY AT GOD NOW?" LELA ASKED. SHE WAS one of the ghosts in the circle that listened as I spoke. The circle had grown by a few. I think the whole graveyard was now in attendance.

I wished Lela and I could have a private conversation, but it was clear she was doing this for a reason. I shook my head. "No. I was almost twelve years old then. I didn't understand why the world had to be so hard."

Pasha sniffed, her eyes looking down. I noticed that her black hair was now in a braid just like Lela's. Her eyes found me and her face hardened. "I'm mad at God," she said. "Why did I have to die? Why did I have to then watch my parents cry and cry? Why am I here?"

"Why are we here?" Esmeralda echoed, her old face looking accusing. "At least you had that Banquo to teach you when you died. We have all been stranded here with nothing."

"I was a good Catholic," a ghost named Felipe said. He looked to be about fifty and had a round, mischievous face more comfortable in happiness than with the frown he wore.

"I confessed my sins. I was loyal to my wife. I know we all have to die, but why am I here?"

More of the same questions peppered me. Why me? Why here? Why a ghost? Why did I have to die like I did? Why was my life so full of pain?

They were my own questions, the ones that had been rattling around in my head since I died, and here they were coming from other people. People who somehow expected me to have an answer.

"I don't know," I said quietly, but no one heard. I turned around the circle and looked at all the faces. Men and women, young and old. They were all in pain about something. They all doubted why they were here. They all wanted answers. Except Lela.

When our eyes met I could see her compassion. What I was experiencing was her doing. She had sparked this conflagration of emotion. She had done this on purpose. What did she want? Did she want me to try to answer? Did she want me to admit how lost I really was?

I turned from the ghosts, thinking of Sister Dominga and how this chaos must be affecting her, worried that it would be increasing her suffering, that I was, once again, not paying attention to her when I needed to. But when I looked at her face, all worry fled away from me.

She was still a wispy mess, her eyes vacant. But on her face was a smile, like she was glad for all of this.

I turned back to the ghosts, their questions finally dying down.

"I don't know the answer," I said quietly.

"Eh?" Esmeralda said, her hand to her ear.

"I don't know why," I said loudly. "I don't know why we had to die the way we did. I don't know why we are ghosts.

According to the Catholic faith we shouldn't be." Everyone was silent now listening to me, as if they expected wisdom to flow out of my mouth. But I had no wisdom for them. "But to answer Lela's question, I am no longer angry at God like I was in Sister Dominga's orphanage."

"Why not?" Lela asked.

I paused, gathering my thoughts, looking back to Sister Dominga. "Because of her. Because of what she taught me. Because she never stopped loving me."

Sister Dominga's smile was gone, but her head twitched slightly, as if she were nodding at me to continue my story.

THE ORPHANAGE HAD A SCHOOL—THE DINING ROOM WAS used for class during the day. Various nuns would come teach us reading, math, history, and religion. They taught all of us together.

The orphanage had a playground, more or less. It was a narrow courtyard between the church and the orphanage with an iron fence between the sidewalk and the courtyard.

On the playground were the remnants of grass that never got the chance to thrive because of too many feet pounding on it. There were some rose bushes, whose thorns kept them alive—a few pokes and the kids learned to keep their distance.

It wasn't much, but it was ours. After a few weeks, Sister Dominga put me in charge of recess. I still had my cast on, but I was starting to feel like myself again.

The older kids were kicking around a soccer ball. Danielle was looking after the younger kids. I stood in the back corner, in the shadows, watching it all.

I had been distracted, wondering once again about the

Muchachos and what they were doing. I still missed that life. Because of my distraction, I didn't notice the altercation until Paco and David were rolling around on the ground, yelling and punching at each other.

Paco was eight, a year younger than David, but was chubby and outweighed him. It was a pretty even fight.

With a sigh, I left my corner and walked over. I thought I had been so smart—let the boys sort it out themselves. That is what had worked for the Muchachos. That should work here.

Only for Paco and David it didn't work. I had let them fight several times, until they were bruised and bloodied. I had endured the scathing looks from Sister Helen and the disappointed look from Sister Dominga.

"Break it up," I yelled as I pushed my way through the other kids who had gathered around. The two boys ignored me.

"She likes me best," I heard David hiss to Paco. Paco currently had David pinned to the ground.

"Liar!" Paco cried, his fist landing square on David's cheek.

I yanked Paco off with my good hand. I had several years on both these boys and was a lot bigger. Paco staggered back, and then came charging towards David, blood dripping from his swelling lip. I stepped into his path and hit him with the flat of my hand in the middle of his chest. He went down hard, grasping for air.

"New rule," I yelled. "You start a fight with anyone for any reason, and I'm going to come end it." I looked down at Paco. "Got it?" He nodded, still gasping for breath. I turned to David who was now standing, rubbing at his jaw. "Got it?" I asked him.

"Yes, Jesús," he said.

"Recess is over," I said. "Everyone in. Time to work on your math homework."

There were grumbles and complaints, but everyone moved towards the door to the dining room.

"Look who's El Mejor now," I heard a familiar voice say. I turned around and saw Rafael standing at the iron fence, his hands gripping two of the bars, his face pressed against them.

I already had a lot of adrenaline running through my veins, but when I saw him more dumped into my bloodstream and my heart thumped loudly in my chest. What would it mean if Mamá knew I was here? Surely Rafa would tell her.

"Rafa," I said, trying to hide my shock.

He looked around grinning. "Not bad, you landed good." He nodded towards where I had just broken up the fight. "Glad to see you remember some of the moves I taught you."

"What do you want, Rafa?"

He smiled, showing his uneven teeth. It sent a chill down my spine.

"Come on, Jesús. Aren't you glad to see an old friend? One that plucked you off the street, taught you how to survive, gave you a place to live."

I took a few steps toward him, looking into his eyes. He was scared about something and trying to hide it.

"It's been a fine reunion," I said quietly. "But I've got things to do, so spit it out."

"I..." Rafael began, but his voice cracked, jumping up an octave. He cleared his throat, the fear widening his eyes. His voice was changing. If Mamá heard his voice like that he would be out. No men with the Muchachos, only boys.

"I need some money," he whispered when he had control of his voice back. "You are going to go in the church tonight and steal something valuable for me."

"Did Mamá kick you out yet? Did she hear you voice squeak like that?" I took another step forward, studying his eyes like Flaco had taught me. "She hasn't yet, huh? What are you doing? Faking laryngitis or something? You are on borrowed time, Rafa."

He reached through the bars, grabbing my shirt and jerking me forward. Our faces were almost touching and I could smell his stinking breath. "Listen to me, you little worm. You are going to help me, or I will bring the corredores back and we will take what we want." His voice broke again at the end, making it sound almost comical, but I knew he was deadly serious.

IGLESIA DE SAN MIGUEL ARCÁNGEL IS NOT A WEALTHY church in a wealthy neighborhood. Most of what seems valuable about it is the building. Stained glass windows, beautifully painted frescos, crystal chandeliers, and the life-sized crucifix. What was there here that I could take?

I slowly walked down the aisle, my hand lingering on each pew as I passed, my eyes wandering high and low. I reached the front of the church and turned around. I couldn't face my namesake on the cross as I contemplated theft.

I wandered towards the front of the church and saw the silver basin that contained holy water and next to it the offering box.

My heart fluttered in my chest. Could I actually take the offering box? Was there enough in it to send Rafael away?

I touched the box; it was made of dark wood with a metal front that depicted a communion goblet in what looked like brass. It was old, the wood and metal stained with age. There was a slot on the top for the offerings and a key in the metal door. It was roughly a third of a meter on each side.

I caught of whiff of sweet incense as my finger probed the lock. It was an old lock, simple. But I lacked the skill to pick it. I could go get a shovel and probably break it open, but I would surely be caught again.

I sighed, my shoulders slumping. The situation seemed impossible.

I heard the scrape of a shoe against the tiled floor and heard a man say in English, "Have you come to confess?"

I jumped and turned to see Father Finnegan. It was late, he looked tired.

"I... Well... I..." I stammered.

The Father chuckled, his warm hand resting on my shoulder. "We are both here, so let's at least give it a shot."

His hand moved to my back and he guided me to the confessional. It seemed tall and imposing as we approached. I studied its ornate wood and heard my heart pounding in my ears. How long since I had been in one? My mother had insisted that I confess my sins regularly. The last time had been the day my parents died.

Soon I was sitting on the hard wooden bench, a lattice made of brass separating me and Father Finnegan. I could smell the oils they used to polish the wood and I could hear him breathing.

A few minutes passed and he cleared his throat. "Any time now, son."

I cleared my throat several times and said, "Bless me,

Father, for I have sinned. It has been... umm... maybe two years—probably more—since my last confession."

I had whispered, like I had been taught, but the sound seemed so loud, like everyone could hear me, like everyone could see me.

"I... During that time I have done what I had to to survive. I have begged, stolen, lied. I have struck other boys and wished my enemies dead." My voice grew louder as I spoke, the words rushing out of me. "I have longed for vengeance against those that killed my family and..." I stopped, my breath coming fast and ragged. "And I have knowingly worked for the cartel so I could survive."

The silence that followed was thick. "Anything else?" he finally asked.

"I am angry, Father. I am angry at God." My hand struck the wall of the confessional, the thump startlingly loud. "I am so angry." I kept hitting the confessional with the side of my fist until my hand began to ache and tears were running down my cheek. "Why, Father? Why does it have to be like this? Why has life been so cruel to me? Why couldn't I just have had my parents and grown up like a normal boy?"

He might have said something, but I was crying too hard to hear him. Before long, I heard the door to the confessional open and his arms were around me, drawing me forth. He was a stronger man than I had thought and I could not resist. Soon he had positioned me in the front pew, and we were both kneeling.

"Our Father, Who art in heaven," he began, speaking Irish-accented English, his voice soft but strong.

I kept my head down as I continued to sob. I felt his warm hand on my back.

"Say it with me, Jesús. It will help. I promise." He paused

for a moment and began the prayer again. "Our Father, who art in heaven, hallowed be thy name..."

He kneeled with me, for how long I don't know. He started the prayer over and over until I was coherent enough to say it with him.

"Our Father, who art in heaven, hallowed be thy name. Thy kingdom come. Thy will be done, on earth as it is in Heaven..."

And then he said it with me over and over until I was calm and my eyes were dry.

"Better?" he asked when we were done.

I nodded my head. "I don't know if I believe it. Was it His will that my parents be murdered? That my mother die giving me a chance at life? That I be witness to it all?"

I looked into his blue eyes and the compassion that I saw made tears flow anew.

"That is a difficult question and one I will attempt to answer. But not tonight. That is enough for tonight."

I nodded and rose.

"I want you to say that prayer when you rise, before you sleep, and every time you feel angry at God."

I bit my lip. "I'll be saying it all the time then, Father."

He nodded and gave me a small smile. "So much the better, my son."

I was about to leave when he grabbed my hand and put a string of rosary beads in it—his rosary beads. My mouth opened to speak, but the look in his blue eyes stopped me. His eyes were so intense, but I could see that he was close to tears. For the first time I wondered at his past and what he had been through. What was a German born, Irish priest who didn't speak Spanish very well doing in Mexico

City? What kind of childhood did he have? What brought him here?

I smiled and nodded. I knew what he wanted—say the prayer and use the beads. Something in his eyes, more than his words, told me that it could help. That it had helped him.

As I left the church, thoughts of Rafael and what he wanted came back to me. I didn't sleep much that night, I just kept saying the prayer, Father Finnegan's rosary beads slipping through my fingers, hoping that it would somehow make a difference.

Chapter 49

"DID PRAYING HELP?" PASHA ASKED, HER USUALLY SMOOTH forehead deeply furrowed.

I nodded. "It took time, lots of it. And it took Sister Dominga and Father Finnegan never giving up on me."

"Maybe *we* should pray."

I looked around, scared. It was like I was that boy again. I hadn't prayed much since I died, and certainly hadn't since finding my killer and seeing him arrested, since this crisis of mine started. Just like back then it seemed like a foreign thing, like if I prayed I would be ignoring all the questions I had, turning my back on all my feelings.

I looked around the little circle. Lela was watching Pasha, a thin smile on her face. Esmeralda was slowly nodding, her face serious. Felipe had his arms crossed, a deep frown on his face.

I chuckled and shook my head.

"What's so funny?" Felipe asked.

"Here we are a group of Catholic ghosts unsure of whether we should pray," I said. Felipe looked offended so I added, "Don't you see the humor in that?"

He shook his head.

Lela cleared her throat, a most intentional gesture as a ghost, since we have no throats, per se, and said, "I am not Catholic, and I have no issue praying."

All eyes turned towards her and I felt excited. Lela was speaking of herself. Offering information. I moved next to her and gestured towards the center of the circle. "Then please, lead us in a prayer," I said.

Pasha clapped her hands together and said, "Yes, Lela. Make it a good one. A happy one."

Lela's eyes narrowed as she studied me, but it didn't last long. With a single nod she stepped into the middle of the circle.

She held her arms wide, her palms up as she slowly rotated, looking at us all.

"Great Spirit," she began looking upward. "We give thanks to you for our existence, for our intelligence, for our love. We honor your creation by walking our path as close to you as we can. We let go of the past and turn our backs on the future, living each moment as fully as we can. We are humbled by the majesty of your creation. May we walk in beauty."

Her head bowed briefly before she returned to the circle, leaving us all looking at Sister Dominga. Her eyes seemed to focus for the briefest of moments as she watched Lela reenter the circle.

"Did you see that?" I said to her. "She seemed to wake up for a moment. Maybe it's not me that can wake her, maybe it's you."

As we tried to wake up Sister Dominga, the dynamic of the group changed. Gone was the shyness or the accusations. In its place was everyone trying to help. The stories had changed everything.

At first Lela repeated her prayer as we all watched, a tight grouping of ghosts focused on Sister Dominga. That didn't glean a reaction, so she started saying other prayers. They were beautiful and poetic. Speaking of the directions, of the sky and the earth and the moon. Speaking of beauty and the "way." They seemed like poetry to me, not quite like the prayers I was used to. They seemed to lack the guilt of Catholicism and didn't talk of hell or damnation.

I found them curious and intriguing—much like Lela herself. But Sister Dominga didn't wake up.

In the middle of this, Banquo popped in. I hadn't seen him since the Cantina.

The rest of the ghosts scattered when he appeared, although I could feel that they weren't far and were listening.

Banquo's gaze quickly took it all in. We caught up briefly, and told him of what we had been doing, and he told me of JJ's struggle in the bardo, how he had willingly gone in to help a man he didn't know named John, how he had been there these many months since I had left. My heart went out to him—and I could tell Banquo's did to, it seemed to trouble him greatly. I wanted to help JJ, but I had my own problems to deal with.

"You changed things at the Cantina," he said after we finished talking about JJ.

My puzzled look was my only answer.

"More souls have left since you did. Some have answered the call. Well done, Jesús. Well done."

He clapped me on the back, but I didn't feel accomplished.

"Valeria?" I asked, catching the narrowing of Lela's

eyes—that was a story I was not looking forward to telling her.

He shook his head and turned to Lela. "How did she die?" he asked, nodding toward the ghost of Sister Dominga.

"She just stopped breathing," Lela said. "When her soul separated, she was like this. Already in the bardo."

I hadn't known that. I hadn't been there and Lela and I had not talked about it. The hooded expression in her eyes warned me not to ask her any questions now.

"Can that happen?" I asked Banquo. "Can a spirit be in the bardo before they die?"

"Yes," he said. "Look around this world, Jesús. Many of the living are walking around in their own bardo. Surely you relate." I nodded and he continued. "But that is not what you were asking. Can a spirit literally be in the bardo before the body expires?" He nodded sharply. "Yes. Given how long it took her to die, it's not really surprising. She was trapped in a dying body, getting pulled into the bardo is easy in those circumstances."

"How do we reach her?" Lela asked.

I knew Banquo well enough to know the answer. "Find what is more important to her than her suffering," he said. "Has she shown any signs of waking?"

"I have been recounting the story of my time with her," I said. "That calms her, just like when she was in her coma. Lela recently said a prayer with the group and that seemed to bring her about for a moment, but we can't repeat it."

Banquo sighed, his index finger rubbing his upper lip as he walked around Sister Dominga. He reached out, his finger briefly touching her wispy form. He walked over to Lela and me. "Tell your story," he said to me. "Say your prayers," he told Lela. "I think you are on the right track."

We both opened our mouths to ask what else he knew, but before we could, his lips twitched into a smile and he popped away, leaving our questions hanging in the air.

Chapter 50

I PACED THE FENCE OF OUR LITTLE YARD AS THE REST OF the kids played. Soccer, dolls, coloring. I knew Rafael was coming, and I had nothing for him. The sun was hot, having just tilted towards the west, and I was sweating. I chewed on my thumbnail and wished my belly would stop roiling.

I had a plan, but I didn't think it was a good one. If I had two good arms, maybe it would work, but with the one, I was doubtful.

Paco and David had almost gotten into it several times, but had stopped themselves. At least something I was doing was working. At least I knew it was about Danielle now. It made sense. Except for me, they were the oldest boys and she was the oldest girl. They were of the right age for this kind of nonsense.

The thought almost made me laugh. I, too, was the right age for this kind of nonsense, but I had never had a life that had room for it. In some ways it made me glad for them. This orphanage let them be young.

I heard the heavy scrape of a foot and turned to see Rafael, grinning as he clutched the iron bars of the fence.

My heart leapt, but I tried to hide my surprise. I had been lost in thought and hadn't seen him approach.

"Hi, Juan," he said, my Muchacho name sounding strange in my ears. I was used to being called Jesús again. "What you got for me?"

I reached into my pocket with my left hand, making a bit of a show of it. I wanted him to think I had something for him. His grin widened and he licked his chapped lips.

"If I do this, how do I know it will be the end?" I asked.

He shrugged. "You'll just have to take my word for it. I'm not planning on staying. I'm going to head north. I just need some funds to get me there."

I nodded slowly, my hand still in my pocket as I approached the fence, the sound of the kids playing an odd accompaniment for my plan. "That's good," I said quietly. "Because after we're done here today, if I see you again, I will kill you."

His eyes widened as my heart thumped in my chest and then he laughed loudly. "You always were a joker," he said. "Juan and Flaco, the mendigo comedians. All I have to say to that, Juan, is try. I taught you what you know about fighting, and I didn't teach you half of what I know. Now, let's see what you've got."

The noise behind me had lessoned, but I didn't turn. I could feel their eyes on me. Rafa's laughter must have caught their attention. I didn't want them watching, but there was nothing I could do about it.

I reached deep into my pocket and grabbed a handful of what was there. I brought it out and threw the fine dirt up into his face. He had been looking closely so he got an eye full, yelling as he stepped back, his hands going to his eyes.

I lunged through the fence with my good hand and

grabbed his grubby brown shirt. I jerked back with all my might, his body hitting the iron of the fence hard. I was hoping to knock him out, but his hands at his eyes were in the way.

I heard shouting and the sound of running feet behind me, but I didn't look. "Never come back!" I shouted. I pulled him against the fence again, this time his hands falling away and reaching through the fence to me.

He swung wildly, his forearm connecting hard enough with my left ear for my head to ring. His eyes were tearing, but I was betting he couldn't see yet. I yanked at him again, this time his head connecting with the iron fence, but not very hard.

His right arm found my cast and he pulled it through the fence and started swinging it back and forth against the bars on either side. It hurt, but I could handle it. I let go of his shirt with my right arm and punched him in the face. It landed, but it didn't have much force behind it.

He continued to bang my cast against the bars, I kept punching out at him. We didn't speak, just groans and grunts. I was fighting for my life and the safety of the people that had given me a home. I wasn't going to stop.

But soon my cast started to break down and the pain went from bearable to excruciating as he banged at my still mending arm.

With a scream, I reached through and grabbed his hair, pulling his head as hard as I could. This time there was a solid thunk as flesh met iron. This time it worked; he let go of my arm, falling in a heap.

I heard people moving and shouting behind me, but it all had no meaning. I had my leg through the fence and was stomping down over and over on Rafael. "Come back here and I will kill you. I will kill you!" I shouted.

Soon a strong hand pulled me away from the fence, but I fought wildly. I swung back with my right fist and felt it connect with flesh. I heard a grunt, but the arms just tightened around me.

I was still screaming at Rafael when I was dragged inside.

Chapter 51

I T WAS F ATHER F INNEGAN WHO HAD GRABBED ME, dragged me to a room, shoved me in and locked the door. It was the same room I had recovered in. Just a bed, a dresser, and a small window. I stalked the floor like a caged animal holding my injured arm to my chest. The pain was not as sharp as it had been, but it was spreading, the ache becoming pervasive, taking me over.

And I had been like an animal. Attacking Rafael, defending my territory, doing my best to preserve my life. They were going to kick me out, I just knew it.

I walked to the open window and peered out. There was the church's small garden three floors below and nothing to hold on to. I might have chanced it with two good arms, but not with one.

I slumped onto the bed, defeated. There was nothing I could do but wait.

"T AKE THIS ," S ISTER D OMINGA SAID . S HE HANDED ME A white pill and a cup of water. Her expression was inscrutable, as usual, but her cheeks were flushed.

I had finally lain down as I waited, the pain from my battered arm getting the best of me. I was sitting on the edge of the bed dizzy. My cast was cracked, plaster flaking off.

"It will help with the pain," she added.

I took the pill and drank all the water. My mouth was dry and sour. "Sister Dominga, listen... I..." I stammered.

"Save it, Jesús. There will come a time for you to explain yourself, but this is not that time." She swept towards the door and for once I didn't smell her clean soapy scent. I smelled sweat and fear. Mine and hers. "I'll be back when that has had some time to work. We've got a ways to walk."

She closed the door and I heard it lock.

I lay down wondering where she was going to take me.

"THEY WERE KICKING YOU OUT," FELIPE SAID WITH A GRAVE nod. "I was an orphan, too. Everywhere I went they would do the same. My uncle, my grandparents, the orphanage. One sign of trouble and out you go."

Esmeralda snorted, pointing her boney finger at him. "Oh, give it up, Felipe. From the stories you've told, you were an unholy terror. You and your fascination with fire. Didn't you nearly burn down your uncle's house?"

The grin on Felipe's face was scary. "I like fire," he said, his hand erupting in flame.

"At least you can't burn anything down now," Esmeralda said.

Felipe started waving his fiery hand in the other ghosts' faces and the circle broke up. It seemed it was time for a break. There were four of us left: Pasha, Lela, Sister Dominga, and me.

"Why did you try to hurt that boy?" Pasha asked, her face drawn tight in concern. "You tried to kill him. Why?"

She had backed up a pace and was watching me closely, as was Lela. "I was wrong to do that," I said. "Even though Rafael had threatened me, had threatened those that had taken me in, I was wrong to do what I did."

"Did you know it was wrong then?" she asked.

I nodded. "I did, but I was scared. We all do some things we shouldn't when we are scared." I turned to Sister Dominga. "You helped me, didn't you, Sister? You always helped me."

"You don't hit kids anymore, do you?" Pasha asked, her voice thin.

I turned to her, but did not approach. "Of course not, Pasha. I would never hurt you. I am sorry my story is scaring you now."

She nodded slowly. "It's not right to hit kids." Her eyes were filling with tears and I suddenly knew something about her. About why she was here. About what had happened to her when she was alive.

I opened myself up to Awareness, letting my perception grow. She had been struck, I knew it. How could I help her? I saw the look of concern on Lela's face. She must have known it too, but she stood silently watching us.

"It was your father, wasn't it?" I asked.

She bit her lip and very quietly said, "Yes."

"Your father can't hurt you anymore, Pasha. You are safe here with Lela and me. We would never let anyone hurt you."

She looked to Lela who smiled and nodded to her and then back to me. "Why?" she asked. "Why did my father hit me? Why did that boy threaten you? Why did I have to cough so hard I died? Why did I have to be like this and watch my mother cry so much?" She was crying now, ghostly tears running down her face, her form going diffuse, flickers of a sickly green running along the edges her form. If something didn't happen soon, she was bardo bound.

Chapter 52

THE MEDICINE SISTER DOMINGA HAD GIVEN ME DIFFUSED the pain but made me nauseous, my stomach churning and roiling, my arm pulsing with dull pain with every heartbeat. I knew they were done with me, I just didn't understand what they were waiting for.

A while later she came sweeping into the room and said, "Come with me."

"I'm sorry, Sister," I said. "For what I did, I am so sorry. Is Rafael OK?"

She studied my face, her mouth drawn into a thin frown. "I don't know. We went looking for him, but he was gone."

"I was... He threatened..." I stammered.

She held her hand up, her palm facing me. "This is still not the time. Come with me." With that she turned and walked out of the room. I followed her down the hallway, down three flights of stairs and out the entrance to the cloister and out on the street.

We were greeted with the sounds and smells of the city. Honking horns, exhaust fumes, the smell of cooking meat from a street vendor. The latter made me want to throw up.

Sister Dominga set a quick pace and I had to do every-thing I could to keep up with her. We headed east into a little bit better part of town. She stopped in front of a clinic and held the door for me. Inside was a crowded waiting room filled with the sick and the injured. People coughing, one man with a bloodied face, a mother with a child lying in her lap as she stroked the girl's head.

She found two open chairs and I sank heavily into one.

I sat next to her and waited. I tried to apologize, to explain why I had done such a desperate thing. But she would not hear a word of it.

I sat there with my pain and regret, worried about what was to come next.

FATHER FINNEGAN'S OFFICE WAS CROWDED. HE SAT behind his messy desk, his eye swollen and blackened from my struggling as he pulled me off of Rafael. I had hit a priest. The thought sat in my stomach like a stone. I sat across the desk from him, my eyes darting to the wound and then away in shame. Sister Dominga and Sister Helen stood against the wall of the office watching me closely.

I had a new cast on, and while I was in pain, it had finally become bearable.

"Who was the boy?" Father Finnegan asked. He spoke in Spanish for the sisters' sake. I felt a brief sliver of pride that his Spanish had improved considerably since my arrival.

I looked to Sister Dominga and she nodded grimly to me. It was finally time to talk about what had happened.

"His name is Rafael. He is the boy that recruited me into the Muchachos."

"What did he want?" he asked.

"He wanted me to steal something valuable from the church and to give it to him. He threatened to bring the corredores back if I didn't and take whatever is of value here by force."

Sister Helen gasped, but neither of the other two reacted noticeably.

"Is this the kind of thing you did when you were with them?" he asked. "Threaten and extort?"

I shook my head. "No, Father. I was a beggar at Chapultepec Castle for most of the time. I was briefly a corredor, but I only made deliveries. Rafa is desperate. His voice is changing and soon as Mamá finds out he will be kicked out."

"Can we expect him to bring his corredores back here?" he asked.

I shrugged. "I don't know. He is El Mejor, they do what he says. I guess he could."

He nodded slowly, his eyes hooded, and said, "This is most unfortunate, Jesús. You understand that there will be consequences to your action."

"Yes, Father. I am sorry for what I did. I know it was wrong. I just... I was desperate. And then as we fought I just got so angry. I am so sorry that I... that I..." I wanted to apologize for hitting him, but couldn't get it out.

Father Finnegan cut me off with a loud sigh. "Your contrition is noted. Leave us now and go back to your room. Pray as I taught you to and rest. We must discuss this in private."

SISTER DOMINGA LOOKED TIRED. NOT IN HER ERECT posture, direct speech, or clasped hands, but in the darkness under her eyes. This thing was finally wearing her down. I was finally wearing her down.

It had been several hours since Father Finnegan dismissed me, and I had been in my room unable to rest. My mind would not let me be. Part of it judging my actions as necessary and proud of it—I had stood up to the mighty Rafael and beat him in a fight despite the handicap of my arm. The other part of me was just plain scared. What would I do? Where would I go? I didn't want to be on my own again.

"I need you to listen to me carefully, Jesús," she said. She was pacing back and forth, the short length of the room, her hands held tightly together in front of her. She paused, sighed deeply, and said, "Guadalupe preserve me, I hope I am doing the right thing."

My stomach dropped and my mouth went dry.

She must have seen my face. "It's OK, Jesús. Relax. You can stay."

I just stared at her. Of all the things she might have said, that was not what I was expecting.

"There are conditions, but if you meet them, you can stay here."

"What? How?" I stammered.

Sister Dominga chuckled. "Believe me, it wasn't Father Finnegan's first choice, but Sister Helen and I stood up for you. Actually..." she trailed off, her eyes staring out the small window to the city that surrounded us. I could hear the usual honk of horns and snippets of voices.

She swallowed hard before looking back to me. She slowly sat down next to me and took my hand. "Things are going to have to change, Jesús. Much will be asked of you. I will be asking much of you. But I believe you are up to the challenge."

"What... what do you want?"

She smiled gently. "You are now my direct responsibility,

Jesús. You will no longer be working in the orphanage. You will take classes there, but you won't work or live there. You will stay here, and when you are not in class you will be under my direction."

"Doing what?"

"Learning your catechisms, cleaning up, doing whatever it is I find for you to do." She let go of my hand and her face hardened. "And you will be very, very busy. There is so much to do."

A mozo, she was asking me to be her mozo, her house boy. The lowest rung of the Muchachos. I didn't really like the idea and I think it showed on my face.

She stood up and faced me, her arms crossed over her chest. "There is more. You must go to Mass every day. You must confess to Father Finnegan every week, you must tell him every sin no matter how small. You must memorize your catechisms and recite them to me. If you ever see one of the boys from your past, you must not talk to them but come find me immediately."

I took a deep breath and did my best to put a smile on my face. As I looked up at her, I could see that weariness again, and I felt a stab of guilt. I did not want to be a burden.

"Your actions now, good or bad, will reflect directly on me. I have taken responsibility for you, Jesús. Do you understand?"

I told her I did, but I really didn't. I felt the burden of it, like a heavy stone on my chest, but I didn't really under-stand.

"What I tell you, you must do. Without question. Without hesitation."

I nodded and swallowed hard.

"You can leave any time you want. Just tell me and we'll

do what we can to prepare you. But if you stay you must understand that this is your last chance. If you break any of these rules, I will escort you out of here myself."

She stood there for what seemed like forever, staring at me. "Do you want to stay?" Sister Dominga asked, her hands on her hips.

I didn't answer right away. I wasn't sure. I wasn't ready to be out on the street, but I didn't know how I would do with Sister Dominga's rules. But deep down, I understood what she was doing for me, the depth of compassion that she was showing. I took a deep breath and said, "Yes, Sister Dominga. I want to stay."

"Good," she said, walking to the door and opening it. "Time to prove it."

Chapter 53

With intent, I slowed things down, taking the ghostly equivalent of deep breaths. I needed to act fast, but if I rushed I would probably do the wrong thing. I looked around.

Pasha crying, haunted by her past, her form flickering with a sickly chartreuse glow.

Lela speaking rapidly, trying to reach the girl, her face tight with concern.

Felipe still chasing Esmeralda around with his flaming hand. They both seemed to be enjoying themselves. The other ghosts close by, but not paying attention to us.

Sister Dominga, her eyes focused on the girl. Did she see? Did she know what was happening? I turned away. I didn't have time for her.

The little graveyard with its wooden fence, weeds, and gravestones.

The single oak tree, it's leaved branches reaching towards the blue sky.

Back to Pasha. I opened myself to what she was feeling. It was like hanging from a ledge, your fingers slipping, the abyss below. She saw no way out, but somehow I had to reach her and metaphorically pull her up. But how?

Abusive father. Beloved mother. Painful and difficult death. A past horrible to remember.

I took another ghostly breath and opened myself further to Awareness, and I saw a doll. A ragged thing with a pink dress made of cloth with small buttons for eyes and thick yellow yarn for hair.

I caught sight of Felipe again, his hand a blazing fire.

I didn't really think about it, I just held the vision of the doll firmly in my mind and reached forward to Pasha.

"It's OK, dear," I said gently, my hand now the doll I had seen. "Look, I found Madeline for you. She has so missed you."

Pasha blinked and stared at the doll, her brow furrowing. She stopped crying and took a half a step back.

"It's Madeline," I said quietly. "Your mother made her for you, right?"

Pasha nodded, her hands clasped over her heart, her ghostly form tightening up, the chartreuse glow dying out.

She looked from the doll to me. "How did you do that?" she asked.

I shrugged. "I just saw her and thought about her real hard. And here she is."

Tears were running down Pasha's cheeks again. At first I thought I had made a terrible mistake, but the smile on Lela's face let me know this was a different kind of tears.

Pasha surged forward and embraced the doll and me. I modulated my form so that we could have that ghostly sensation of touch.

"Thank you, Jesús. Thank you. You are not like my father."

"No, Pasha, I am not."

She pulled away, her hand still on the doll. "Can you teach me how to do that?"

"Of course," I said.

Behind me I heard Sister Dominga sigh.

WE WERE BACK IN FATHER FINNEGAN'S OFFICE. I WAS beginning to hate the place. It's musty, booky smell starting to make me nauseous. It was here that they brought me when the difficult discussions needed to happen.

Father Finnegan sat behind his desk, his fingers steepled as he watched. The swelling was gone from his eye, but it was still rimmed with a dark purple. Sister Dominga stood in front of one of those bookcases, her hands clasped in front of her. And Detective Ruiz sat in a chair next to me, his pen poised above a small pad of paper.

Detective Ruiz was middle-aged with a noticeably receding hairline and a mustache, his black hair peppered with grey. The mustache reminded me of my father, which didn't help the mix of emotions I was feeling about what they wanted me to do.

"We can't ignore the threat that boy made," Father Finnegan said from behind his dark wooden desk.

Sister Dominga didn't say anything, but her face spoke volumes. It was time "to prove it." They wanted me to tell this policeman all about the Muchachos, where they lived, what they did.

Ruiz had tired eyes, dark circles hanging under them. He looked like the kind of man that was constantly overworked. His foot twitched and he kept blinking. I didn't like him. I didn't trust him.

But at that point in my life, I didn't trust anyone. Except Sister Dominga—she had saved my life. She was hard on me, but her caring was clear.

I shifted in my seat, trying to avoid everyone's eyes.

"We can put a stop to how they are using boys like you," Ruiz said. The Spanish word he used for boy was "chico." I bristled at the word. I wasn't a little kid, I was a Muchacho. Except I wasn't anymore, was I?

"What... what will happen to them?" I asked.

"The adults will go to jail," Ruiz said. "The children will be cared for."

"How will they be cared for? Where will they go?" I kept thinking of Flaco. He wasn't alive anymore, but there were other boys like him there. Mamá was using them, but at least they had a home. In many ways, I still missed her and missed it.

"Trust me," he said. "There are orphanages, good places like this, all over the city."

"You can trust Detective Ruiz," Father Finnegan said. "He has been coming to this church since he was a boy. This is his community too."

Ruiz nodded and smiled. I didn't like his smile, and he was so close I could smell his breath. It was sour like he didn't brush his teeth or he was ill.

"The boys will be cared for," Sister Dominga said. "I promise you."

"How the cartel is using them is disgusting," Ruiz said. "This is a new trend. They use children to move their drugs. They know they can move through the city easily. Who stops a street kid? They don't care what happens to the children, they just discard them and get another one if there is a problem. Just like they did to you, Jesús. It makes me sick. Please, help me stop them."

As he spoke, I found myself staring into Sister Dominga's brown eyes. I could see the pain. She had started the orphanage here. She was the one that wanted to care for children. She gave me a small nod and I felt my resistance crumble.

I turned to Detective Ruiz and told him what he needed to know. Not everything, but enough. The abandoned building, the secret entrance, the basics of what we did there.

He scratched on his pad the whole time I spoke, a small smile on his face. And then he left.

Sister Dominga was happy with me, but I was left with this sinking feeling in my stomach.

MY NEW LIFE AS A MOZO FOR SISTER DOMINGA WAS ALL consuming. Up before dawn studying the catechisms. She constantly quizzed me on the ones I was supposed to be learning. I then went down to the church and swept the floor and dusted off the pews and altar, that crucifix watching me the whole time.

After a while, the church started to become a place of comfort for me. Right then, not because of any religious feelings, but because of the quiet. The space was so big, so quiet, so peaceful, I couldn't help but feeling some of that peace. As my time passed with Sister Dominga, she offered to take that duty from me several times, but I always asked to keep it. In ways I still don't understand, it helped me.

After cleaning the church I would rush to class with the orphanage kids. They had all eaten, but Sister Helen always had some food for me. I sat at the back of the room and didn't interact much with the rest of the kids. After what happened with Rafael, they gave me a wide berth. Except for David and Paco, they seemed to look up to me.

I only attended the first half of school, the sisters that taught giving me more work to do on my own. After a quick lunch standing in the kitchen, while the rest of the kids were around the table, I went and found Sister Dominga and did whatever she told me to do.

Sometimes it was cleaning bathrooms, which she taught me how to do and made me repeat if I didn't do it correctly. Sometimes it was polishing the thurible that they burned incense in at Mass. Sometimes it was accompanying her on errands and carrying packages for her.

It was on one of these errands about a week after I spoke with Detective Ruiz that Rafael found us. His face was pale except for the yellowing bruise on his left cheek, a bruise that I had given him. His head was down as he walked the sidewalk, his hands shoved deeply into his pockets. I held a large basket filled with groceries we had just bought. We were walking down a busy street about a kilometer from the church.

I stopped dead when I saw him, Sister Dominga nearly running into me. "What is it?" she asked.

Rafael heard her voice and looked up, his eyes widening. I sucked in air when I saw his eyes. They were not the bold confident eyes of the Rafael I knew. They weren't the eyes of a boy anymore. They were the haunted eyes of a man who has seen too much.

His breathing came in rabid gasps as he pointed and stammered, "You... you... you did this."

I felt my stomach drop and was afraid. When we had fought, I had been the animal, now, he was.

"You!" he screamed as he launched himself at me, his arms outstretched.

Chapter 54

"You heard it too, right?" I asked Lela as we studied Sister Dominga. She was the usual gape-jawed, bardoed-out ghost we had been seeing. But where did that sigh come from? As sighs go, this one had seemed to be one of relief.

"Yeah," Lela said, nodding her head. "I heard her. I didn't see it though. I was focused on you and Pasha."

I turned back and looked at the girl. She was gazing at me with this look of adoration on her face. Thinking of her past made me angry. That my small act of kindness could generate such a reaction spoke to how poorly men had treated her in her life.

She wanted me to teach her how to turn her hand into a doll but had understood when Lela and I had excused ourselves.

"Sister Dominga," Lela said softly. I turned back, my eyes lingering on Lela. The more time I spent with her the more her unusual features seemed beautiful to me—that sharp nose and narrow chin with those blue, blue eyes of hers. "Grandmother," she continued. "My name is Lela. I am the daughter of your son. Although we never met, I felt your passing was growing near and came to be by your side. I..." She faltered, her eyes finding mine. They looked on the verge of tears.

"Sister Dominga," I said, looking away from Lela to the nun. "It's Jesús, I'm here and I need you. I need to talk to you about what has happened to me since I died. I hope you got word, and I am so very sorry it has taken me so long to come find you. When I was young and so confused, it was your steady faith that showed me the way. It was your unwavering love that helped me heal. It was your nurturing that helped me make something of myself. Please, Sister Dominga, please come back to this world."

I felt the whisper of a touch and looked down and saw Pasha. "Hello, Sister Dominga," she said, first smiling at me and then looking at the sister. "You don't know me, but I need you too. I need you to help me understand why I had to die so young. Why my father had to be so mean. Why I am in this graveyard and not in heaven. Can you please come and talk to me? Can you please help me too?"

For a sliver of a moment, Sister Dominga's eyes seemed to focus on Pasha.

The other ghosts had quietly gathered around us. Esmeralda stepped forward and said, "Sister, come back to us. We all need you. Jesús has shown us there is more to being a ghost than this graveyard, more than this long lonely existence. I don't understand either, why we are here. But maybe you can help us. Please come back."

"I am nobody, Sister," Felipe said, crossing himself as he approached. "But if you can hear me then come back out of that terrible place you are in. We need your wisdom. Please, Sister, please."

One by one the rest of the ghosts approached and made

a plea. I glanced at Lela and saw tears streaming down her face; the same was happening to mine. We had not been there long, but these people had become dear. I was humbled by their outpouring of love.

I studied Sister Dominga as this went on. Each time someone spoke, her eyes would seem to flicker into focus for a moment, but never for long.

After everyone was done, the silence was thick and heavy. I sighed, at a loss as to what to do. "Pssst," Pasha whispered.

"What is it, Pasha?" I asked.

"She wants you to finish your story," she said. "Unfinished stories are a terribly lonely thing. Once you finish your story she will come back."

"How do you know?"

She shrugged. "I just know."

I looked to Lela who shrugged her shoulders.

RAFAEL HAD TAKEN ME BY SURPRISE—THAT HE WAS THERE at all and the fierceness of his attack. His eyes were wide and wild. Gone was the controlled Rafael I had known, and in his place this wild beast.

He charged me, his hands reaching for my face. The basket got between us, I was still holding it, and he brought both fists down and knocked it out of my hands. Vegetables, bread, and canned goods went rolling into the busy street. I took a step back, holding my left arm, still in a cast, in front of me.

"Rafa, I'm sorry for the beating I gave you. I—"

He marched forward, spittle flying from his mouth as he spoke. "You told them, didn't you? You told them where we were. You told them how to get in." He was breathing heavy, and I kept backing up. I saw a glimpse of Sister Dominga standing on the sidewalk, a look of surprise on her face.

"I'm sorry, Rafa. You threatened the church. I had to tell the police."

He laughed, a snarled, bitter sound. "It wasn't the police that came, you fool. It was the Equis cartel. Men with guns. Men without mercy. Men who like to kill."

"What? I... I don't understand. I didn't talk to the cartel, I talked to a detective."

Rafa shook his head. "You always were a bit naive, weren't you? Your detective ran off and told our enemies. They came and cleaned house." He stopped, his face going blank for a moment, his hand over his mouth. "I wasn't there. It was late, past dinnertime. I had gotten delayed. I was in the tunnels and heard their voices and hid. They passed me, smoking and laughing, like they'd just gotten off a day's work in the factory. I got a glimpse at their leader. He was big and mean looking, his right eyebrow half scar. I've heard of him. They call him *Tiburón*, the shark. He is well known in the cartel."

My heart was beating in my chest and my breath came in ragged gasps. That was the man that killed my family. It must be him. "What... what happened?" I asked. I didn't want to know the answer, but couldn't stop myself from asking it.

Rafael's lip twitched up and then he laughed. It was more like the bark of a scared dog. "They're dead, Jesús. They're all dead. Tiburón came with his men. He killed them all." He paused, his hands balling into fists. "They didn't see me, and after they left I went in and found them all. Not one alive. Not Mamá, not anyone."

With a cry like a wounded animal, he rushed me, knocked me over and was on me, his fists pounding into my face and body. I couldn't fight back, I didn't have the will. They were dead, they were all dead.

Because of me, they were dead.

Chapter 55

BEATING NUMBER THREE WAS THE HARDEST TO RECOVER from. Not because of the injuries, but because of the guilt.

Sister Dominga had dragged Rafa off of me before he could inflict any permanent damage. She wasn't a small woman and was very strong. He stood there glaring at her after she did it, his fists balled. For a moment I thought he was going to hit her and I struggled to get up—I couldn't let him hit a nun. But his fists relaxed and he ran off.

My head was swimming and I rolled onto my side and vomited. Sister Dominga picked me up and for the second time carried me to the hospital, saying "mercy" with each step. But it wasn't the physical wounds that plagued me, it was the spiritual ones.

Yet again, things so incomprehensible had happened in my life that I couldn't imagine the reason. I couldn't envision a God that would let this all happen.

"I think I should leave when I'm better," I told Sister Dominga. I hadn't been in the hospital long, no broken bones this time, and was back in my little room in the cloister. Sister Dominga was sitting on the edge of the bed feeding me that salty brown broth one bite at a time. I could have fed myself, but the look in her eyes insisted she needed do this.

Her eyebrows knitted together briefly and she nodded once. "If you must, but I wish you wouldn't."

"Why, Sister? Why do you care about me? Why do you keep looking after me?" I asked. My encounter with Rafael had stripped me of any guile, left me saying exactly what I was thinking.

Her eyes got faraway for a breath or two before she brought another spoonful to my lips and said, "Because I must." There was more there, but that was all that was forthcoming.

"Why does God let these horrible things happen?" I asked. It was one thing to live in a place like Mexico City and know of the violence and tragedy that goes on every day. It was very much another thing to be a part of it.

She sighed and put the spoon in the bowl, the metal clattering against the porcelain. "Most people might say it is not God, but man and his free will. That God wants the best for us, but man's sin makes that impossible."

"And what do you say?"

She smiled briefly and her eyes welled up with moisture. "I say, Jesús, that I don't know. It is not for me to understand why this life is so difficult. What is for me to do is to have faith in God. To do my best to walk the path He has laid out for me. To know that I will sin but that He will forgive."

I stared at her as she spoke. There was something about her. She was sad, but something else was shining through. Something stronger than the sadness and the doubt. Something that I knew I needed.

"It's simple, really," she said, "and easier. The ways

of this world are just too much for someone like me. I can't understand them. But my little world here." She looked around the room we were in—sunlight flowing in the window, the dresser and bed, the small crucifix on the wall. "This world I understand. In this world I can make a difference."

She pulled the sheet up, tucking it gently around my body, a kind smile on her face. "You are too young to understand this now, but knowing is often its own trap and can get in the way of real faith." She took the soup and headed towards the door.

"Sister," I said before she reached it.

"Yes, Jesús?"

"I... I think I understand. Those things you said, that is your faith. Not knowing and being content with that. Not understanding but knowing there is a purpose in it somewhere."

She nodded. "Yes. Exactly." She paused and studied my face. "I couldn't survive in this world without it."

Chapter 56

THE SILENCE IN THE GRAVEYARD WAS ALMOST A TANGIBLE presence, like another one of the ghosts. It surrounded me in the darkness. My story had gone on until the sun had gone down and before the moon had come up. The glow of Mexico City reflecting off the cloudy night sky lit our gathering.

I looked around and no one was looking at me, each lost in their own thoughts. It had been so long since I had let my mind wander back to that time, that I had forgotten. That simple way that Sister Dominga let go of her expectations of how the world should be and took it as it came.

She found her place and did her best to make this world better, but she didn't fight the battles she didn't have a chance of winning.

"Is that the end?" Pasha asked quietly.

I shrugged. "There is more to my story, but I think that may be the end of this one. My change was not instantaneous, but her clearly articulated faith transformed me. It was this quiet, little moment, but the reverberations of it colored my entire life."

"But your Muchachos," Esmeralda said. "So terrible."

I nodded. "Indeed. I had much to grieve over that and over my parents' death. Over the suffering the cartels have created, and continue to create. But she had given me a way through. A way to let go. I spent four more years at the orphanage, until I was sixteen."

"And what of that terrible Detective Ruiz?" Felipe asked. "He sold those boys out to the Tiburón."

I smiled as I remembered. "It wasn't him, but someone else in his department. He did his best to make things right. He ended up telling me about someone who would later become very important in my life."

"Who?" Pasha asked.

"His name was Big Ed Quinn. He was an Australian man living in Mexico City and working as a bounty hunter. I was his apprentice, he taught me my trade."

"More stories, yay!" she said.

I shook my head. "Not today." I was done with my story for the time being. I could feel it. I turned to Lela who had been silent this whole time, her eyes on Sister Dominga. I nodded to her and she stepped forward and we both stood in front of the ghost of Sister Dominga, the rest of the ghosts arrayed behind us.

"What happened to you?" Lela whispered. "You are different."

"I remembered what Sister Dominga taught me."

"And that is?"

"The essence of faith is trust. I may be a ghost and that may not make sense, that may not align with what my religion taught me, but I don't have to figure out if they are wrong, and if they are, if that undermines the whole religion. I don't have to come up with a cosmology that embraces

Catholicism and a ghostly afterlife. I just need to hold strong to what I believe and trust."

We stood silently staring at Sister Dominga. Her eyes were wide, her form diffuse and cloudlike, her jaw moving in a silent wail. She was still in the bardo. It was time to get her out.

"Should I go in?" I asked Lela. Remembering what Banquo had told us that JJ did for Tamara's fiancé, John.

"He has been in there for almost a year," she said. "You might not ever come out."

I nodded and sighed. Even though I was trying to trust that there was a reason for Sister Dominga's state, it grieved me terribly. The two are not mutually exclusive. "What do we do?" I asked.

"I don't know," Lela said. "She's shown signs of waking up several times, but only for a moment."

"What is more important to her than her suffering?" I said.

"What?" Lela asked.

"That's what Banquo always says about the bardo. You have to find something more important to them than their suffering." A thought occurred to me and I looked at Lela pointedly.

"Why are you looking at me like that?"

"Maybe you can be more important to her than her suffering," I said. "You are of her blood. Maybe she doesn't understand it. Maybe you need to really explain it to her."

Her eyes narrowed as she looked me up and down. Lela had been very stingy with her story, and even though I desperately wanted to hear more, I honestly thought it might help.

Knowing now that Sister Dominga had had a child, she

made more sense to me. She started the orphanage and spent her life helping kids in desperate need, like me. She had been a mother to us all and before her stood her granddaughter. If she knew it, truly knew it, how could she resist coming out of the bardo?

"OK," she finally said. "What do I do?"

I took a deep ghostly breath and opened myself up to Awareness. I tried to let the thought of Lela reaching Sister Dominga get bigger. I stepped back so I could see them both easily. The resemblance hit me. The broad, flat face, the narrow chin, the shape of the eyebrows. It was suddenly as clear as day. If only I could get Sister Dominga to see it.

"Take her hand," I finally said. "And take my hand, and I'll take her other hand. We three are family."

She gave me the look again but complied, modulating her left hand and joining it with Sister Dominga's right as I did the same. We then joined our two remaining well-formed hands.

I gasped once the connection was made. I could feel Sister Dominga's bardo experience. No words or pictures, but the strong tide of emotions. Shame. Regret. Longing. Lela's eyes were wide; she must have been feeling it too.

"Speak to her," I said to Lela. "Tell her about you. Who you are. How you came to be here."

She composed herself and began.

"Hello, Grandmother. My name is Lela May Sykes, and you are my father's mother." Lela's eyes were focused on Sister Dominga's vacant stare.

"I don't know much about your past, but I know a little. You were born in Juárez, Mexico, in 1936. Your father was a politician and served on the city council. Your mother was the daughter of a powerful man who ranked high in the Juárez Cartel.

"It was not as bad back then as it is now. The drug trade did not take as many lives, but on the border in Juárez, it was a dangerous place.

"You grew up rich and privileged and at sixteen met a charming, young, blue-eyed American man. You loved him and you thought he loved you. But when you became pregnant, he disappeared. When your pregnancy began to show, your father spirited you away to a nunnery where you carried your son to term. You gave him up for adoption and became a nun."

Even if I had been alive, I wouldn't have taken a breath, wanting to hear everything. Lela's eye color now made sense, as did Sister Dominga so doggedly running her little orphanage.

"My father was adopted by the Sykes who lived just across the border in El Paso, Texas. His adopted parents were simple people, both of them teachers. They named him Anthony.

"He was a happy boy but ran into trouble as a teenager. Drugs, easily obtainable in El Paso, took him for a while. His parents eventually got him into rehab and he got clean. He went to college, became a teacher, and eventually got a job teaching in Shiprock, New Mexico, on the Navajo reservation.

"He had the blue eyes of his father, and that is what caught my mother, Shima. She fell for those blue eyes just like you did. I was born in 1983 out on the reservation west of Shiprock. My childhood was good. I grew up around three different cultures: Navajo, American, and Mexican.

"Anthony's adopted parents had been Hispanic, so he grew up speaking English and Spanish. I grew up speaking Navajo and English and Spanish, the words and the cultures mixing in my young mind.

"When I was eight, my mother was diagnosed with cancer. When I was nine, she died, and my father did not do well with it. He found his way back to drugs and alcohol. He left when I was ten.

"My grandfather, a Navajo shaman, raised me. He taught me the Beauty Way. He taught me of the animal totems, of the directions, of nature.

"I died in 2008 when I was on a vision quest. In far northwestern New Mexico, I was hiking alone through the desert along a deep canyon. My foot slipped on some rock and I fell to my death.

"My grandfather is still there on the reservation. Even though I am a ghost, he can see me sometimes and we still talk.

"A few months ago, as I prayed, I kept seeing your face, knowing you needed me. I am here, Grandmother. I am the daughter of your son. Please come to me. I want to meet you, Grandmother."

The graveyard was still and hushed, all ghosts focused on Sister Dominga. Expectant. Waiting.

Nothing happened. My heart sank. I felt for sure that Lela could pull her out of it. That knowing that she was here was more important than her suffering.

Lela, Sister Dominga, and I were still connected. I could feel Lela's disappointment, the effort it had been to share what she did. That connection helped me understand her better. She was more comfortable alone in the desert than in a crowd, more herself with the sacred than the mundane.

And I could feel Sister Dominga. The weight keeping her in the bardo was the guilt of her youth, her pregnancy and her lost son. A child she had only seen for a moment right after he had been born. She felt guilty about her relationship with her father.

Instead of helping these emotions calm, Lela's story had amplified them. I felt her guilt and regret spill over to me. My parents murdered, my Muchachos slaughtered. A life devoted to my religion, to justice, to doing the right thing, and here I was a ghost.

The feeling was insidious, a dark blight of emotions inviting me down into its depths. Promising me escape. I felt myself slipping.

Lela was feeling her own guilt and regret. It was about her parents. Her mother dead at a young age, her father losing himself to drugs and abandoning her.

We three were feeding into each other, spiraling down. I looked at Lela and our eyes met. She was scared, her form going wispy, something I hadn't seen from her. I glanced at my own form and it was very diffuse. I tried to tighten it up but couldn't. The emotions were too much.

The other ghosts were there, but didn't know what to do. They watched in horror as we slipped towards the bardo, something they must have seen before with other occupants of the graveyard.

I had to do something.

"Our Father..." I croaked and then couldn't continue. It was too much, just too much. How could I be expected to stay balanced with what I had been through? All of it fresh from remembering. How could I go on in this ghostly life? What could I possibly hold on to?

The graveyard started to fade and I could see my mother

struggling with Tiburón, trying to buy me time to survive. Her eyes wide, blood running down her mouth, a bruise blossoming on her cheek from his blows. She was going to die. I was going to watch her die this time. The bardo claimed me. I was lost.

"Our Father," I heard a young girl's voice shout. "Our Father, who art in heaven."

My slide into hell stopped. I could see my mother and Tiburón, but I could see the graveyard too. Pasha had started the prayer.

"Come on, everyone," she said, her young voice strong. "We have to help them. We have to!"

The ghosts, our new friends, gathered close, and I could feel their ghostly hands touching me as we had taught them. They were touching Lela and Sister Dominga too.

"Our Father, who art in heaven," they began, Pasha's voice the loudest. "Hallowed be thy name."

The bardo receded just a bit. Seeing my mother, even like this, was something so hard to leave.

"Thy kingdom come, Thy will be done on earth, as it is in heaven."

I found my voice and started praying with them, with my new friends, my new family. They gave me the strength to fight just a little bit more. Their love and caring was stronger than my shame.

"Give us this day our daily bread. And forgive us our debts, as we forgive our debtors."

Lela's form was firming up and she was praying with us to. Family, this new family, was more important than my suffering, than her suffering.

"And lead us not into temptation, but deliver us from evil. Amen."

The bardo was gone and we all stood there connected. I felt emotions flowing: relief, gratitude, love. Lela smiled at me, her eyes going to Sister Dominga and back to me.

I turned and looked at Sister Dominga. She smiled widely, her eyes in focus, her form firming up.

"Our Father," she began nodding to us to join her in saying the prayer again. And we did.

Chapter 57

THE FEW DAYS WE SPENT WITH SISTER DOMINGA WERE sweet. Simple days in that little graveyard on the southern edge of Mexico City, nestled in rolling hills with its uncut grass going to seed and the single majestic oak tree. We spent time together, time with her alone, and time gathered in groups.

It was good to be ghosts for those days. We had nothing to do, nowhere to go. So we talked and prayed and shared and loved.

We said "Our Father" a lot, and I remembered those rosary beads that Father Finnegan had given me. Just like I had done with Pasha's doll, I altered my form so that I often had rosary beads in my hand, feeling the ghostly comfort of them sliding through my fingers as we prayed, as we grew closer, as we grew stronger. I thought of Father Finnegan often, my heart full of gratitude for the prayer and the beads. It has made such a difference in my life and in my death.

"I believe what I experienced was purgatory," Sister Dominga said, her face youthful and bright. We were walking the borders of the graveyard, just the two of us. She must have seen the doubt in my face. "My regrets, my mistakes, they assailed me. It was the cleansing fire, Jesús. I know it."

I bit my lip and nodded. "The ghosts that taught me call it the bardo. Many ghosts go there, some never come out. But I have not been there. The only time I heard its call was when we finally reached you."

She smiled kindly, almost apologetically. "I would not wish it on anyone. But, you know, this," she said, spreading her hands to encompass the graveyard and the land around us. "This may be purgatory too. This whole ghost experience."

I sighed, remembering how upset I had been that I didn't hear the Call after JJ and I brought my killer to justice, before I had remembered the lessons Sister Dominga had taught me about faith and trust. "I will trust, Sister. I will. But we were told that we would be judged at the moment of death."

"Ahh," she said as she stopped and looked closely at me. "But who is to say you weren't judged? Perhaps your ghostly nature is judgment that you are not ready for the kingdom of heaven."

I laughed. I wasn't sure that it fit with all that I had seen, but I laughed out of relief. How easy it was for her to see her way through. "But, it doesn't matter, does it?" I asked.

"No. Not at all. All that matters is our faith in God and our trust in His plan."

I stopped as I felt doubt creeping in again. "But what about all the terrible things that are done in the name of religion? In the name of an unquestioning faith?"

Sister Dominga smiled gently at me. "That is not faith. That is hate or greed or fear. That is not His will and you know how to tell the difference."

"I do?"

She nodded. "His will for us is to love, to be merciful and generous, to care for others more than ourselves. You know this."

I smiled and nodded, looking down at my shoes. So simple for her. "But I still doubt."

She smiled broadly. "That is good. Let your doubt test and strengthen your faith." She put her ghostly hand on my shoulder and I looked up into her kind brown eyes. "Even your namesake doubted. On the cross he felt forsaken, that moment enshrined in our church, that moment of pain and doubt captured in that statue. It serves as a lesson to all of us. We all wish to be perfect, Jesús, but none of us are, and He does not expect us to be."

I smiled and nodded.

"Faith can be a simple thing," she said, "but that does not mean it is easy."

SOMETHING CHANGED WITH LELA DURING THOSE DAYS. Spending time with her grandmother was a joy to her, but her attitude towards me changed. She looked at me differently.

Not like after I disappeared into the Cantina, where she was wary of me. Not even like when we were touring the city visiting historical ghosts, when she was shy but engaged. Now, she was all there, unreserved, unrestrained.

It was magnificent.

"What are you thinking?" she asked me one night when we had a moment alone next to the big tree. It was a moonless night, getting on towards dawn, the graveyard lit by the yellow glow of Mexico City to the north.

"I'm thinking about how I never in my life, and certainly not in my death, expected to meet someone like you."

Her cheeks flushed red in an unconscious mimic of what would have happened if she were alive. "I hope that is a good thing," she said quietly.

I reached for her face and said, "It is the best." I just wanted to touch her. I stopped short because her eyes went wide and I felt an odd sensation behind me.

I turned and saw Sister Dominga. She was beginning to glow with an inner light.

Pasha and Esmeralda were with her and the rest of the ghosts were moving towards her.

"The Call," I said, knowing that is what the glow had to be. I was not sure what I was feeling. I was happy for her, sad that she was going, and a bit jealous. I had never heard the Call myself, the lack of it had sent me on this adventure.

"She's leaving," Lela said, the sadness in her voice clear as a bell.

I found myself slowly flying towards Sister Dominga. I wasn't doing my normal "walking" routine, but I moved towards her without trying, like she was exerting some sort of gravitational pull on the rest of us ghosts.

She wore a blissful expression on her face, her head turned down, looking at Pasha, her hands clasped in front of her in prayer. Her white robes and coif were pure white and a dazzling light emanated from her. Except for the color of her clothes, she looked like the classic image of Our Lady of Guadalupe. The one that had been miraculously imprinted on Juan Diego's cloak in 1531.

Soon I was there and I was vaguely aware that Lela wasn't. She had been moving towards her, but at a slower pace.

"It is time, dear ones," Sister Dominga said. "He is calling us home."

"So soon," I said.

She looked up and smiled at me. "I am ready, Jesús. I am done with this life. Do you hear that? It is so beautiful."

Pasha nodded vigorously and started to take on a glow herself, as did Esmeralda, Felipe, and the rest of the ghosts. I could hear what sounded like music, but faintly. A beautiful melody I couldn't quite put my fingers on, played by instruments I couldn't name. The most beautiful thing I had ever heard. It made me weep at its beauty.

"All who want to," she said, raising her voice, "can come now. He calls for us all, His arms open and waiting."

With that she started to slowly fly around the graveyard, all of us ghosts drawn along in her wake. She went to each bardoed ghost and whispered something to them and touched them on the forehead, like she was a priest delivering a blessing.

I almost cried out when she did this to the first one. It transformed from a barely formed shape of a human with a mouth open in agony, to a middle-aged woman with sparkling eyes and rosy cheeks who took on Sister Dominga's glow and joined the group. She had pulled the woman out of the bardo with such ease.

The music became louder and I looked down and saw that my own form was beginning to glow. I felt a peace deeper than I had ever thought possible. I had no doubt heaven was the source of this music.

One by one Sister Dominga attended to the bardoed ghosts. Not all were transformed by her touch, but many were. Soon she was done and the group of us were in the center of the graveyard near the tree.

She looked at Lela and said, "Will you come with us, Granddaughter?"

With a start, I realized I had forgotten about her. The Call was so intoxicating there wasn't room for anything in my head but that.

She stepped forward and shook her head. "It is not my time, Grandmother. I have more that I wish to do here."

Sister Dominga smiled broadly. "Yes, you do. I can see that."

Lela came closer, but stopped about three meters away from Sister Dominga. "I am so glad we got a chance to meet."

"As am I," Sister Dominga said. "Thank you for helping me."

Lela nodded, but didn't speak.

"Now, my children," Sister Dominga said. "Open yourself up to His Call, let it fill you, and soon you will be in His arms."

One by one the ghosts started to glow brighter and brighter until suddenly they were gone and only Pasha and Sister Dominga were left.

Pasha's eyes found mine and she said, "It's so beautiful, Jesús. You hear it, don't you?"

I nodded, unable to speak.

She looked around the near empty graveyard. "Maybe I should stay. Maybe I should go watch over my mother." She looked up at Sister Dominga. "Can I do that? Will God be mad at me if I do that?"

"Of course not, Pasha. God will delight in your desire to serve."

Pasha looked at me again and said, "But it can be so hard here." I saw the pain in her eyes, the toll her young life had taken on her. She turned to Sister Dominga again. "Will He think less of me if I don't stay?"

"No," Sister Dominga said, "this is your choice."

She smiled, her eyes once again locking with mine and then she was gone in a brilliant flash of light.

The music became louder and I began to sense it more fully. It was like I could not only hear it, but feel it, and taste it, and smell it. Its beauty was beyond anything I had ever experienced.

"Now you must decide, Jesús," Sister Dominga said. "Are you ready?"

I looked at Lela, but her head was down and I couldn't read her expression. There was so much to explore with her. I looked back at Sister Dominga, light and bliss radiating from her face. This was it, the thing I had been waiting for since the moment I died.

I hesitated, looking from Lela to Sister Dominga. I opened my mouth to ask her what to do, but couldn't get any words out.

"Trust, my dear Jesús. Trust in Him and trust in yourself. You know what to do."

I thought of JJ and Banquo and my friends in Tucson. Was I ready to leave them? The answer was a clear, yes. They would be fine without me.

I looked again at Lela; she somehow seemed so small. Why didn't she want to go? What did she have left to do? Her head slowly rose and her iceberg blue eyes locked with mine. Those amazing eyes called to me.

I took a deep ghostly breath and turned back to Sister Dominga. "I... I will miss you. You have been saving me since the day we met."

"I am grateful that you let me," she said. "You are a good

man, Jesús. Never forget that. Always follow your heart no matter the cost."

I nodded.

"Trust, you must always trust." And with that she was gone, the music of the Call was gone, and the graveyard suddenly seemed small and dark.

NEITHER OF US MOVED OR SPOKE FOR THE LONGEST TIME. For my part, having experienced the Call and having it gone was a shock. It was like the world had gone black and white on me, all the color and depth of it drained out.

What had I done?

The remaining ghosts in the graveyard, all in the bardo, seemed to feel it too. They began to moan and wail together. Even though Sister Dominga hadn't been able to pull them out of the bardo, her presence, the Call, had comforted them.

"Why?" Lela finally asked, her voice a rough whisper.

I looked down and saw my form was diffuse and I consciously tightened it up, making it as solid and clean as I could. Appearance Matters, as Banquo would say. I took two steps to her, some few meters still between us. "For you," I said. The words thrilled me and scared me at the same time.

I had stayed for her. For those eyes. For the mystery that she still is.

Her eyebrows came together as she studied me, her head cocked slightly to the side. Her father had abandoned her, but her grandfather had been her teacher. She had mixed feelings about men, I got the impression that she was trying to decide which camp I fit into.

"Me? Why me?" she asked.

"Because I've never been in love before," I heard myself say. The words just came out. I had been aware of my growing feelings for her, but they hadn't coalesced into the word "love" yet. Not consciously.

Her mouth opened and closed. She squinted her eyes and looked closely at me, the blue of those eyes seeming like they reached into my soul. I felt doubt and fear creep into my stomach. What if she refused me? What if I was stuck here without her and without the Call?

I had refused heaven for her, could I be here without her?

Tears sprung to her eyes and her form went a tad diffuse along the edges, quite a loss of control for Lela. She took a step forward, her mouth moving, but no words escaping.

I thought back to the romantic movies I had seen. How I should be saying some grand speech, comparing my love for her to the moon or something. JJ could have done that, but I just stood there, staring at her.

She had become more beautiful to me. Her petite, lithe form, her flat face, her piercing blue eyes. Those looks, at first unconventional, were now the epitome of beauty.

"I... You..." I stammered, trying to get some of these feelings out in words, but I failed utterly. We stood there in that neglected graveyard on the edge of Mexico City staring at each other.

"You stayed for me?" she said quietly, almost as if she were talking to herself. As if it was the most unbelievable thing in the world.

"Yes," I said. I had no more words.

And then words didn't matter. She closed the distance between us, wrapped her arms around me, and pressed her lips to mine.

This was no flesh-kiss. This was something else,

something I had never imagined possible. There was the dim ghostly sensation of her body against mine, of her lips pressed to mine, but that was not the core of the experience. It was connection, pure and simple. The essence of what a kiss is with all the distractions of the physical gone.

The first wave was emotions. I could feel what she was feeling. Relief, happiness, and love. She loved me too. It frankly surprised me. With all the stories I had told, the reality of my past that I had bared, I doubted that I could be loved. And I felt my love for her, my fascination with the mystery she is, the beauty that I see in her every move, that all flowed back to her.

The words we couldn't say were replaced with something much more powerful.

The second wave was bliss. Not quite like the Call, not that strong, but something even more intimate. Knowing, truly knowing, the depth of her feelings for me and mine for her. Knowing I was not alone in this strange ghostly world. Knowing that I had a friend and companion.

It was honestly too much for me. Somewhere in my heart I didn't think I deserved it, deserved her, that my sins were too great for something this precious in my life. I began to pull away, but she didn't let me, she held me tighter, kissed me harder.

And then the third wave hit and I saw things. Tall red-rock sentinels rising up out of the New Mexico desert. Her grandfather, his face an eroded landscape just like the desert, smiling at her. Her mother, her face drawn in concern, telling Lela that she was dying. Her father, when she was very young, playing ball with her outside a traditional Navajo hogan, his piercing blue eyes dancing. A lynx standing in new fallen snow, mountains sharp and craggy rising up behind it.

Images fled past quickly. I didn't understand everything I saw, but it was like she was showing me who she was. Like I had done with my stories, but much faster, much more vivid. She was giving herself to me, letting me see her, letting me know her.

The more I saw, the more love I felt for her.

And then it was over. The sun was rising and Lela stood smiling in front of me.

"I love you," I said.

She nodded, her smile widening. "Yeah... I can tell."

Epilogue

THE ROAD STRETCHED OUT BEFORE US, THE LAND DROPPING off, the desert laid out like an enormous brown blanket in front of us, Mexico City now far behind us.

After that kiss we hadn't said a word, we had joined hands and started walking. We were about three meters above the ground, cars and trucks passing below us. We took a step at a time, carefully and intentfully, our hands clasped together.

My walk to Mexico City had been much like this. I had taken those months and step by step made my way south, except I had been alone and confused. I was neither now.

North was Tucson, JJ and Banquo and my friends there. North was New Mexico and Lela's grandfather, and somewhere, she hoped, her father. Those two men were a big part of her staying when Sister Dominga offered her the Call. She wanted to be present for her grandfather's passing, and she wanted to find her father and see if those wounds could be healed.

So we walked north, the silence an unspoken agreement between us.

Soon, though, I stopped, let go of her hand, and broke the silence. I wanted our unspoken agreement to be made explicit. "I need to go back to JJ. If he is truly stuck in the bardo, I will have to try and help."

"I know," she said with a smile. "We will go together."

The word "together" rang around my head. I hadn't had a partner of any kind since I had ended my apprenticeship with the bounty hunter Quinn. It felt good.

"Thank you," I said.

"But we can take our time, can't we?" she asked. "I would like to be 'us' for a while before I meet the rest of your friends."

I laughed, the sound of it surprising me. It had been far too long. I laughed for the joy her request gave me. I laughed for the relief I felt no longer questioning everything. I laughed because I was happy.

"Yes, Lela. Of course. I spent a long time walking south. I found some very interesting and very old ghosts that you will love meeting. More of your 'living' history."

"Yes! Yes!" she said, as she clapped her hands together, her enthusiasm like that of a little girl's. "And Quinn, you must tell me of this Australian man that taught you to be a bounty hunter and how you brought the dreaded Tiburón to justice."

"It would be my most distinct pleasure," I said.

She took my hand and we resumed our long walk together.

Author's Note

Thank you so much for reading. What follows is an excerpt from *Drawing the Dead,* another book in this same ghostly world, and then acknowledgements and a bit about me.

But, before you proceed, I have a favor to ask you. If you've enjoyed this book, then do me the honor of spreading the word. Write an honest review on Amazon (just a few sentences is fine), loan the book, or tell your friends. Word of mouth is the best endorsement a book can get, and only you can do that. Thank you!

For more ghostly adventures pick up *Life After,* a collection of short stories that features a brand new ghost trying to solve his own murder. And keep your eyes open for another ghost book coming soon.

If you want to know as soon as new books come out please sign up for my email newsletter. Go to RobertJMcCarter.com, you'll see the signup offer on the home page. As of this writing I am giving away ebooks of the first episode of my Superhero/Love Story series.

Want more adventures in the world of Of Things Not Seen?
The following is a sample of Drawing the Dead.

Chapter 1

DOUBT FILLED THEIR EYES, AND HOPE AND FEAR. BUT LIKE all of Madam Valarka's clients, there was mostly desperation. The man and woman sat at the small round table across from her, their hands clutched tightly together as they watched her draw. It was to be expected. What followed would be either an amazing miracle or a huge disappointment. There was no middle ground.

A single light illuminated the silk festooned table in the otherwise dim room. The man and woman huddled close, leaning into the light as if afraid of the surrounding darkness. The room was silent and the air smelled of sage and sandalwood.

Madam Valarka paused, smiling at her clients, trying to put them at ease. Her heavy makeup, hoop earrings, jangling bracelets, and silks covering her slim body added to the mystical atmosphere. Valarka was a gypsy, and even though they sat in a small room above a bookstore in Sedona, Arizona, this was her domain.

A photograph of a smiling young man with unruly brown hair sat upside down to her left and in front of her was the portrait she was creating. Valarka always worked upside down. That way her clients could see their loved one clearly, but mostly because that was the way her grandmother taught her.

"It draws on a different part of the brain," the older woman had said. "I know it feels strange to do it this way, but it works."

She hadn't believed her grandmother, of course, and had tried drawing from a right-side-up portrait, but only once. That was all it took.

Valarka searched through her pastels finding the three shades of brown she needed for the hair. The silence wasn't good, so as she outlined and started filling in the hair, she asked, "Tell me more about Cole, what kind of child was he?"

"Oh..." the woman began, her shaking hand brushing at her hair. "He was such a boy. When he was just a toddler he would love to go outside and play in the dirt."

"And eat bugs," the man added with a thin chuckle. "That boy loved to eat bugs, he'd stick anything into his mouth."

They continued on, with occasional prompting, telling little stories and anecdotes about their son. Inevitably, each story would lead them back to the motorcycle accident and his death.

Each time she would prompt them again, taking them back to birthdays and vacations and other fond memories. Madam Valarka took these in as she worked the pastels, blending with her fingers, bringing the portrait to life. She moved from the hair, to the nose, to the lips, and finally back to the eyes.

She spent a lot of time on the eyes. They had to be perfect. They were brown, like his hair, soulful and expressive.

She worked hard, giving them depth and feeling, framing them with their heavy lids and long lashes.

The man and woman stopped talking, but she didn't prompt them to start again. She was almost done. She let her fingers guide her, choosing black, and began working it in around the face, filling in the blank portions of the paper. When she had first started drawing the dead she would have been scared by the choice. Black was often not good a sign. But, she had learned to trust. She had to trust.

"Okay," she said, putting her pastels away. "I think we are ready to try this."

"If... if it works. How much time will we get?" the woman asked.

"Just a few minutes," Valarka answered with a smile. "Just a few."

"That..." the woman said, tears forming, "that would be wonderful."

"Okay, I need each of you to place the fingers of your left hand on the bottom of the portrait, and I will do the same on the top. Only those touching the portrait will be able to see what happens."

Madam Valarka placed her hand so that her index finger touched the top of the young man's head.

"Now," she continued, "I want you to take a deep breath and see Cole on this page. See him alive and well and healthy."

She looked at them and saw they were holding their breaths. "Breathe, deeply," she continued. "See your son as smiling and happy, and alive." She led them, breathing deeply in and out, focusing her gaze on the portrait, feeling the energy build, feeling the portrait grow warm under her fingers.

When the moment was right, she leaned down and gently exhaled onto the drawing of Cole.

At first nothing changed, but slowly the picture began to look more three dimensional as the eyes came alive. The woman gasped and the man said, "Oh my God!" as the drawing began to move.

Fully alive on the paper, Cole's mouth opened and he said, "Mom? Dad?"

Chapter 2

Viki Dobos, known to her clients as Madam Valarka, sighed. Her clients left happy, having talked with their dead son, and she was exhausted. It took a lot to draw the dead.

She said a brief prayer of thanks that began the ritual that marked the close of her long work day. She felt grateful to have served and grateful that nothing untoward had happened.

The forces she dealt with were powerful, and things could go wrong... things had gone wrong.

After the prayer, she cleaned up. One step at a time, in the proper order, just as her grandmother had taught her.

First, she swept up all the stray pastel crumbs and put them into a jar. These she would dispose of in the desert in the way she had been taught.

Second, she folded up the colorful silk scarfs that covered the table, and packed them and the rest of her gear into her case, making sure each pastel, each piece of equipment was in place. She put the jar with the pastel crumbs in last, shut the case, fastened the hasps, and locked it. The tiny key she put in the heart-shaped locket around her neck.

She paused, a small smile on her lips, as her hand rubbed the old, stained leather of the antique, hard-sided cosmetic case. It had two brass hasps, a small lock, and a handle on the top.

The case, which she had inherited from her grand-mother, had been customized to hold her gear. Something newer, something with wheels, might serve her better, but it connected her to her grandmother and rooted her in their tradition; connected her to her past.

Third, she cleaned the area, wiping down the table, and vacuuming the carpet and the chairs.

Fourth, she walked around the room clockwise four times, singing the Romani song her grandmother had taught her.

Lastly, she went into the little bathroom and attended to herself. She removed the silk from her head, the large hoop earrings, and slowly removed the heavy makeup—too heavy for her taste—from her face. She went in Madam Valarka and came out Viki.

Without her makeup, Viki no longer looked like a gypsy, but like a normal woman in her late thirties. She had a slim body, brown hair pulled into a ponytail, and hazel eyes. Her clients would not recognize her.

Case in hand, she was ready to go home for the night. She longed to draw a bath, light a candle, and immerse her body. She was about to leave when she saw the note slipped under the door.

"V, I know you are at your limit for the day, but please talk to the waiting gentleman. He doesn't want you to draw, he has an offer for you and has paid full price for the privilege of asking."

It was signed in a looping scrawl, "Reg."

Viki sighed, what now?

SHE OPENED THE DOOR AND FOUND WHAT SHE COULD only describe as a "gentleman" waiting. He was tall and thin with long fingers, short grey hair, and brown eyes. He was impeccably dressed in an expensive suit.

"Ms. Dobos," he said in a genteel British accent as he rose and offered his hand. "My name is Alexander Wells. I am so grateful you have agreed to see me."

She hadn't agreed, but she couldn't refuse him. She felt fate nudging her along. She nodded and said, "Please come in, Mr. Wells."

She signaled for him to sit down as she unlocked and opened her case, pulled out a vibrant blue silk, and spread it on the table. She then retrieved a deck of cards from her case and sat across from him.

"I thought Mr. Anderson had explained," he said. "I don't require a reading, just a few minutes of your time."

"Yes, Reg did explain. But I need to find out who you are first."

"I am sorry, but there is some urgency to the situation."

She held up her hand. "Please, Mr. Wells. This won't take long. You have paid to see me—we will do at least this."

Viki had finished with her day, finished with clients; she needed something to bring her back to center so she could be present for his request.

She deftly shuffled the oversized cards and handed them over. "Pick one card." Alexander looked puzzled, his hands at his side. "They don't bite, I assure you, Mr. Wells. Just pick a card and we can get to what you came for."

He snatched the card on the top of the deck and handed

it to her. Viki nodded and smiled, and turned the card over. It was a simply, but elegantly, hand-drawn card with the word "Mercury" at the top. The card depicted a round orb with a figure of a man in front of it with winged shoes.

"Ahh..." Viki said. "Mercury, messenger of the gods. See, I do need to listen to you, Mr. Wells. Do you bring me a message from the gods?"

Alexander laughed briefly. "Well, sometimes he thinks..." He trailed off, cleared his throat, and continued. "Excuse me, Ms. Dobos. I didn't say that."

"I'm sorry? I missed that last part," Viki said with a grin. Alexander smiled. "Please, Mr. Wells, what is it you came here to talk to me about?"

"My employer would like to hire you for the next two weeks—"

"Ohh, I'm sorry, I have a lot of appointments, I can't just leave them."

"—for $2,000 per day."

Viki felt a cold sweat spring to her forehead as she put her hand over her mouth. This no longer seemed like a gentle nudge fate was giving her, but a giant push.

Chapter 3

"WHAT THE HELL, REG, WHAT IS THIS? WHO IS THIS GUY?"
Viki asked. She had excused herself, and left Alexander in
her workroom and come downstairs.

Reginald Anderson stood behind the counter of the
Sacred Vortex shop. He was a big man with long grey hair
pulled back in a ponytail, sharp grey eyes, and wore a green
silk shirt. "Calm down, V," he said, his voice deep and even.

"Calm down? Two grand a day? What is this?"

"Look, I've been checking his story out. He works for a
very wealthy Russian named Mark Kosov. Kosov is one of
those crazy-rich guys that made his money the old-fashioned way—by beating his competition to a pulp. Now he
wants to give it all away. He's signed onto Bill Gates's and
Warren Buffet's 'Giving Pledge.'"

"That's a lovely story, Reg. But if he is paying two grand
a day, he is going to want something."

"The guy is for real. I can't find anything bad about him
since he cleaned his act up about twelve years ago. Maybe
you should talk to his man and find out more.

"Besides, two thousand a day for fourteen days is a lot of money. How can you turn that down?"

Viki inhaled, as if winding up to say more, but slowly exhaled and stomped back up the stairs.

"I APOLOGIZE, MR. WELLS. IT'S JUST THAT THE AMOUNT you have offered is a lot of money."

"I understand, Ms. Dobos, but the matter is urgent, and my employer thought it a reasonable compensation for the inconvenience."

"And what, exactly, does your employer, Mr. Kosov, I believe..." Alexander nodded. "What exactly does he want me to do?"

Alexander looked down at his steepled fingers before continuing. "To tell you the truth, Ms. Dobos, he didn't tell me exactly what he wants. All I know is that it involves your rather unique gift and your presence at his house in Hawaii."

"He wants me to draw for him? In Hawaii?"

"Yes."

"Why didn't he just come with you? I could draw for him here for a lot less money."

"I am sorry, but I am not sure. I do know that he has his reasons. He always has a reason."

Viki sighed and got up. "I am going to need to think about this. Can you come back in the morning?"

"I am sorry, Ms. Dobos, but the offer expires today. I have a plane waiting for us at the Sedona Airport and I was instructed to head back this evening with or without you."

VIKI LEFT ALEXANDER WELLS AGAIN AND WENT OUTSIDE to think. The British man had been gracious about it, but she could tell he was agitated, he kept fidgeting and checking his watch. It was late January and cold. Viki pulled her sweater around her as she paced in front of the Sacred Vortex. She reflexively reached for a cigarette and silently cursed when she didn't find one. Five years later and the habit still wasn't totally gone. She missed Boston and how sure of herself she had been then. How with a few minutes with a cigarette her tension would fade.

The money was enticing, she had to admit it. It took a busy week for her to make two thousand dollars. Why not go to Hawaii for two weeks and make twenty-eight thousand? She could really get ahead, maybe start looking for a house. Not in Sedona, of course, she would never have enough money for a house in Sedona, but maybe down in the Verde Valley. That would be enough for a down payment on a small place. She could start a garden, or—

"V," Reg said as he sauntered out. "The butler is getting anxious, so what's it gonna be?"

"I don't know, Reg. The money is nice, but this doesn't feel right."

"Oh come one, V. You've barely left Sedona in the seven years since you got here. You've only been back to Boston once to visit your family. I know you and your mother aren't tight, but... she's your mother."

Viki's shoulders tensed at the mention of her mother. Memories of how they had fought flickered past. Fighting over her gift, over her lifestyle, over her lack of a husband, over her abortion. With her grandmother dead there was nothing left for her in Boston.

"Don't you think it's time for you to step out a little?"

Reg continued. "Have an adventure? And, God forbid, maybe some fun?"

"And what if I do? What if I lower my guard? What if it's like Boston all over again? What if someone dies?"

Reg frowned. "That wasn't your fault. You didn't know."

"Yeah, well maybe I should have. My gift should help people, not kill them."

"And what, just because you've got a gift, just because you're sometimes psychic, you think you should know everything? Be able to avoid every mistake? Is that what you're doing in that little room above my bookstore charging tourists a tenth of what your worth?"

"Reg, please..." Viki crossed her arms and looked down at her feet.

"No. I've got something to say and you need to listen. Remember when we met?"

"Yes," Viki replied. "You came to Boston, I drew your mother. You invited me to come draw at your bookstore."

"That reading changed my life, V. And the readings you do change lives every day. But back then you had started coming out of your shell, you wanted to find a way to help more people, even those you couldn't draw for. You weren't afraid. You weren't hiding then."

"I am not hiding," Viki said quietly, her gaze meeting Reg's.

Reg smiled thinly and shook his head. He gently touched her shoulder. "Yes you are. I do all the public stuff, and I am happy to, but this gift of yours could reach so many more people. Maybe this Kosov guy can be a start of something for you."

Viki turned, shrugging his touch off and walked several paces away.

"And make so much more money, you mean," Viki said.

"Yes, V, more money. And what the hell is wrong with that? You help more people, you earn more money. Sounds like karma to me."

"Mark Kosov, he's going to ask me to do something I shouldn't do. I can just feel it, Reg."

Reg shrugged. "So set your boundaries and go for it. If it doesn't look good once you get there, walk."

"But, my cat, who's going to take care of her?"

"I already called Jamie, she said she would be happy to look after Bast."

"But my appointments—"

"I'll reschedule."

Viki sighed and wrapped her arms around her chest, shivering at something other than the weather. Reg was right, she had been hiding, afraid to use her gift and afraid not to use it. Afraid to leave the safe little world she had created. What would her grandmother think? She felt change coming, and she knew she needed it.

More than anything she needed change.

"Okay, I'll do it. And, Reg, you'll get your usual twenty percent of this."

"Ahh... No need, V," Reg began, as he looked at his shoes. "I've arranged so my cut is separate from what they are paying you."

Viki laughed, "Of course it is."

She shook her head and walked back into the bookstore wondering about what was to come.

That's the end of the sample. To find out what happens next, pick up a copy of Drawing the Dead. For more information go to: RobertJMcCarer.com/Books/DrawingTheDead

Acknowledgements

THIS WAS A HARD BOOK TO WRITE. EACH BOOKS HAS ITS challenges (*Shuffled Off* was my first novel, and rather accidental, but very intimidating; *Drawing the Dead* had a female protagonist, which terrified me; *To Be a Fool* made me worry I couldn't live up to the innocence of *Shuffled Off* and get JJ into interesting new territory), but this book was especially challenging. It veered into territory I was less familiar, both literally (Mexico City) and intellectually (Catholicism). But, for me, the stories I write are the ones that won't leave me alone, and this one wouldn't leave me alone.

In *Shuffled Off* there is one paragraph the sums up Jesus's backstory, and when I was writing *To Be a Fool* and he exited for most of the book and came back with Lela, I wanted to know that story, to know more of his background beyond that meager paragraph.

This book was also difficult for personal reasons. Much of the two-year delay in getting this finished was taken up in caregiving for my mother and then dealing with her death. I've faced my share of loss, just like my characters, and this was a tough one.

Don't get me wrong, the challenges are not a bad thing. After all, why put the energy into a novel if there isn't some new things to discover, a new path to follow? It just means I have more people to thank than usual, so here we go.

Extra special thanks go to my Spanish language editors, Susana Acosta-Cavert and Adrian Reyes. They helped me stray into this less familiar territory, making sure my Spanish was correct, and ferreted out issues with my depiction of the Catholic religion and the Mexican culture.

As always, great thanks to my amazing team of beta readers: Roni Hornstein, Chris Kalinich, Aleia O'Reilly, and Eliot Schipper. Time after time they all catch so many of my mistakes and elevate each and every book.

Great gratitude to my amazing proofreader, Diana Cox (*www.novelproofreading.com*). She's my safety net in all of this, catching all the little things everyone else missed.

Thanks to Jennifer Star, the long ago winner of my "Name the Ghost" contest, who gave me such great inspiration for Lela. And thanks to Mark Carol and Christine Stephenson who graciously donated to charity (the wonderful Further Shore that my wife runs) for the rights to name Father Finnegan. I really appreciate all your support!

I also did a bunch of research and got a lot of help from these books: *Mexico City: An Opinionated Guide for the Curious Traveler* by Jim Johnson; *Catholicism for Dummies* by John Trigilio and Kenneth Brighenti; and *Mexico: What Everyone Needs to Know* by Roderic Ai Camp. And I spent many hours in Google street view cruising around Mexico City finding real world locations to help me dial in the setting.

Huge gratitude to my loving and amazing wife, Aleia. Without your support, none of this would be possible. You inspire me.

And finally, thank you dear reader for coming along on this journey of faith and love!

About the Author

ROBERT J. MCCARTER IS THE AUTHOR OF FIVE NOVELS, three novellas, and dozens of short stories. He is a finalist for the *Writers of the Future* context and his stories have appeared in *Adomeda Spaceways Inflight Magazine*, *Everyday Fiction*, and numerous anthologies. His short stories have been published alongside such luminaries as Brandon Sanderson, Peter S. Beagle, Jody Lynn Nye, and David Farland.

He has written a series of first person ghost novels (starting with *Shuffled Off: A Ghost's Memoir*) and a superhero / love story series (*Neutrinoman and Lightningirl: A Love Story*). Ten of his short stories were published in *Life After: Stories of Life, Death, and the Places In Between*.

He lives in the mountains of Arizona with his amazing wife and his ridiculously adorable dog. Find out more at RobertJMcCarter.com.

Books by Robert J. McCarter

Novels in the "Ghost's Memoir" world:
Shuffled Off: A Ghost's Memoir, Book 1
Drawing the Dead
To Be a Fool: A Ghost's Memoir, Book 2
Of Things Not Seen: A Ghost's Memoir, Book 3

Books in the Neutrinoman and Lightningirl Series:
Meteor Attack!
   Lightningirl and Neutrinoman, A Love Story. Episode 1
Toxic Asset
   Lightningirl and Neutrinoman, A Love Story. Episode 2
Protocol X
   Lightningirl and Neutrinoman, A Love Story. Episode 3
Season 1 (Omnibus edition of Episodes 1 - 3)
Off Book
   Lightningirl and Neutrinoman, A Love Story. Episode 4
   (Coming soon)

Short Stores and Collections
Life After: Stories of Life, Death, and the Places in Between
Probability: Resolve
The Turing Test Will Be Televised
Ghost Hacker, Zombie Maker

For a complete list, go to RobertJMcCarter.com